P9-CCV-091

SPY RUNNER

WRITTEN AND ILLUSTRATED BY

EUGENE YELCHIN

HENRY HOLT AND COMPANY
NEW YORK

Henry Holt and Company, *Publishers since 1866*
Henry Holt® is a registered trademark of Macmillan Publishing Group, LLC
175 Fifth Avenue, New York, New York 10010 • mackids.com

ISBN 978-1-250-12081-6
Library of Congress Control Number 2018945030

Our books may be purchased in bulk for promotional, educational,
or business use. Please contact your local bookseller or the
Macmillan Corporate and Premium Sales Department at (800) 221-7945
ext. 5442 or by email at MacmillanSpecialMarkets@macmillan.com.

First edition, 2019 / Designed by April Ward
Printed in the United States of America by
LSC Communications, Harrisonburg, Virginia

1 3 5 7 9 10 8 6 4 2

For Steven Malk

1

Every morning the students of Mr. Vargas's class pledged allegiance to the flag. They stood behind their desks with their hands over their hearts and their eyes on the flag, and they said with one voice—*I pledge allegiance to the flag of the United States of America, and to the Republic for which it stands, one Nation indivisible, with liberty and justice for all.*

Among them was a boy named Jake McCauley, and he, too, stood behind his desk with his eyes on the flag and the palm of his hand pressed to his heart. His palm was always a little sweaty because the classroom was hot, even in the morning with all the shades down.

Jake McCauley was proud to be an American. He was proud of the flag and he was proud of liberty and he was proud of justice for all, but when he pledged allegiance, he would only pretend to say the words like the others. Instead, he would whisper to himself his own secret pledge. It went like this—*I pledge to save my dad from the Russians and to bring him home so my dad and mom and I can be a regular family like we're supposed to be in America.*

This all happened a long time ago, in the year 1953, when the dads of some of Jake's friends from Mr. Vargas's class were fighting in the war in Korea. You could listen about that war on the radio and then talk about it at school with your friends. And Jake did, but his heart was not in it.

Here is why.

His dad still had not returned from the old war, the big one, the one with the Nazis. That war had ended a million years ago, or at least it felt like a million years to Jake. He had just turned twelve in December.

Why his dad did not return from that war was explained in the letter Jake's mother kept in the drawer beside her bed. The letter was from the United States Air Force, and it said that Jake's father went MIA, which meant *missing in action*. Missing in action did not mean Jake's father had been killed, of course. It only meant that the air force did not know where he was.

Once, Jake heard a program on the radio about American GIs imprisoned by the Russians and forced to work in the mines above the Arctic Circle. GI stood for *galvanized iron*, from which some of the army stuff was made, but Jake believed that the American soldiers were called GIs because they were as strong as iron. His dad was surely as strong as iron, and he could surely survive working in the Russian mines until somebody would rescue him.

Jake wrote a letter to the radio station asking them who could help him rescue his dad. When nobody answered his letter, Jake knew that even if his mom had checked it for spelling, he could not have counted on the radio station for help. He could not count on anyone and would have to save his dad all by himself. He even had a plan for how he would do it.

2

"Class, I have inspiring news," Mr. Vargas said when everyone sat down after the Pledge of Allegiance. "As we all know, our brave troops are fighting Communists in Korea, but we also have Communists here at home, in America. Mr. Hirsch, our principal, has proposed that once a week, the father of one of the students visit each classroom to share his method for fighting the threat of Communism. Today, Duane's father, Major Armbruster—"

"What's Communism, Mr. Vargas?" said Trudy Lamarre from the front row.

Jake elbowed his desk buddy, Duane Armbruster, whose dad was to visit them today, and peeped in his ear, imitating

Trudy, "What's Communism, Mr. Vargas?" Duane did not reply, and Jake shook his head, adding in his own voice, "Who is she kidding?"

"Who can tell us what Communism means, children?" said Mr. Vargas.

Jake's hand shot into the air. "Ask me, sir! Ask me! I know!"

"Go ahead, McCauley."

Jake sprung to his feet and, filling his lungs with air to shout, realized that he did not know the answer. Communism was bad all right—that was all you heard on the radio, or saw in the movies, or read about in comics—but he did not know how to explain it. He glanced at Duane, hoping for help, but Duane was looking away on purpose.

"It's the Russians, sir," Jake said. "They cooked it up."

"Cooked what up?"

"Communism, sir."

He felt his ears burning and knew that they were turning red. The Communist flag was red, and also red was a large chunk of the right hemisphere on the world map hanging beside the blackboard. The red on the map was Russia, where his father was locked up in the mines.

"What the Russians do, sir, is this," Jake said. "If they catch an American GI, for example, they send him to dig for uranium in the top secret mines above the Arctic Circle.

The Russians need uranium to make A-bombs so they can drop them on us, sir."

He felt everyone gaping at him, waiting for what he would say next. He wanted to tell them that at this very moment his dad was digging for uranium in one of those mines, whacking at the permafrost with a pick in his hands while a Russian guard was aiming his machine gun at him, but the mocking eyes of his classmates stopped him.

He shrugged and said, "I heard it on the radio, sir."

"Well." Mr. Vargas sighed. "We can't trust everything we hear on the radio, McCauley, can we now?"

"We can't?" Jake said, astonished.

Mr. Vargas glanced up at him quickly, and Jake could have sworn that the teacher looked frightened.

"A good try, McCauley," Mr. Vargas said, as if he were apologizing for something. "You can sit down now."

Jake plunged into his chair and elbowed Duane again. "Don't expect me to save your bum when it's your turn, buddy."

Duane did not look back at him and did not answer, and Jake peered at him out of the corner of his eye, confused by Duane's odd behavior.

"Well, Trudy," said Mr. Vargas, "perhaps I can explain." He stepped closer to Trudy Lamarre's desk, cleared his throat, and said quietly, "In theory, Trudy, Communism is a society in which everything is shared; there's no private property."

Jake's hand shot up again.

"What is it now, McCauley?"

"Can you speak a little louder, sir?"

Mr. Vargas nodded and went on in the same hushed voice. "The homes and the farms and the factories belong to everybody equally. Nobody owns anything, but at the same time, everyone owns everything."

Jake leaned into Duane. "Why the heck is he whispering?"

"In this way, Trudy," Mr. Vargas continued quietly, "people can work for themselves and not for somebody else, you see?"

"No, sir," said Trudy Lamarre. "I do not see. If I didn't have something, I would work for it, but if I already had everything, why would I work?"

"You'd work your fanny off, no matter what!" Jake shouted, and when the classroom quaked with laughter, he looked around, smiling.

"McCauley!" said Mr. Vargas.

"What? She's never even had an A minus," Jake protested. Trudy Lamarre had beautiful red hair and eyes that made him stutter: deep, dark brown eyes. Jake despised her.

"I wish you'd work a little harder, too, McCauley."

Mr. Vargas flung a nervous glance at the door, as if worried that someone might barge in at any moment. "Well, you see, Trudy, the idea of Communism is . . . And it's only an idea, you understand? The idea is that everyone works for the common good, and everyone gets paid for their contribution, but only as much as one needs, no more and no less, you see? Everyone's equal."

"And why is that bad?" said Trudy Lamarre.

Then there was a knock on the door. What happened next was so amazing that no one in the classroom even remembered to laugh. Instead of answering the door, Mr. Vargas darted to his desk and sat down, then changed his mind and sprung up and rushed to the door, then changed his mind again and wheeled toward the blackboard and snatched a piece of chalk and began writing: *Today's Topic: The Threat of Communism.*

When the door cracked opened and the principal stuck his head in, Mr. Vargas glanced away from the blackboard and, clearly faking surprise, said to him, "Ah, Mr. Hirsch. We didn't hear you knocking. Stand up, children. Major Armbruster is here."

3

It was no secret that Jake held Duane's father in the highest regard. Major Armbruster looked like a real American hero, and every time Jake had imagined his own father, he had always looked like the major—tall, broad-shouldered, and square-jawed.

"It's your dad!" Jake whispered excitedly to Duane when Major Armbruster, clad in blue air force dress pressed and starched to perfection, briskly marched into the classroom and, extending his right hand for a handshake, headed straight for Mr. Vargas.

"You may sit down, children," said Mr. Vargas, grimacing in pain from Major Armbruster's mighty handshake.

The students crash-landed in their seats.

The major scoped the classroom, zeroed in on the desk that his son was sharing with Jake, and smiled in their direction. He had a beautiful smile, and his teeth were even and white. Everyone turned and gaped at Duane. Duane blushed, keeping his eyes glued to the lid of the desk before him.

"You are just in time, Major," said Mr. Vargas. "Trudy here had a question about Communism. Would you care to explain to the children what it really means?"

"The very reason I'm here, sir," Major Armbruster said in a voice as crisp as his air force dress. "Let me show you, young lady, what this Communism thing is all about."

The major snapped up the chalk and began writing in square capitals, each letter exactly the height and the width of the one that came before it. Jake watched the major's every move and, listening to the chalk knocking against the slate, whispered to himself word by word what the major was writing: "Communism—equals—destruction—of—the—American—way—of—life."

Major Armbruster scanned the classroom to ensure that everyone had had a chance to read what he had written, then in one decisive sweep, erased *of the American way of life*. "Communism equals destruction," he announced, screeched a line below the words, slammed the chalk down, and marched to the world map beside the blackboard.

"Here's Russia," he said, and stuck his finger into the

large chunk of red. "See how it's spreading in all directions? The Communist bosses in Moscow are planning to take over the world. If we let the Russians succeed, they'll bring their Communism to America—a terrible, merciless destruction of our way of life."

"What would they do, sir?" Trudy Lamarre said nervously.

"Glad you asked, young lady," the major said. "What do we value most in America? Freedom. Truth. Justice for all. We are not afraid to think and talk as we please, correct? The first thing the Russians will do, they'll take that away. You follow me?"

"Does everyone follow Duane's father?" said Mr. Vargas.

"Freedom of speech, you say?" went on Major Armbruster, even though Trudy Lamarre had not said a word this time. "I guarantee you'd wish you never had it. There'll be such spying and snooping and wiretapping going on that if you dare to whisper even one word against the Communists, you'd be arrested, imprisoned, *killed*!"

"Killed?" gasped Trudy Lamarre.

"Excuse me, Major," Mr. Vargas said carefully. "What can each of us do to prevent such a terrible thing? You, personally, sir. What do you do? The children would like to know. Right, children?"

Major Armbruster flashed his beautiful smile in Duane's direction. "Why not ask Armbruster Junior? Stand

COMMUNISM =

ESTRUCTION

up, son, and tell your classmates what your daddy does in the United States Air Force."

All in one motion, the entire classroom swung to look at Duane again, and once again he did not move. Jake leaned forward and twisted his neck to look into Duane's face. What was wrong with him today? Did Duane not know how lucky he was? If Jake's dad stood there for everyone to see, Jake would be so happy and proud, but Duane could not even look at his father.

"Duane?" prompted Mr. Vargas. "Would you like to tell us about your father's contribution to the fight against the threat of Communism?"

Impatient, Jake kicked Duane's foot under the desk. "Get up, bud, get up."

Duane's face broke out in red patches. He stirred, lumbered to his feet, and, awkward and slouched and a little chubby, stood without speaking.

"Say something, bud," Jake whispered, but Duane, who would talk Jake's ear off bragging about his father when he was alone with Jake, was struck dumb with the major present.

Jake noticed the major's beautiful smile fading away, and Mr. Vargas's face rumpling like he was ready to weep, and his classmates' eyes shining as if they were about to burst out laughing, and even though he had promised not to save Duane's bum when it was his turn, Jake punched his arm into the air and cried, "Ask me, sir! I know!"

"All right, Duane," said Mr. Vargas. "You can sit down."

Duane dropped into his chair, and before Mr. Vargas could object, Jake leapt to his feet. "United States Air Force Major Armbruster is the head of security at our air force base." He drummed out the very words Duane had used boasting about his father that morning. "His mission is to protect American know-how from Russian spies."

"Well, McCauley, Russian spies?" Mr. Vargas said with a skeptical smile. "In our city?"

"It's no joke, sir," snapped the major, narrowing his eyes at Mr. Vargas. "We have concrete evidence that Communist agents have infiltrated our air force."

Mr. Vargas swallowed something in his throat and said, "Did they, now?"

"Yes, sir. As well as the army and the navy. Not to mention our government, entertainment, press, youth groups, and schools."

"Schools?" said Mr. Vargas, turning whiter than chalk.

Major Armbruster looked at him severely. "Communists are everywhere."

And then the bell rang for recess, and all at once, the classroom exploded with laughing and shrieking and scraping of chairs. The kids, forgetting about the threat of Communism, charged toward the door past their white-faced teacher and past the stone-faced major, and spilled into the hallway, happy and wild.

4

No one could ever beat Jake at speed. His and Duane's desk stood by the window in the back of the room, nearly the farthest desk from the door, but Jake was always the first one to fly into the hallway at the sound of the bell.

Not this time. This time he stayed behind, watching Major Armbruster shake Mr. Vargas's hand, then slap him on the shoulder and march out the door held open by the smiling principal.

When the door behind the major closed, Mr. Vargas said, "Phew," and turned to the blackboard and wiped it clean, careful not to erase COMMUNISM = DESTRUCTION in the major's steady capitals. Then Mr. Vargas returned to his desk, pulled out a chair, sat down, and began writing in his ledger.

Jake was the only one who remained in the classroom besides Mr. Vargas, and he sat quietly, listening to his teacher's pen scrape lightly in the silence. Soon he grew bored and, leaning toward the window near his desk, moved the shutters aside.

The window looked out onto the school's parking lot, where at that very moment Major Armbruster turned away from the principal toward his motorcar. His motorcar was beautiful: a brand-new Cadillac in a blue finish with chrome-plated trim sparkling in the sun. The major sunk into the driver's seat and closed the door. The principal rose on his toes, waving after the brake lights flashing briefly as the Cadillac swung out of the lot.

"What is it you want, McCauley?" came Mr. Vargas's voice.

Jake dropped the shutters and spun around. "What?"

Mr. Vargas closed the ledger and put it in his briefcase and snapped the briefcase shut. "Is it about your homework?"

"No, sir."

Mr. Vargas rose and took his hat off the hook on the wall and fit it on his head. "What is it about, then?"

Jake blinked at him. "Communism, sir."

Mr. Vargas was on his way to the door, but the word *Communism* stopped him cold. "What about it?" he said cautiously.

"Well. It's what you said about dads, sir."

"What is it that I said, McCauley?"

"You said that dads would be coming every week like Duane's dad did today? Talking about fighting the threat of Communism? The way they do it? That's what you said, sir."

"All right. I did say that. What's wrong with that?"

"Well, sir. I was just wondering. Could my mom come?"

"Your mom?"

"Yes, sir. Tell everybody how she fights it? Communism, I mean."

Mr. Vargas pinched his hat off and wiped his forehead with the back of his hand. He seemed relieved. "I'm sorry, Jake. I should have included mothers. Of course." He looked at the hat in his hand and smiled a foolish kind of a smile that Jake did not like at all. "Especially your mother, McCauley. She's always been a role model in our community. An upstanding citizen, your mother." When he looked up at Jake's face, his foolish smile instantly vanished. "I'll tell you what, McCauley. I'll write your mother a note inviting her to our classroom. Would that be good?"

Mr. Vargas hung his hat back on the hook and set his

briefcase on the floor beside his desk and sat down to write a note.

Suddenly, Jake did not want Mr. Vargas to write to his mother. Why did he talk that way about her? And why did he smile like that? He had seen Jake's mom only once, when she and Jake ran into him at the grocer's. Mr. Vargas talked to her for two minutes, if that. How did he know that she was an upstanding citizen and a role model? He did not know anything about her.

Mr. Vargas put his pen aside and folded the note. "I don't need to remind you, McCauley, that your mother has made many sacrifices for you. Never remarried, for example." He held the note out to Jake. "You better take good care of her, McCauley. After all, you are the only man in the family since your father was killed in the war."

Jake felt his heart leap. "How do you know my dad was killed?"

"What?" Mr. Vargas said, startled. "I thought—"

"My dad is MIA," Jake cut him off. "Missing in action."

"I'm sorry, Jake. Missing in action. Of course. Please take this to your mother."

Mr. Vargas began to rise, holding up the note, but Jake was already turning, already running to the door. "No, sir. My mom's too busy to come."

5

On the way home, Jake, sitting loosely on his bike, knees bopping up and down, hands deep in the back pockets of his jeans, rolled steadily along, looking neither left nor right but straight ahead. Beside him, Duane pedaled in sudden spurts, slowing at times, then catching up again.

The sky was specked with hazy daylight clouds, but to the west, the sun began its steady slide behind the mountains, pitching the boys' shadows across a two-lane blacktop that stretched ahead of them in one straight and endless line.

"What did you talk to Vargas about?" Duane said, and when Jake did not answer, Duane caught up to him, weaving alongside Jake's bike. "Shucks, Jake, what's eating you, bud? It's your roadster, right?"

He leaned over the gleaming bars of the latest make of Schwinn Phantom in two-tone finish with chrome-plated fenders, a recent present from his father, and studied Jake's battered ancient roadster. "Hear that squeaking, bud? It's your chain. The links must be rusted."

Jake did not bother to look at the chain squeaking between his pumping feet. Of course the chain was rusted. He had inherited this prehistoric roadster from his father, who had put a million miles on it before Jake was even born.

"A rusted chain could lead to a serious problem, Jake," Duane declared, as if reading from a bicycle manual. "You might injure yourself. If I were you—"

A crashing roar drowned his advice. The front wheel of Duane's perfect Schwinn wobbled, and Jake swerved to avoid Duane ramming into him. A giant shadow spread over the boys, dousing the setting sun.

"Superfortress!" Duane hollered over the roar. "B-29!"

The enormous bomber was passing so low over them, it seemed to Jake that if he rose on the pedals and stretched up his arm, he could touch its darkened belly. Balancing his bike in place, he watched the B-29 fold its silvery flaps after takeoff.

"Did I ever tell you about the B-29s?" Duane hollered. "What the Russians did?"

He had, of course, a few times, but knowing that Duane would tell it again, Jake did not answer, watching the B-29 breach the mountain range and, sparkling in the sun, melt behind the shimmering haze of the waning day.

"My dad said the Russians got ahold of a couple of our B-29s during the war with the Nazis," Duane went on when they were riding again, "and took them apart piece by piece and built their own bombers exactly the same! Exactly, bud! Called reverse engineering. But they gave theirs a different name, of course, TU-4 or something, so we wouldn't know they had stolen from us. The Commies, right? Always cheating."

Jake nodded, pedaled silently for a while, and then he said, "What about the fellows who flew those B-29s? What happened to them?"

"You mean the crews?" Duane shrugged. "My dad didn't say. I bet the Commies shot them all."

Without noticing it, Jake was pedaling harder, as if trying to outride the terrible fear that his dad might have been on one of those B-29s downed by the Russians. Strangely, he knew Duane's father's rank and his position in the air force but not his own dad's. He had always imagined him to be a B-29 pilot. If not a pilot, then at least a gunner.

"Are you coming to the parade on Friday?" Duane called after him, trying to keep up. "The American Legion, remember? I'll be riding a float with my dad. You know what kind of float? B-29! Yes, sir! Like the one we just saw. Superfortress! Dad took me to the AFB—the air force base? To see them building the float in the special hangar. Because it's humongous, bud! Humongous!"

Jake stepped on the pedals, but Duane managed to keep up, talking excitedly. "But listen, bud, that's just a parade float, right? Not a big deal. My dad is going to start teaching me to fly real aircrafts at the base. Don't tell anyone, but my dad said we'd be testing a top secret bomber. He wants me to know how to drive it in case of an emergency."

Jake stole a glance at Duane. My dad this. My dad that. Why did he not brag about him in class? Swallowed his tongue in front of everybody. Could not even look his father in the eye. Was Duane afraid of him? Afraid? Could you be afraid of your own father? Jake did not know.

The boys lived in a suburb that sliced the desert into a grid of recently paved streets. The homes sprawled to the southwest, but at its eastern border, a chain-link fence with no beginning and no end kept the suburb from spreading. Beyond the fence lay an enormous empty lot of dry caked mud and cactus huddles. Beyond the lot began the air force base where every male grown-up in the boys' neighborhood served.

"Later, bud," Duane called out, swinging into the clean-swept driveway of the three-story house, the largest home on their street. "See ya in the morning."

On the front lawn, Major Armbruster, in his full air force dress, stood watering the grass. Out of the corner of his eye, Jake watched Duane duck under the spray from the water hose, disappear behind the blue Cadillac parked in the driveway, and reappear again beside the porch. The American flag, billowing from one of the posts, obscured Duane for a moment, and when the flag cleared the view, it was just the Schwinn Phantom leaning on its kickstand. Duane must have entered the house. Jake glanced back at Major Armbruster, saw him looking in his direction, and quickly turned away, ashamed to be caught spying.

It pained Jake to feel envious of Duane. Not of Duane's stuff, but of his having an American hero for a dad. But Jake knew even this was not the truth. The truth was, of course, that being an American hero had nothing to do with his envy. Jake was envious of Duane for simply *having* a dad.

Jake turned into the next driveway. Passing a mesquite tree, he caught hold of a rusted chain drooping from the tree branch and pulled himself atop a tire swing. The roadster bounced over the buckled concrete, collided with the house wall, and fell on its side. Spinning on the tire swing, Jake frowned at his mother's bruised prewar Chevy. The way her motorcar was parked looked as if she had been in an awful hurry to get into the house. The garage door was lifted, but the Chevy had not made it inside, angled halfway in, halfway out, the driver's door flung open. Her shoe lay on its side below the clutch. Five feet away, the heel of her other shoe pointed up from the brown grass. The front door of the house was not fully shut, and on the threshold, his mother's purse lay slumped on its side. Spilled keys, coins, and a compact mirror shone brightly against the doorstep.

6

Pressing his mother's purse to his chest, Jake stepped into the hallway and closed the door behind him. The window shades, drawn to keep the house cool, kept away the fading daylight, and the murky hallway suddenly felt ominous to him.

"Mom?" Jake called uneasily. "Where are you?"

His mother did not answer, but the sound of water running in the kitchen reassured him. Jake bounded up the hallway. The water was gushing into the sink from the open faucet, but his mother was not in the kitchen. Jake peered in suspicion at two glasses gleaming on the Formica counter. One had its rim stamped brightly by his mother's lipstick, but who was drinking from the second glass? Few visitors came to their home, and besides, his mother was not the kind to leave the faucet open, park her Chevy on the lawn, or run around without shoes.

The wall phone hanging by the kitchen doorway shrilled over his ear. Startled, Jake spun around and stood staring at it. The telephone continued ringing. Jake lifted the handset and pressed it to his ear.

"Hello?"

Behind the faint crackling in the wires, someone was wheezing on the other end of the line.

"Who is this?"

"Give me Shubin."

"Who?"

"Shubin."

"Wrong number, sir. There's no one here by—"

Click. The line went dead. Jake shrugged and set the handset down. The phone shrilled again at once. Jake swiped the handset and pressed it to his ear.

"Yeah?"

Wheezing on the other end.

"Listen, sir," Jake said, "I told you—"

Click. The wheezing fellow hung up. Jake looked at the handset and carefully set it back into the cradle, expecting the phone to ring again. It did not.

With a gunshot pop, a floorboard cracked in the attic. Jake's heart leapt in fright, and he let his mother's purse fall to the floor. Lifting his face to the ceiling, he listened to the muffled voices upstairs. What was she doing up there? Who was she with?

Before Jake was born, his father had built himself a study in the attic, a small, cozy room with a square window cut through the pitched shingled roof. His mother stayed away from there and never mentioned it, as if the study were a secret. When Jake was little, he had not known it existed, but now, when his mother was not home, he would often climb the creaky stairs to be with things his father left behind—his air force jacket and his books, his navigation maps and his brass desk calendar swiveled to the day he went to war. One day before Jake's first birthday.

He heard something heavy dragged across the floor in the attic, bolted out of the kitchen and through the hallway toward the staircase, but halfway up the steps, he saw the attic door fly open and halted at the sound of his mother's voice: "Easy does it, mister. I don't want you hurt."

"I don't get hurt, angel," a raspy voice replied.

She was up there with a man!

Jake stood, afraid to move, and when he heard his mother laugh, a queasy feeling made his belly tighten.

"Is that a fact?" said her voice. "Let's keep it that way."

Jake's mother, Mrs. McCauley, barefoot, laughing, her hair a mess, backed out of his father's study, hauling a large trunk. Facing the doorway, she stretched her left foot behind her, searching with her toes for the first step below the cramped landing. When her foot found the step, she began turning. The trunk pivoted, and a man Jake had never seen before appeared holding the other end.

"What did you keep all this junk for?" the man rasped, chuckling.

Mrs. McCauley glanced over her shoulder down the staircase and, seeing Jake standing there, dropped her end of the trunk. It surprised the man. The trunk slipped out of his hands and crashed onto the landing. "What the hell?"

"Hello, honey," said Jake's mother.

The man looked past her in Jake's direction. The only thing Jake could tell for certain about the stranger standing in the dim light of the landing was that he wore spectacles. Two radiant crescents gleamed on either side of his nose.

"Is that Jake?" the man said hoarsely.

Mrs. McCauley looked up at the man as if she was expecting him to continue, but he did not say anything more.

"What's in the trunk?" Jake said.

"Your father's things, Jake. I will explain."

"He's tall," the man said, and looked at Mrs. McCauley.

"He's twelve. Why don't you two shake hands?"

The man hesitated for a moment, moved around the trunk, and stepped down into the slanted light filtering through the slats of the shuttered window. Mrs. McCauley pressed her hips against the banister to let him pass and briefly smiled at Jake. The man squeezed between Mrs. McCauley and the wall, careful not to brush against her, halted one step above Jake, and held out his hand.

Jake looked at the narrow, ropy hand, long tobacco-stained fingers, broken nails, and then beyond it, at the face behind a pair of crummy spectacles with a wad of dirty tape around the bridge of its frame and one split lens. He could not see the eyes sunk deep in the shadows behind the glinting lenses. The man's nose was bent a little to one side, probably broken, and the ashy gray skin of his face was so deeply lined, it made Jake think of scars. The face was thin, too thin, and his colorless hair was thin, too, with an ashy gray scalp visible through it.

"Shake hands, honey," Mrs. McCauley said. "What are you afraid of?"

"I'm not afraid."

This thin man seemed so insubstantial in the faint light of the staircase that Jake would not have been surprised if he had suddenly vanished, leaving behind the smell of stale tobacco and unwashed clothes. Jake would not have minded if he had vanished, but the stranger stood there, holding out his hand, and when Jake took it, the man's powerful grip came as a shock.

"Shubin," the man said in his raspy voice.

Shubin? Where had Jake heard that name?

"But you can call me Victor if you want."

"What kind of name is that?"

"Victor Shubin? Why, it's a Russian name."

"You're a Russian?"

"My mom and dad were. Guess it makes me one."

Jake remembered the wheezing voice on the phone. Shubin? The phone call was for him!

"Mom? Can I talk to you in private?"

Jake wrenched his hand out of the man's grip and fled downstairs. When Mrs. McCauley came into the kitchen after Jake, he shut the door and whispered, "Who's that guy, Mom?"

Mrs. McCauley walked past him toward the sink and turned off the running water. "He told you, Jake," she said. "You can address him as Mr. Shubin for now."

"What do you mean *for now*?"

"While he's staying with us."

"Staying with us?"

Mrs. McCauley collected the water glasses off the counter and put them into the sink. "I'm renting out your father's study in the attic, Jake," she said in a casual tone, as if it were barely worth mentioning. "It will be Mr. Shubin's room."

"What?" Jake stared at her in astonishment. "How could you do this, Mom? He said that Dad's things were junk!"

"You know we need money, Jake. Your father's air force pension and my salary are not enough to cover our expenses. We have to rent the room."

"Yeah, but why to him?"

"My boss, Mr. Hoover, has highly recommended him."

"Your boss, Mr. Hoover? The guy who makes window blinds? How does he even know him?"

"He's been helping Russian refugees ever since the end of the war, Jake. You know how terrible that war was on the Russians. Those who chose freedom need another chance."

"But, Mom, if he's Russian, why does he speak American so good?"

"English, Jake, not American. And it's *so well*, not *so good*. I guess he studied it a little harder than you do at school."

"We can't have a Russian in here, Mom! Duane's dad said today that if the Russians come, there'll be such spying and snooping and wiretapping going on that if you dare to whisper even one word against the Communists, you'll be arrested, imprisoned, and killed!"

"Don't be ridiculous, Jake. Mr. Shubin is not a Communist."

The hallway floorboards creaked, and Jake's head swung in the direction of the door. "Who is it?"

The door cracked open, and the Russian poked his head in. "Oops. Sorry. I didn't mean to interrupt."

Jake swiftly turned his back to him and whispered to his mother, "Not a Communist, Mom? Why is he snooping around, then?"

Mrs. McCauley spread her arms to stop Jake from running out, but he was too fast for her. By the time the screen door slammed behind him, Jake was already leaping over the hedge, crossing the property line into the Armbrusters' backyard.

7

The handful of gravel sprayed against Duane's second-story window, and when the window remained closed, Jake scooped another handful and pitched that, too. This time, the pebbles knocked against the window frame and bounced back. Jake ducked, bracing himself against the wall. He sidled stealthily toward the rear of the house, hoping to slip in through the kitchen door without Duane's folks spotting him. He had done it before.

Mrs. Armbruster was in the kitchen.

"What are you standing there for, lamb?" she said, smiling at Jake through the screen door. "Come in, lamb, come in."

Jake stepped into the blinding lights of Mrs. Armbruster's

gleaming kitchen, instantly drowsy from the sweet smell of her cooking and the hum of her convenient appliances.

"The boys are in the TV room," said Mrs. Armbruster, and stirred something bubbling in a chrome-plated saucepan. A cloud of steam rose, obscuring her hefty shape. She sailed out of the cloud toward the Frigidaire, opened it, and took out a casserole. "You go right in, lamb. They're watching a movie." Her ample hip bumped the Frigidaire's door, and it closed with a soft and pleasant thump.

"Thank you, ma'am," Jake mumbled, and, conscious that she was watching him, slowly stepped out of the kitchen. The moment he was out of her sight, he took off running. He sped over the perfectly polished floors of the perfectly furnished rooms, passed through the rainbow-colored light bouncing off the cut-glass chandelier, and slid to a stop in front of the door behind which music was playing, the kind they used in the movies when something bad was about to happen.

"McCauley?" said Major Armbruster from the couch when Jake opened the door. "Grab a seat, son. It just began."

Jake was dying to tell Duane about the Russian, but he did not dare to disobey the major. He walked in and sunk into the opposite end of the couch from where Duane was sitting. The major sat in the middle. Before them, a twenty-one-inch Philco TV, the first television set on their street, beamed from a polished console.

The major sat erect, with his elbows propped on his knees. Jake leaned casually behind his back, trying to attract Duane's attention by rapid winking and nodding toward the door. Duane noticed, but he kept his eyes fixed on the TV. When Jake redoubled his efforts, the major looked at him in alarm. "Are you all right, son?"

"Yes, sir," Jake said. "Sorry, sir."

He looked at the TV screen, but could not focus on the movie, thinking about the Russian at his house. Besides, the movie was confusing. The jittery music kept playing, but on the screen, everything looked perfectly normal. People riding on a train somewhere, reading newspapers. Regular Americans on the way to work. The sound did not go together with the picture at all.

"What's this all about?" Jake said, baffled.

"One of those fellows is a Russian spy," said Major Armbruster.

"Oh, yeah?" Jake said, instantly interested. "Which one?"

"We don't know yet."

"It's the one in the hat," Duane said. "That one, way in the back reading the paper."

"You're way off, Junior," said Major Armbruster.

Just as he said it, the movie moved in close to show the fellow Duane had pointed out. With a hat worn so low that only the tip of his nose was visible below the brim, the fellow looked plenty suspicious. Jake thought of the Russian again. How could his mom let that man into his dad's attic? Was he going to sleep up there, too?

"Watch this, Dad," Duane said. "He's sitting on the dead drop."

"On the what?" said the major.

Duane rolled his eyes, frustrated by always having to explain spy stuff to his dad. Duane knew a lot about spies from the comics.

"It's where one spy leaves something secret for another spy to pick up without them ever being seen together. Called a dead drop."

The major turned to Jake, grinning. "Ever heard of such a thing, McCauley? Dead drop?"

"Yes, sir. It's in the comics."

The major shook his head. "Comics," he repeated, and turned back to the TV screen.

The fellow in the hat that Duane said was a spy was still reading the newspaper, but his left hand sneaked down beside his knee, scraped something from under the bench he was sitting on, and came up again folded into a fist. The movie showed his hand real close the moment he opened his fist. A tiny black film cartridge with twin chambers lay in his palm.

Duane turned to his dad with a superior smirk on his

face. Jake, grabbing the opportunity to catch his eye, ducked behind the major's back, furiously wagging his head toward the door. Duane frowned and looked away.

"I always say you can learn things from watching television," said Major Armbruster. "It's educational."

"Yes, sir," Jake agreed. "Better than going to school."

Major Armbruster guffawed and, twisting toward Jake, slapped him on the shoulder. "Better than going to school?" he repeated, laughing. "You're a riot, McCauley."

Pleased that the major liked his joke, Jake laughed, too, but he laughed a little too hard. Duane turned to them, glancing anxiously between Jake and his dad laughing together. Noticing it and instantly ashamed for playing up to the major, Jake brought a fist to his lips, pretending to be coughing.

Meanwhile in the movie, the spy was sneaking about the hallways and hiding in the shadows and eavesdropping on telephone conversations, but Jake had trouble paying attention. That Russian, that Mr. Shubin, with his cracked spectacles and his ropy hand with yellow fingertips, kept floating up before his eyes, and soon the Russian spy in the movie and the Russian his mom had brought to their house became confused in Jake's mind.

"Junior?" He heard Major Armbruster's voice. "Shoot to the kitchen and tell Mother we'll be wanting iced Coca-Colas. Bring some nuts and such."

Jake leapt up eagerly. "I'll go, too, sir!" he shouted, hoping to be alone with Duane so he could tell him about the Russian.

"Sit tight, son," said Major Armbruster. "Junior will go."

"Yes, sir." Jake sat down, watching Duane shuffle out of the room with his eyes fixed on the TV until the door shut behind him.

In the movie the jittery music was up again. The spy was slinking down the street, glancing from under the brim of his hat to check if he was being followed. Beside Jake, the major's regulation army oxfords were planted side by side on the white-carpeted floor. Two little blue squares, the reflections of the TV screen, flickered in the round patent leather toes. Within each square, the tiny upside-down spy was clearly visible. Watching the reflections in the major's shoes was far more interesting than watching the screen because the spies seemed to be in competition, and it looked to Jake that the one on the left was a little sneakier than the one on the right.

"McCauley? Mind if I ask you something?" The major crossed his legs, and both spies vanished.

"No, sir."

"I've been thinking about this morning. About Junior standing in front of his classmates."

"Yes, sir?"

"I'll be frank with you, McCauley, it worries me. Is he always that way at school? Quiet-like?"

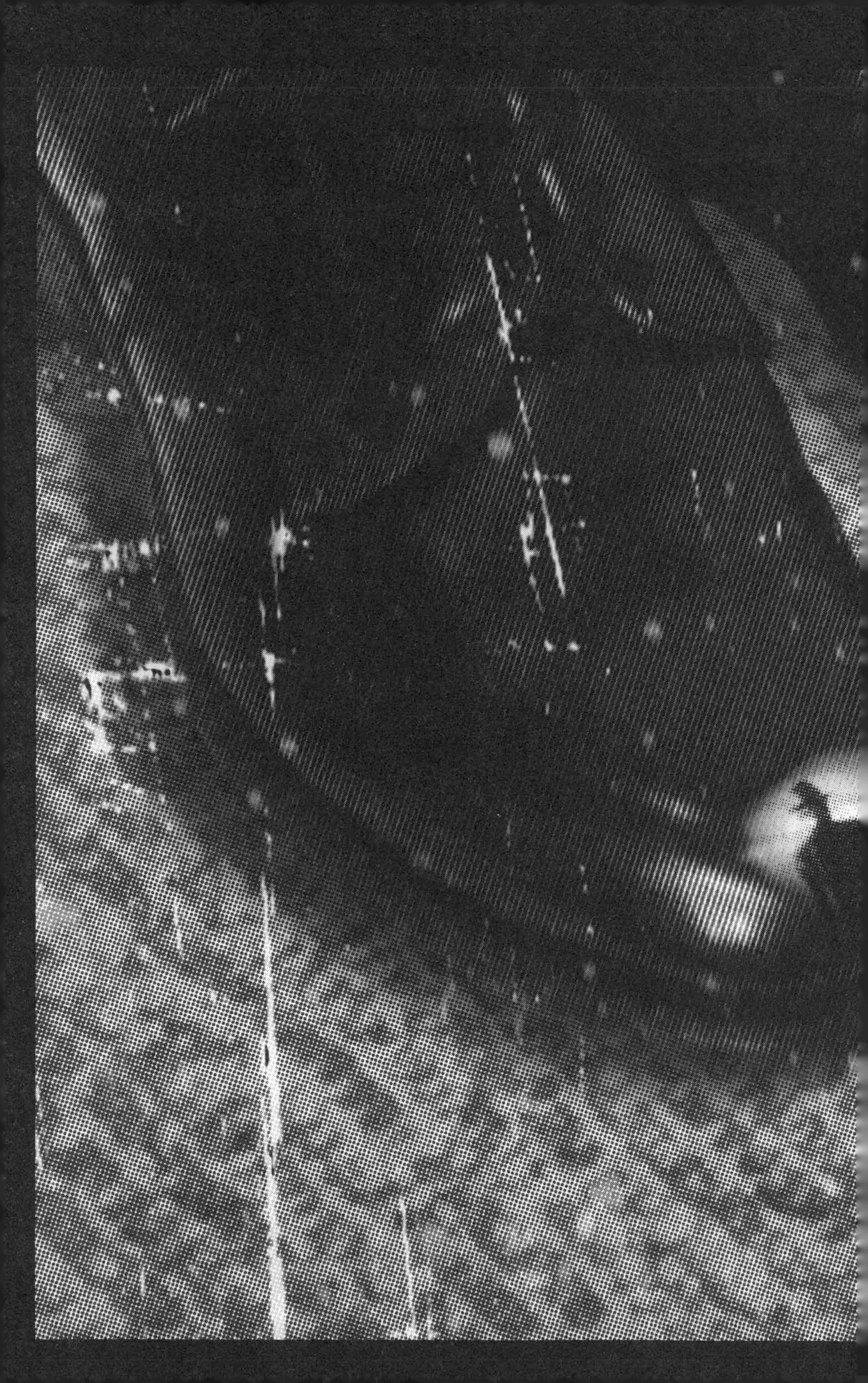

"No, sir. He talks like most everybody."

Major Armbruster's radiant green eyes burned into Jake's face, and he could tell that the major was skeptical of his answer.

"Duane is real smart, sir," Jake assured him. "His grades are good."

The major's green eyes slipped off Jake's face, and he sat back, peering gloomily at the TV. "Oh, McCauley, McCauley, it's not his grades I worry about."

"What is it, then, sir? I don't understand."

"How could you? You're loaded with character, McCauley. You've got spirit, son; you go after things, but Junior—"

The door opened, and Mrs. Armbruster walked in with two Coca-Cola glasses and little plates on a shiny tray. Duane slipped in behind her, but hovered in the doorway, his eyes darting back and forth between Jake and the major, clearly trying to guess what they were talking about while he was gone.

"What are you doing in here, Mildred?" the major snapped, annoyed. "I told *him* to bring it."

"He'd spill it, honey," said Mrs. Armbruster.

"Where's the third Coca-Cola?" the major said, looking at the two glasses on the tray.

"I don't want any," Duane said, and slinked back to his seat.

Mrs. Armbruster held the tray before Jake. "Thank you, ma'am." He took one of the glasses.

The major waved the tray away. "I ain't thirsty."

"I'll set it down on the side table, boys," said Mrs. Armbruster. "Maybe you'll change your mind or Jake will be wanting another. Dinner's coming."

She sailed out of the room and carefully closed the door behind her. They went back to watching the movie, but Jake, taking hurried icy pulls through the straw, was only pretending to watch it. The conversation with the major had confused him. Jake should have thought of smarter answers to his questions. He should have made the major feel good about Duane. But what was there to feel bad about? There was nothing wrong with Duane. He was Jake's best friend since kindergarten and he had read more comics than anyone in their whole school, and if that stupid spy on television was not caught real soon and that movie was not over and done with so that he could tell Duane about the Russian in his house, Jake was going to explode. His patience, always in short supply, was quickly running out.

"Watch him now, Dad," Duane said. "He's going to photograph the top secret stuff."

Jake glanced at the major, expecting him to say that Duane was wrong again, but the major kept silent. Jake looked back at the screen, where the spy was sneaking into some office. Jake could not tell what kind of office because he did not have enough time to make out the words on the frosted glass door.

Moving in and out of shadows, the spy approached a massive steel box. It was a safe like the one they had in the Valley National Bank downtown. The movie showed the round combination lock close when the spy's black-gloved hand turned it clockwise, then counterclockwise until the safe's door swung open. The safe was empty inside save for one cardboard folder. The folder looked like the folders Mr. Vargas used in their classroom for special projects, but when the spy took the folder out of the safe, the jittery music went up a few notches.

"Told ya," Duane said smugly. "Top secret."

And sure enough, when the spy set the folder under the glowing circle of the desk lamp, you could read TOP SECRET stamped in the upper right corner.

The major peered at the TV with such a glum expression that Jake felt guilty he could not defend Duane better, and he promised himself he'd say something really nice about Duane to the major the first chance he got.

When he turned back to the screen, the spy was leaning over the folder so that the desk lamp lit his face from below. A line of beaded sweat glistened above his upper lip, and on his bristly chin each tiny hair cast an upward shadow.

"He's got a Minox," Duane said.

"He's got a what?" the major said.

"Minox is a spy camera, Dad," Duane said, rolling his eyes.

The spy in the movie brought a tiny camera up to his eye and went on snapping away at the top secret folder, quickly turning the pages and glancing over his shoulder at the door.

"Geez, Duane, you could really tell about spies," Jake said, looking at Major Armbruster. "Doesn't he though, sir? Duane knows a lot about spies?"

Jake expected the major to agree with him, or at least to smile, or to nod, or to do something that would show he felt better about Duane because he knew so much about spies, but instead the major said, rising from the couch, "That's a lot of hooey, boys. We don't allow for such things."

"It's a movie, Dad," Duane said.

"No need to tell me that, Junior," snapped Major Armbruster. "I should know the difference."

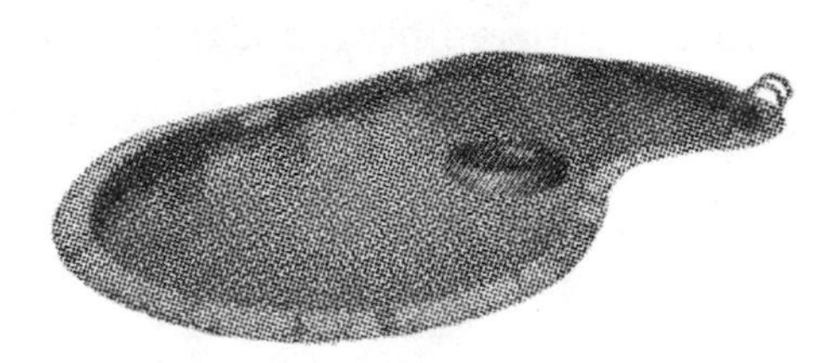

8

The instant the door closed after Major Armbruster, Jake scooted toward Duane and breathed into his ear, "You're going to die when I tell you!"

"Don't block the view, okay? Can't you see I'm watching a movie?"

"Forget the movie, bud! My mom took a renter in."

"So?"

"So? Are you nuts? She rented out Dad's old room upstairs. He's a Russian."

"Who's a Russian?"

"The guy Mom took in. He's from Russia!"

Duane's eyes darted past Jake to the door. "Keep your

voice down, you fool. He hears you, he'll blow his top. He already wants to take me out of school."

"Why?"

"He says Vargas is a Communist."

"Oh, yeah," Jake said, amazed. "The way he talked about Communism today, he probably is."

"He was lucky my dad didn't hear him," Duane whispered. "But it's what he said about radio that makes him suspicious."

"Radio? What did he say about radio?"

"Heck, McCauley! Where were *you*? He said we shouldn't trust what they say on the radio." He tiptoed to the door, peeked out, and whispered over his shoulder, "Can't talk in here. Let's go in the back."

The air felt cool and moist outside. The evening was coming. Creeping close to the wall, the boys sneaked around the Armbrusters' enormous house, ducked under a low-hanging bougainvillea, deep purple in the dwindling light, and looped around the grassy knoll below which was a fallout shelter that cost more than Jake's whole house. After Jake was allowed to visit the shelter last year—a deep cement bunker furnished with comfortable beds and stocked with food and water—he had always felt uneasy at the sight of its steel-riveted door. Any day, the Russians might drop the A-bomb on their town, but unlike the wealthy Armbrusters, Jake and his mother had no place to hide from the atomic fallout.

Behind the shelter, Duane took a sharp left to the kidney-shaped pool, where he halted and wheeled round so abruptly, Jake nearly tumbled into the water.

"Your mom took a Russian in?" Duane whispered. "Why would she do a thing like that?"

Jake shrugged. No use explaining money trouble to Duane; he would never understand it. "It's not her fault," he said. "Her boss made her do it. A fellow named Hoover. He's in the window shades business."

"Window shades? Who are they kidding, bud? But it's a shady business, all right. A cover for the den of spies, if you want to know my opinion. Guess why that Russian moved into your house."

Jake looked at him anxiously, already knowing the answer. Their neighborhood was at the edge of the air force base where secret aircrafts were tested. "Why?" he said anyway.

"Because we live right next to the air force base, you dummy."

"So what?"

Duane's eyes opened wide. "So what? You want to get my dad in trouble?"

"Your dad? The Russian has nothing to do with him."

"You're not paying attention, bud." Duane glanced up at

the house, scanning the second-story windows, then turned back to Jake. "My dad is cleared on all the classified stuff. He's got top secret files all over the place. What if your Russian sneaks in to take pictures of them? With a Minox? Like in that movie just now? Who'd be in trouble then?"

Jake felt a sudden shiver passing through his body and he wrapped his arms around himself. It was definitely getting cooler. "Would he do that?" he said.

"Sure he would."

"What if he doesn't have a Minox?"

"That's what you should find out. Did you go through his stuff yet?"

"What stuff?"

"His suitcase. First thing you do is look inside the lining. It probably has a false bottom. He's got to keep his tool kit hidden."

"What tool kit?"

Duane rolled his eyes. "You're just like my dad, McCauley. I'm not giving you any more of my spy comics; you're learning nothing." And leaning close to Jake, he speedily recited, "A shortwave radio. Invisible ink. Does he have an umbrella? Careful when you open it. Shoots bullets. He's got to have poison, too. Check the heels of his shoes for secret compartments. Look for photographic equipment. Cameras, film, stuff like that. Come on, bud, use your brain."

Every word Duane whispered stung him, as if somehow

it was *Jake's* fault that his mother took in that Russian. What if he really *was* a spy?

With a sharp click, the pool lights came on, startling Jake. Duane was leaning heavily into him, pressing Jake to the edge of the pool. Lit from below by the underwater lights, Duane's face looked spooky, and his eyes, radiant green as his father's, shone brighter than usual. Jake took a deep breath and pulled away from him. "I can't go through his stuff."

"Why not?"

"My mom would kill me."

"Forget about your mom! It's your duty to fight the Communists."

"He may be a Communist, but he's no spy."

"All Communists are spies, McCauley. My dad says you can be around someone for years and never guess he's a spy, but I can always tell them! Always! My dad says that I am really good at—"

Abruptly Duane stopped and narrowed his eyes at Jake. "What did he talk to you about while I was gone? Did he talk about me?"

"Who?" Jake said, pretending not to understand.

"Come on, bud," Duane said. "What did my dad say about me while I was gone?"

"What did he say?" Jake shrugged. "I don't remember." He flinched under Duane's intense gaze and turned away to stare into the glowing pool. A black inner tube turned lazily in the water, thumping against the tiles.

"You don't have to tell me," he heard Duane's voice beside him. "I know. He'd rather have *you* for his son."

"WHAT?"

When Jake spun around to say that the major would never want any such thing, his foot slipped on a wet tile. Falling, he reached out to Duane to steady himself, but Duane took a quick step back, and Jake belly flopped into the pool. The water went into his mouth and up his nose. His eyes were open when he fell, and the underwater lights confused him. Instead of rising to the surface, he dived to the bottom and smashed his fingers into the blue concrete.

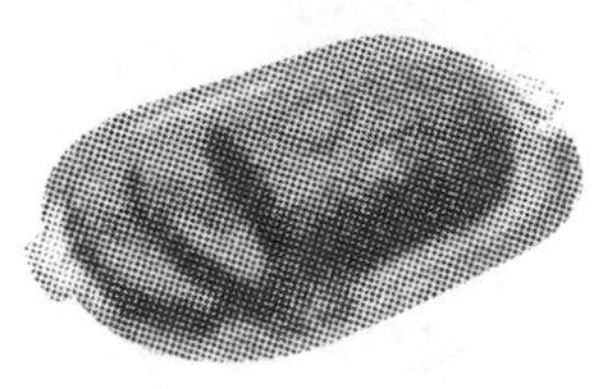

9

It was dark when Jake stamped wet footprints on the steps leading to the back porch of his house. The door was not shut all the way, and the light in the kitchen drew a swarm of night bugs to the mesh of the screen door. Jake had cupped his hands over a huge shaggy moth when his mother's voice rose from the kitchen.

"It's hard on him growing up without his dad, and it's hard on me, too. I've been doing this alone for too long."

Jake froze, feeling the moth's wings throb under the moist palms of his hands.

"He's a good boy, a very good boy, and he means well, but he always manages to get himself in trouble. His teacher, Mr. Vargas, called the other day, complaining. He said that

Jake is too impulsive. He said Jake gets these rash ideas and he can't stop himself, he has to carry them out. Must be all those comics he reads. Spy comics, by the way."

Jake opened his hands, and the moth flew up and bumped against his cheek. He swiped at it.

"And the way he rides that old bike?" his mother said. "He's covered in bruises. He's just plain reckless."

A chair creaked.

"You're making too much of it," Shubin's voice piped through the screen. "The kid's eleven."

"He's twelve."

"Right. He's twelve. Boys are like that."

"Maybe in Russia they are, but not here. I've tried everything. I put clocks in every room, made a chart for him when he needs to get up, go to school, eat, do his chores, every little thing, and still he forgets everything. He's always in a hurry, and he's always late. He's not quite . . ."

"What?"

"I don't know," said Mrs. McCauley. "He's different."

His mother and Shubin looked up when Jake swung the screen door open. They were seated at the table, dinner was served, and they were eating it, at least Shubin was, but when he saw Jake, his loaded fork halted halfway to his mouth.

"What happened, honey?" said Mrs. McCauley. "You're all wet."

Before he could answer, the screen door bounced back and whacked Jake from behind. He was not looking directly at Shubin, but he spied the Russian's left hand flying up to cover his mouth. Was he laughing at him?

"You must have been playing with Duane," said Mrs. McCauley, smiling. "Well, it's all right. Why don't you go and change into dry clothes, honey, and come back while the meatloaf is still warm?"

His mother's meatloaf was nowhere near Mrs. Armbruster's cooking, but it was the best thing she knew how to make, and now she was giving it to the Russian. Jake stood speechless, shocked by her betrayal.

"I should have told you this before, honey," said Mrs. McCauley. "From now on, Mr. Shubin will share *all* our meals." She exchanged glances with Shubin, then looked at Jake again. "Please don't just stand there, Jake. Go into your room and change your clothes as I said."

Jake did not move. The sound of his mother's cold and measured voice, the voice she used when she was annoyed with him, had always made Jake uneasy, but her speaking to him in that voice in front of the Russian felt even more like a betrayal than feeding him Jake's favorite meal.

"What is the matter, Jake?" Mrs. McCauley said. "Did you not hear me?"

Deliberately, Jake was only looking at his mother and not at the Russian, but out of the corner of his eye, he caught

Shubin making a quick and urgent gesture, moving his left hand side to side as if erasing something off the blackboard, or maybe trying to erase Mrs. McCauley's growing anger.

Jake's sodden shirt and jeans stuck to his skin, his high-tops felt slushy inside, he was cold, and all he really wanted was to change into dry clothes and have a bite of his mom's meatloaf, but having that man watching him made it impossible. Jake had to say something to him first, something clever, and something insulting, but absolutely nothing came to his mind, and he remained in place without speaking.

"You stop this silly behavior at once, Jacob McCauley!" his mother said. "Go into your room and change your clothes."

"I don't want to get in the way, ma'am." Shubin laid his fork over his plate and began to rise. "I think I better—"

"Sit down!" Mrs. McCauley shouted, and slapped the table so hard the plates leapt up.

Shubin dropped into his seat and snatched his fork again.

"I would like you to be present for this, Mr. Shubin," said Mrs. McCauley.

The way she said it was confusing. Jake knew that his mother was angry with *him,* yet there was something in her voice that told him that she was also angry with Shubin.

In the gaping silence that followed, the dishes in the cupboard began to rattle, tinkling softly at first, then violently knocking one against the other. A butter knife slid off the edge of the counter and clanked to the floor. A ceiling fixture blinked on and off and on and off again. A rolling thunder rumbled through the kitchen walls as some enormous thing roared over the roof of their house.

"What was that?" said Shubin.

"Don't answer him, Mom!" Jake dashed across the kitchen toward the hallway door. "He's trying to fool us!"

"What are you talking about?" said Mrs. McCauley, glancing at Shubin.

"*He* knows what I am talking about!" Jake stormed out and slammed the door behind him, but opened it at once and stuck his head back in. "And guess what, Mom? I'm not *different*. I'm an American! He's the one who's different, okay? He's a foreigner! So stop telling him stuff!" And then he slammed the door for good.

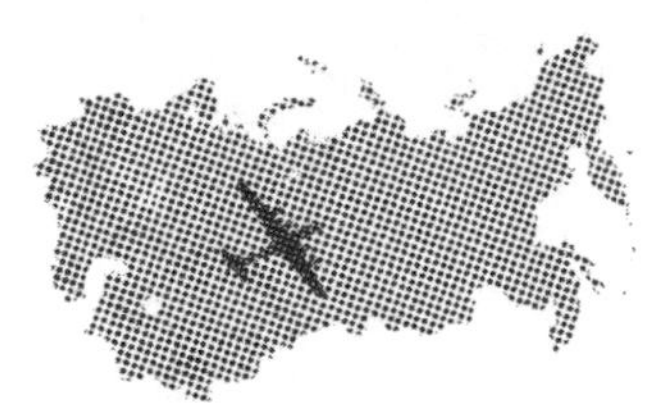

10

According to his mother's chart, a list of rules to which Jake had agreed, scrawling his signature in the bottom right corner, he was supposed to be asleep, but it was past midnight and he was nowhere near sleeping. He lay in the dark, aiming his Eveready flashlight at the model of the B-29 Superfortress suspended from the ceiling on a fishing line. Slowly spinning in the light beam, the plane looked real.

Jake raised the flashlight until the bomber's shadow slanted onto the large map tacked to the facing wall. Once folded into his father's *Great World Atlas*, the faded map was coming apart at the creases. A dotted line that Jake had drawn on the map ran west to east, from North America to Europe. Tossing the blanket aside, Jake stood up on his bed

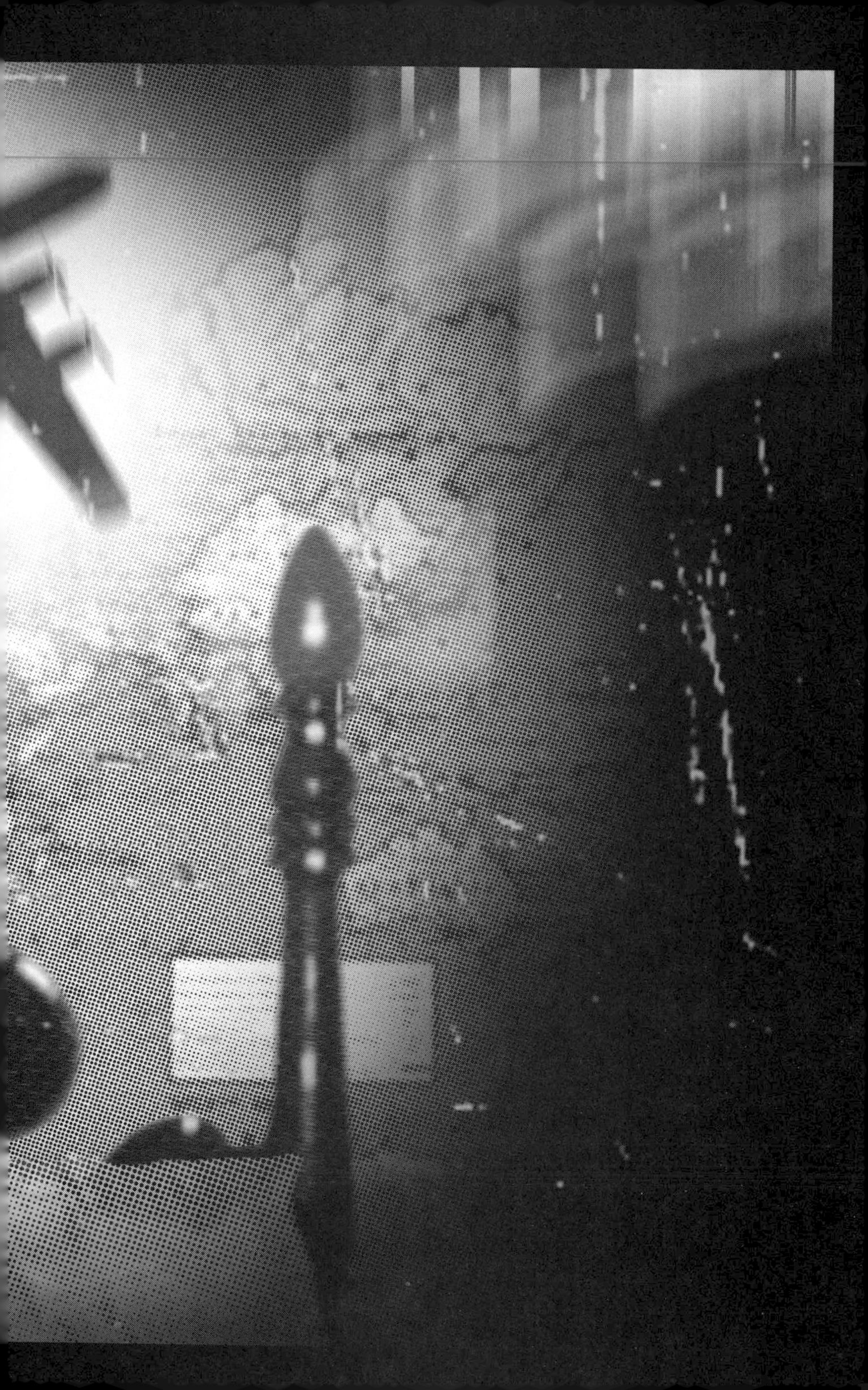

and, balancing upon the mattress springs, moved the light beam past the model bomber so that its shadow tracked the dotted line.

"Come in, Delta Alpha Delta One," he whispered. "Off the ground at twenty-four hundred hours. Roger that. Over and out."

He flew the bomber east from Arizona toward West Virginia, then left the coast north of Delaware Bay. To stretch fuel, he slowed down over the ocean, but ninety miles off the Irish coast, his wing tanks were running dry. He lost visibility and began drifting sideways, but broke through the heavy fog over London into the crisp and clear skies. Crossing the English Channel, he had engine trouble. Outside of Berlin he smashed into a cold front. The weather behind the Iron Curtain was always awful. Entering the Russian airspace, he picked up a load of ice on both wings and plunged into darkness.

"Calling Delta Alpha Delta One," he whispered, blinking at the shadow of his model bomber against the red-colored portion of the map. "Come in. Come in. Delta Alpha Delta One? Where are you?"

Every time Jake entered the Russian airspace, a faint sickness came over him. He knew that every morning at school during the Pledge of Allegiance while whispering his secret pledge to save his dad he was lying to himself. He could not save him. He was only a boy playing a game with a shadow of a toy over an old faded map. To save his dad, he would have to fly a real B-29 all the way to the Arctic Circle, where the top secret uranium mines were surrounded by guard towers and barbwire with electric current coursing through it. How could he possibly do it, if he had never even been inside the Superfortress's cockpit, let alone learned how to fly the real thing?

He heard footsteps in the hallway, then up the stairs to the attic.

The Russian!

He clicked the flashlight off and dropped onto his scrambled sheets. The door creaked open overhead, creaked closed. Shubin walked into his father's study. His footsteps were so loud, it seemed that he was in the room with Jake. With every step he took, the whole house shuddered, causing the model bomber to give little shivers on its fishing line. Jake shivered, too. On a breath of chilled air, a sick-sweet scent wafted into the room through the open window. Jake slapped the sheets beside him, looking for his blanket. It must have fallen off the bed. He rolled onto his side, snatched the blanket off the floor, and rolling back, glimpsed a dark shape behind the open window.

A man stood in the driveway.

Jake froze, hanging off the bed and clutching at the blanket. The moon was not out yet, and the man's large head and sloping shoulders, all that Jake could see of him above the windowsill, were black against the blackness of the night. The air hummed with the crickets' choir. Jake's heart pounded against his chest. The man's head moved slightly as if to look at Jake, and something flashed in its lower portion, gleaming a burnished yellow, as if the man smiled at Jake with teeth of pure gold.

Next, the doorknob squeaked, slowly turning. The door creaked open. Jake flung the blanket over himself, hiding. He screamed when someone touched him.

"Honey! What's the matter?" His mother pulled the blanket off his head and cradled him into her arms. "You're shivering." He felt her dry cool hand on his moist forehead. "I knew it, you're warm."

All at once, as if the moon were waiting for his mother to save him, the room grew lighter. A shaft of moonlight fell through the open window, shaping itself beside her feet into a slanted square. Above the crook of his mother's elbow, Jake could see the open window. Where the man with gold teeth stood a moment ago, a thick clump of hackberry swayed gently over the moonlit driveway.

"Oh, honey. Why don't you ever listen to me? I told you to change out of your wet clothes. You could catch pneumonia." Holding Jake close, his mother glanced about the room. "Better keep the window shut."

"Don't go there, Mom!" he cried, and tried to catch her by the arm, but she was at the window already. The windowpane swiveled and the reflection of the empty driveway streaked across the glass. The man was gone.

"There," said Mrs. McCauley, and then she latched the window.

Shubin's shoes banged across the room upstairs.

"Why is he stomping like an elephant?" she said. "He'll keep you up all night."

She hesitated for a moment, staring at the ceiling, then came back, sat down on the bed beside him, and lifted something off the floor. "I warmed up some meatloaf. You must be starving." The edge of the dinner plate glinted in her lap. "Let me feed you," she said. "Tell me if it's hard to swallow."

Jake leaned away from the coming fork. "I'm not sick, Mom. And I'm not hungry. It's just . . ."

"Just what?"

He nodded toward the window. "Someone was standing out there just now."

Mrs. McCauley looked over her shoulder at the window, then turned back and studied him. "Someone was standing in our driveway?"

Jake nodded.

"Who?"

"I don't know. Some guy with gold teeth."

"Gold teeth?"

She set the plate down on the floor, went back to the

window, unlatched it, and looked out, turning her head in all directions. Then she looked at him over her shoulder. "Do you want me to tell Mr. Shubin?"

"No!"

She returned, forgetting to shut the window again, and sat at the edge of the bed. "You sure you saw someone there?"

Jake looked past her at the moonlit hackberry framed by the window. "I don't know. Maybe. Maybe not."

His mother smiled, or he thought she smiled; she was just a shape against the moonlight. She took his hands in hers and held them pressed together between her palms, which were cool and soft and pleasant.

"You came to my room once in the middle of the night," she said, "just standing there, breathing, staring at me in the dark. I nearly had heart failure."

"Oh yeah? How old was I?"

"Four, I think. Four and a half."

"What did I say?"

"You said that there was an airplane waiting outside of your window. You were going to fly to Russia to look for your dad, and you wanted me to come along."

He tried but could not remember watching her sleep and felt a pang of regret but it passed quickly. It did not matter what it was like *then* because she was beside him *now*, making him feel safe. He wanted to tell her about his toy airplane, and his wall map, and his plan to save his dad, but suddenly she let go of his hands and shifted away from him. He watched her profile etched against the moonlight, still close to him and yet somehow far away. Her thin, nervous fingers were doing something in the dark, and although all Jake could see was a faint glint of her wedding ring, he knew what she was doing. She always twisted her wedding ring when she was upset about something.

"What's wrong, Mom?"

"Nothing, baby."

"It's not nothing, Mom. It's something. Tell me."

She was silent.

"It's that Russian, right?" And speaking hurriedly before she could interrupt him, he went on, "I saw a movie at Duane's house? About this Russian spy. He lied to everyone and he spied on everyone and, you know what else he did, Mom? He broke into someone's office and took pictures with his spy camera of some top secret stuff. And guess what, Mom? He looked just like that Russian upstairs, I swear, whatever his name is, Shubin or something."

His mother turned to him abruptly. Her eyes glistened so intensely in the dark that Jake didn't feel safe anymore. He felt frightened.

"Let's go to the police tomorrow, Mom! Let's go to the FBI! Let's turn him in, Mom! You think that when we were in the kitchen he didn't know it was a B-29 flying over our house? He did, Mom, he did! He knows we live next to the air force base. That's why he wants to live with us. We must get rid of him."

"No, Jake!" she cried. "Listen to me—"

Suddenly, the floorboards in the attic ceased creaking, as if their Russian tenant had stopped to hear what Mrs. McCauley was about to say to her son.

She peered at the ceiling for a moment, then leaned close to him. "Shubin is not a Communist spy, Jake," she whispered, "but it would be safer for us if you don't—"

"If I don't what?"

"If you don't talk about him to anyone. Not to Duane, not to anyone at school."

"Why?" he said, puzzled. "Why would that be safer for us?"

She leaned even closer, and he felt her lips brush his ear. "You know how people are about the Russians these days. Nobody likes them."

11

The model B-29 was the first thing Jake saw when he opened his eyes in the morning, and while he watched it slowly spin, twisting and untwisting the fishing line that fixed it to the ceiling, he wondered why he felt so miserable, but when the shadow of the bomber slanted across the map hanging on the wall, he remembered: a Russian by the name of Shubin had moved into his father's attic.

Imagining Shubin sleeping in his dad's neat old army cot made Jake sick to his stomach. He listened intently for any sounds from the attic, but the racket of the morning birds outside was too loud. Jake climbed out of bed and, tugging on his still-damp jeans, glimpsed the reflection of the driveway in the open windowpane. Last night in that driveway he saw a man standing under the hackberry tree. A man with gold teeth.

Jake hesitated, then cautiously approached the window. When he looked out, a small pearly dove flitting from a bird feeder startled him, and he quickly stepped back into the room. From there, Jake watched the feeder, a shiny yellow box shaped like a miniature house swaying from the hackberry branch, exactly where he had imagined the man's gold teeth flashing at him in the dark.

Jake began breathing again. How could he have mistaken the hackberry tree for a man and the bird feeder for his mouth full of gold teeth? It was Shubin's fault, of course. Having him up in the attic made Jake terribly suspicious.

He closed the window, latched it securely, and looked at the clock on the dresser. He was late. His mother had gone to work before it was his time to get up, and he had either forgotten to set the alarm clock last night or had managed to sleep through its ringing this morning. He finished dressing in a hurry and was halfway out of the front door when a startling thought stopped him cold. His mother said that it would be safer for them if he did not tell anyone about Shubin. What did she mean by *safer*? What kind of danger were they in?

He left the front door open and went back into the house. Quietly, he crossed the hallway toward the staircase and stood, looking up at the door to his father's attic.

The door was closed. He waited, not knowing what he was waiting for, and after a while, he crept up the staircase and pressed his ear to the door. He expected to hear Shubin snoring, but what he heard was silence. He listened for a minute, then drew away from the door. Trying to be as quiet as he could, he took a step down. As his foot landed on the stair, the door behind him slowly creaked open.

Jake froze with his hand on the banister, then cautiously looked over his shoulder into the open doorway. The morning light came into the room from a square window above his father's cot. The cot stood neatly made, as if Shubin did not sleep in it last night. Jake stepped back up on the landing, moved to the doorway, and peered into the empty room.

All of his father's wonderful things were replaced by the Russian's dreary belongings. A stack of sickly gray socks and a stack of sickly gray boxers were folded on the shelf where his dad's history books used to stand, and in place of his air force jacket, an ugly woolen coat with greasy elbows slung off the wall. His dad's beautiful glass globe with the light inside was gone, and the brass calendar was gone also. Instead, the Russian's personals—a bar of soap, a toothbrush, a comb, a safety razor—lay side by side on a towel spread at the foot of the cot.

Jake stepped in closer, gaping in disgust at the safety razor. Tiny black hairs stuck to its rusted edge reminded him of the Russian spy's bristly chin in the movie he saw at Duane's house. Instantly nauseous, he looked away and saw a suitcase slumped behind the door. Duane's voice, breathless and excited, rang through his head: *First thing you do is look inside the lining. It probably has a false bottom.*

No, Jake was not going to snoop. Leave the snooping to the Commies. He stepped back toward the door, but before he knew what he was doing, he was kneeling over the suitcase and unfastening the lock. His hands trembled with excitement. Would it not be amazing if he could expose Shubin as a Russian spy? Jake saw his name in the newspapers, front page, sensational news, and he thought of Duane dying from envy, and he thought of Major Armbruster shaking his hand, and he thought of his mom begging his forgiveness for taking in spies, and for some reason he even thought about Trudy Lamarre, the redhead from his class.

He threw the lid open. The suitcase was empty. He felt through the lining and knocked on the top and the bottom and knocked on the sides. Just in case, he yanked at the handle. Nothing.

He left the attic, ran to the kitchen, and came back holding a butter knife. He tried to make a neat cut in the suitcase lining, just wide enough to squeeze his hand in, but the knife was dull, and when he pushed in the blade, the lining ripped along the bottom edge. He tried to lift the lining, but he pulled too hard and the whole thing came off. There was nothing in between the leather and the lining. He turned the suitcase round and slashed the lining on the inside of the lid. He was not careful anymore, hacking at the fabric roughly. When he ripped the rest of the lining away, there was nothing below it either.

He rose and stood with the knife in his hand, gaping at the mutilated suitcase. Then he raised his head and looked around the room. Next, he surprised himself by snatching every stitch of Shubin's belongings and shoving them back into the suitcase where they came from.

12

Jake burst into the kitchen with the bulging suitcase under his arm, tossed the butter knife into the sink, kicked the screen door open, leapt over the back porch railing, and, dropping to his knees, shoved the suitcase under the porch into the dark and weedy hollow.

A loud crack and then another, closer, came from the street below the house. *Someone needs to fix his muffler* flashed through Jake's head. He darted to where his roadster leaned against the wall, tossed one leg over the crossbar, stood on the pedals, and flew down the driveway, sloping toward the street. Pedaling hard to build up speed, he leaned way back and yanked on the bars. The front wheel left the ground.

Shooting into the street in a perfect wheelie, he heard another loud muffler crack beside him and felt rather than saw a brown Ford pickup truck speeding at him from the left. The truck's passenger-side mirror whacked at the spokes of his bike's airborne wheel. The bike spun, flinging Jake to the ground, and crashed on top of him.

The Ford screeched to a halt, shifted gears, and, spewing clouds of smoke, sped in reverse. Jake sat on the curb beside his bike, frowning at a dark spot blooming below his left knee's denim. The truck came to a stop beside him, and a heavyset man scooted from the steering wheel toward the passenger-side window. His face, bloated and flushed, hung above the rim of the door. A pair of beady eyes, sunk behind the puffy folds, looked down at Jake with curious intensity.

Jake could not be sure, but it seemed to him that behind the stench of gasoline and rubber smoke, he caught a whiff of that sick-sweet odor he had smelled last night on the breath of midnight air. He waited for the man to say something and when he did not, Jake said, to be polite, "It's all right, sir. I'm okay."

The man nodded, curling his thick upper lip into a frightful grin. His teeth were capped in gold.

Something happened in the pit of Jake's stomach. An icy hand snatched at his insides, and while the man scooted back behind the steering wheel, and while the engine whined, and while the tires spun in place, the icy hand held tightly on to Jake's insides. The truck fired a burst of sparks out of its muffler and squealed around the corner and out of sight.

Jake sat quietly on the curb, longer maybe than he had ever sat before without moving. No, it was not the hackberry bush with the yellow bird feeder he saw outside of his window last night. He saw that man. That very man.

Jake rose carefully, carefully lifted his bike, and carefully walked it up the street toward the Armbrusters' house. He must tell Duane everything. About what Jake had done to the suitcase, and about the man with gold teeth, and about his mother telling him to keep Shubin a secret. Duane would know what to do. He was smart. It was because of Duane, of course, that Jake nose-dived into the pool, but Jake was not going to hold a grudge against him, the only person Jake could trust.

He left his bike by the curb in front of the Armbrusters' house, walked up the gravel path, climbed the front porch steps, and rang the doorbell. In the sudden gust of wind from the desert, the American flag to his left snapped against the post.

"What do you want?" said Mrs. Armbruster, opening the door.

Her voice sounded so harsh that at first, Jake did not recognize her. "Who? Me?" he said, surprised. "I want Duane."

"Go away." She slammed the door.

Astonished, Jake gaped at the door slammed inches from his nose. He rang the bell again and, just in case, stepped back a little.

"What?" said Mrs. Armbruster, opening the door.

"It's me, ma'am, Jake McCauley. Don't you recognize me?"

She didn't answer.

"Where's Duane?"

"What do you want with him?"

"What do I want, ma'am? We always ride to school together. You know that."

"He's left already."

Jake stood, speechless, gaping at Mrs. Armbruster. She began closing the door, but halted, frowning at something on the ground. He followed her gaze. From under the rolled-up leg of his jeans, a red streak was making its way onto the rubber mat below his feet. His knee was bleeding.

"Sorry, ma'am." Jake smeared the pooled blood across the word WELCOME with the sole of his sneaker. When he glanced back up at Mrs. Armbruster, the expression on her face was different.

"Wait here, lamb," she said in her regular voice. "I'll get a Band-Aid."

"Thank you, ma'am," Jake said. "But I'm late already. I better go."

He turned away and walked to the curb where his bike stood leaning on the kickstand.

"Jacob?" called out Mrs. Armbruster.

He turned around.

"Is it true that your mother let a Communist into your house?"

Jake thought about it. He did not really know. He got on his bike and swung into the street and pedaled away, feeling the whole time that Mrs. Armbruster was watching him until he turned the corner.

13

It was late in the morning and there should have been motorcars and trucks on the blacktop shimmering across the desert floor, but the road was empty. Jake had never ridden to school without Duane before. The spooky emptiness surrounding him brought forth the nagging feeling that the bad things that had begun to happen since Shubin's arrival were only the beginnings of worse things yet to come.

At last a city bus passed him, working hard to climb uphill. The driver leaned out of the window and looked at Jake without expression. A row of empty windows rattled by. In a low growl of gears, the bus mounted the slope, then dipped out of sight. Jake was squinting into the distance, waiting for the bus to show up ahead, when the sound of another vehicle gaining on him from behind caught his ear. He did not turn around, expecting the motorcar to pass him. It did not. Jake listened to the engine's steady hum behind his back. Soon he was convinced that the gold-toothed fellow who nearly drove him over in front of Jake's house was now following him in his truck. Jake could never outride the truck on his roadster, but he panicked and dashed forward. Strangely, the truck neither tried to catch up with him nor cut him off. It took Jake a while to gather courage to glance over his shoulder. When he did, he saw not the gold-toothed fellow's truck behind him but a two-door Buick, black, not one of the latest models.

Jake exhaled in relief, slowed down, and looked over his shoulder again. He could not make out the driver behind the sunlit windshield, but the way the Buick dawdled at about a hundred yards behind him made Jake instantly suspicious. The nagging feeling that worse things were yet to come returned to him at once. The Buick was tailing him on purpose. To test it, Jake slowed down, rolled for a while in lazy half circles, then quickly glanced over his shoulder. The gap between his bike and the Buick remained the same, about a hundred yards. Jake stood on the pedals, leaned forward over the bars, and hauled fast, but the same hundred yards remained between them.

Certain now that he was under surveillance, he tried to show to whoever was driving the Buick that he was not afraid to be followed. He switched to one steady speed, fast but not too fast, hoping that if he could only stop looking over his shoulder, the Buick might somehow disappear, but he kept looking, and the Buick kept following him at a hundred yards behind.

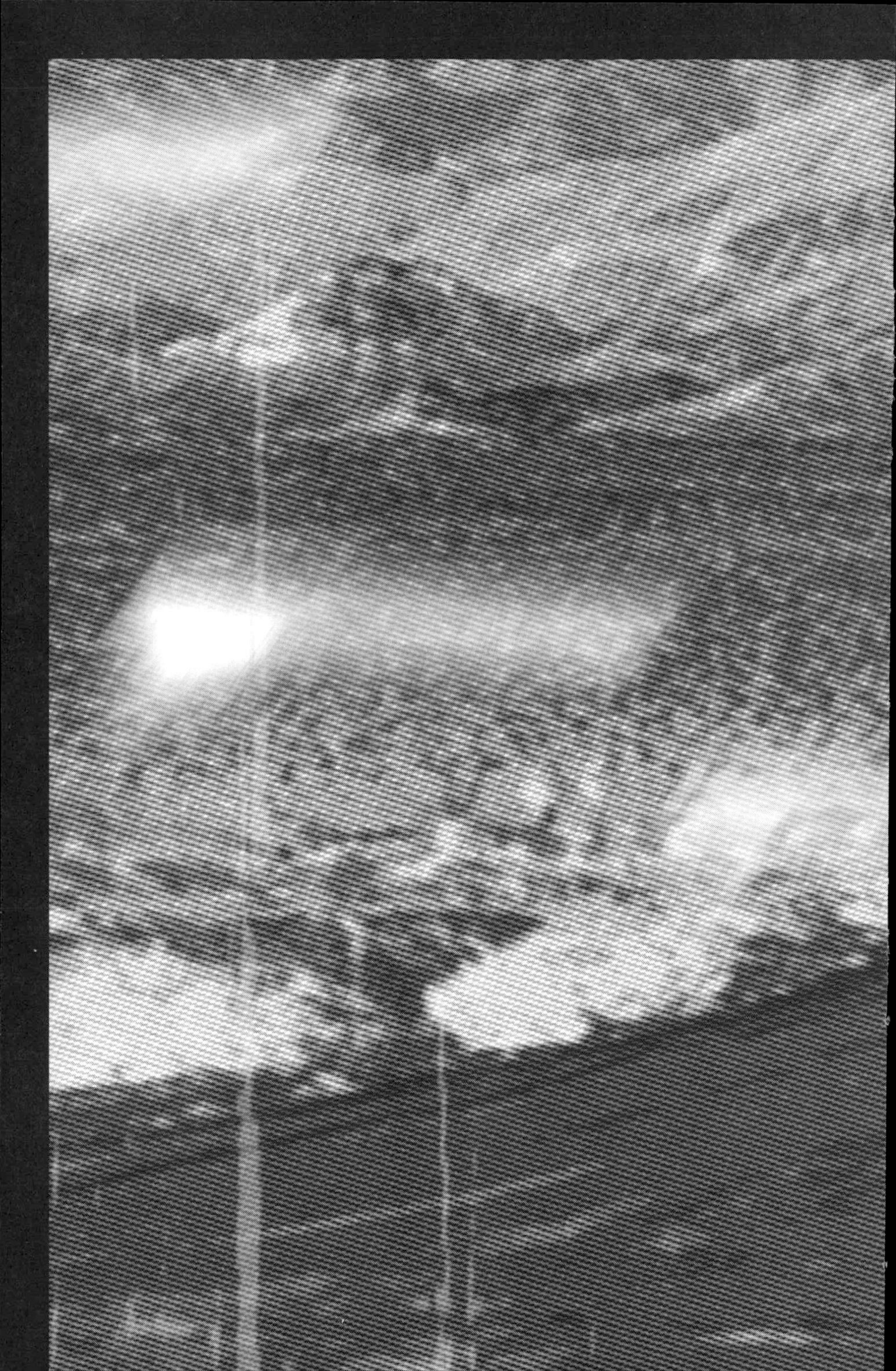

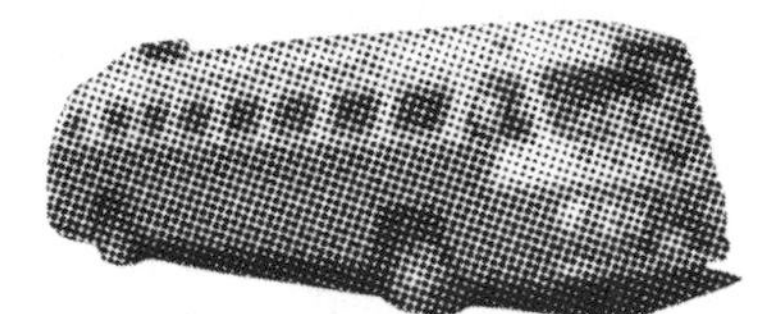

14

Then up ahead, Jake saw the same city bus warped in the haze of the shimmering heat. It rose over the sloping blacktop and dipped out of sight. It rose again, closer. The bus had made it by then to the end of the line and was doubling back downtown. The driver was in no hurry, and it took the bus a long time to pass Jake in the opposite direction. By the time they were side by side, Jake had a plan.

The bus driver looked at him, bored, and looked away. As the bus rumbled past, Jake made a sharp U-turn into the cloud of exhaust uncoiling behind it. His rear tire slid on the turn; the bike fishtailed and leaned close to the ground. Jake swung his bars to the right, kicked at the blacktop with his left foot, and came up level. He did not wait to see if the Buick would also make a U-turn, but sped around to the right side of the bus to shield himself from view. If he could stay covered until the bus stopped downtown, he would have no trouble losing the Buick there.

Jake could ride fast—that part was easy—but he had no room to ride in. The bus was crowding him toward the ditch to his right. Besides, the motor smoke was so noxious that everything before Jake's eyes became awash in tears: the bus, the blacktop, and the ditch all blurred together. Bouncing over the blacktop's crumbling edge, the bike was bucking like a bronco, and Jake rode standing to avoid the jabbing seat.

Speed had never failed to cheer him up, and this ride was so crazy and so fast that soon Jake's heart was pounding not with fear but with joy. He made his roadster leap over a wide crack in the concrete and, for one thrilling and breathtaking moment, he floated suspended in midair. Jake's face lit up with a smile.

On landing, his bike's rusted chain snapped in two, and while Jake's feet cycled loose and useless pedals, he lost control of the bike and fell sideways into the moving bus. His shoulder slammed into the greasy rivets, and he began sliding down. Powerless, he saw the rear tire of the bus: black, enormous, spinning, smoking, flinging pebbles, growing larger and larger, rapidly closing in. If he hit the blacktop now, that monstrous tire would make a pancake out of him. He dropped the bars, twisted toward the bus, and shoved with both hands off its blackened sidewall. In a dizzying flash, he saw his roadster bouncing into the gaping ditch, he saw the bus slanting away, he saw the crumbling blacktop rising, and then the sun hit his eyes, blinding him.

Next thing he knew, he was sitting in the ditch, coughing up dust. A dozen feet away, his bike lay on its side, wheels spinning. Jake rubbed dirt out of his eyes, climbed up to the edge of the ditch, and cautiously peeked out. The bus was rumbling away in the distance. The Buick was nowhere in sight.

"Come in, Delta Alpha Delta One," Jake said. "Mission accomplished. Over and out."

He wished that Delta Alpha Delta One—which stood for his *dad*, of course—could see him at that moment. How smartly he outran that Buick, how fast he was, how brave. When Jake was proud of something he had done, he had often seen himself as if from some distance, as if he were watching himself through his father's eyes.

"Delta Alpha Delta One," he repeated, and felt something lodged behind his cheek. His tongue moved the object to the front of his mouth, and he spat it out. A tooth lay in the palm of his hand. He stuck his finger in his mouth and found the hole and gently poked at it. The edges of the hole were sharp and hurt a little, and when he took the finger out, it was bloody. He spat the blood and wiped his lips and stuck the tooth into the pocket of his jeans.

By the time Jake found a spare pin in his messy saddlebag, fixed the chain, straightened the wheels, and hauled the roadster out of the ditch, the black two-door Buick with its motor running was waiting for him a hundred yards down the road.

15

The first thing Jake saw when he swung into the school's parking lot was Duane's Schwinn Phantom neatly stowed inside the bike rack. Behind Jake, the Buick that had followed him as he rode away from the ditch until he arrived at the school slowed to a stop and stood idling across the street. Forcing himself not to be in a rush, he set his bike into the rack alongside Duane's Phantom, strolled leisurely up the pathway toward the school's front door, skipped up a few concrete steps, drew the door open, and only as he slipped into the hallway did he let himself peek over his shoulder.

The Buick was gone.

Jake bolted up the hallway, cool and dark after the blazing sun outside. The hallway was lined with bruised metal lockers. Most of the lockers were closed, but some doors swung open, and Jake slammed the doors shut with his fist as he ran. Each time he hit one, a hollow thud rolled through the hallway. The linoleum was freshly waxed, and Jake took corners sliding on one foot, then ran again, leaping over a water pail left behind by the janitor.

He halted beside the door to Mr. Vargas's classroom to catch his breath and stuck his finger into the hole left by the tooth that was now in his pocket. The hole still hurt a little, but not too bad, and there was no more blood. He beat the dust off the front of his shirt and the knees of his jeans, took a deep breath, and as quietly as he could, slipped into the classroom.

The window blinds were tightly shut, and the ceiling lights were off. The classroom was dark. He could not see his classmates, but in the stifling air of the room, he felt the heat of their bodies and of their common breath. While he waited for his eyes to adjust to the dark, something began rattling in the back of the center aisle, and a flickering ray, beaming thinly out of the movie projector, cleaved the darkness and lit up a bright white square to his right.

"How kind of you to show up at last, McCauley," Mr. Vargas's voice rose from the dark. "Go sit down."

Dipping in and out of the light beam, Jake went down the aisle, glancing left and right at his classmates. To his surprise, no one looked at him, and no one greeted him as he passed. Everyone's eyes were fixed upon the screen. He glanced over his shoulder, worried that he was missing something important, but the movie had not begun yet. White scratches and numbers were flashing inside the flickering square.

He dropped into his seat and nudged Duane's elbow. "A car just followed me," he whispered. "No kidding. A black Buick." He pulled his tooth out of the pocket of his jeans and pushed it across the desk toward Duane. "Tried to make a run for it, but busted a chain just like you said. Couldn't lose them, but look—cracked a tooth."

Duane moved his elbow away and, paying Jake's tooth zero attention, kept his eyes on the screen. Jake studied his profile for a moment, confused.

"Listen, bud," he whispered, "I nose-dived into the pool, okay? You didn't. So it's not *you* who ought to be unfriendly."

"Settle down, McCauley," said Mr. Vargas from the dark.

"Yes, sir." Jake nodded in the direction of Vargas's voice and leaned into Duane again. "No false bottom in his suitcase."

"McCauley!" said Mr. Vargas.

Jake shoved the tooth back into his pocket, peered at Duane for a moment, then turned to the screen when someone's voice crackled in the movie, "How prepared are we if Russia should attack?"

A gray bomber was flying low over the frozen sea. The bomber looked exactly like the B-29 Superfortress, but it carried a star on its fin. *TU-4* flashed through Jake's mind. What did Duane call it? Oh, yes, reverse engineering. He leaned into Duane to tell him that the bomber on the screen was one of those knockoffs the Russians had made, but instead he heard himself whisper, "What's the idea leaving for school without me? Your mom—"

"McCauley!" cried Mr. Vargas. "I'm giving you one last chance."

"Yes, sir. Sorry, sir."

Jake narrowed his eyes at Duane, who still refused to look at him. *Well, fine.* Jake could play this game, too. He scraped his chair far away from Duane's, leaned back, and, folding his arms against his chest, peered at the screen. Who did Duane think he was anyhow? He would have to beg Jake to tell him about the crazy chase he had with the Buick. Could Duane do it on his perfect Schwinn? Not on his life. Thinking about the Buick made Jake uneasy, and once again the feeling that worse things were yet to come began to nag at him. To distract himself, he tried to focus on the screen, where, inside the cockpit of the Russian bomber, the goggled and leather-helmeted crew was leaning over their instruments. *"Target in sight, Comrade Commander,"* one of them crackled. *"Set detonator,"* another fellow crackled back. *"Detonator set,"* the first fellow answered. *"Release safety." "Safety off."*

The movie began showing New York City—the skyscrapers, the Statue of Liberty, people crossing the street in a hurry, women in the park rolling babies in strollers, stuff they always showed when they showed New York. Then up in the gray, grainy sky above the skyscrapers, the Russian bomber came into sight.

"Nuclear device fused for ground burst, Comrade Commander," the first voice crackled again.

"Stand by for the bomb release," the second voice responded.

At that moment, something stung Jake on the cheek. His hand darted to his face, and he turned around, startled. No one was looking at him, but on the desk beside his elbow, he saw a wadded paper ball. Jake looked in the direction from where it might have been fired. Eddie Cortes. Or Tony Gonzales. Both sat still, watching the movie. He unrolled the ball, smoothed the rumpled paper, and stared at the words scrawled in red pencil.

Jake McCauley is a Communist!

A second paper ball thumped against his neck. He swung

around and glared at Vernon and Dean. They were watching the movie. Crumpling the note in his fist, Jake glared at Duane's profile. Even in the dark, he could see Duane's cheeks flare up.

"You dirty traitor," Jake whispered. "You told them about the Russian in my house."

Something flashed from the direction of the screen. The light bounced off the ceiling, and the darkened room throbbed with blinding brightness. At the sound of the blast, a dull thud went through Jake's chest as if someone had punched him in the solar plexus. On the screen, above a boiling stem of flame and smoke, a huge white ball was swelling to a giant mushroom. With astonishing timing, the school siren went off in the hallway.

"It's a drill, children," Mr. Vargas said calmly. "Duck and cover."

When Jake turned back, Duane's chair was empty. Jake plunged to the floor. Duane was gone. Jake looked around, trying to spot him through the bodies scrambling below their desks.

"Stay down until the alarm is turned off, children," said Mr. Vargas. "Remember, you're safe under your desks."

The mushroom cloud on the screen lit up the room in snatches of bright flashes. For an instant, Jake caught sight of Duane crawling through the aisle on hands and knees.

Jake sprung up and, slicing through the projector's light beam, fell on top of him.

"McCauley!" cried Mr. Vargas. "What do you think you're doing?"

Duane was on his back, flailing his arms, and Jake, straddling his chest, leaned away so as not to be hit in the face. He caught Duane's right hand by the wrist and held it, unsure of what to do with it. His burst of anger had passed. Duane yanked his hand from Jake and when he let it go, Duane's fist bounced back, whacking himself hard on the nose.

"Mr. Vargas! Mr. Vargas!" Trudy Lamarre screeched from under the desk beside them. "Come here! Quick!"

Someone pulled Jake off Duane. Eddie Cortes pounced, punching Jake in the belly and chest. Other boys fell on top of him.

"Give it to the Commie!"

"Let him have it!"

"Dirty Communist!"

Jake thrashed under the blows of the boys' sharp fists and knees and elbows. The siren blared. Mr. Vargas hollered. The screen throbbed in flashes. Jake's foot shot from under Vernon sitting on his legs and kicked the table holding the projector. The mushroom cloud on the screen froze in mid-explosion and slid sideways, bubbling to a boil. The film, stuck in the projector's gate, was melting. At its center a gaping hole spread rapidly, devouring the A-bomb mushroom.

The siren broke off abruptly. The ceiling lights went on. The boys scattered, leaving Jake rolled into a quivering ball in the aisle.

"McCauley?" cried Mr. Vargas. "What have you done to Armbruster?"

"He whacked him on the nose, sir," said Trudy Lamarre. "I saw it."

Duane was sitting on the floor with his chin up and his hand pressed to his nose to stem the bleeding, but the blood was everywhere, running down his arm, soaking the front of his shirt, and spotting his knees.

"I've had enough of you, McCauley," said Mr. Vargas. "To the principal."

16

The principal's office was on the second floor, but Jake was in no rush getting there. His knee was bleeding again, and his belly felt funny from Eddie's punches. He slumped on the floor, cooling his sweaty back against a metal locker. Sharp, hollow sounds of a basketball game came from behind the double doors to the gym at the end of the hallway. Shrilling whistles, shrieking voices, sneakers squeaking over the varnished floor. At each thud of the ball, dust motes hovering inside a sunbeam slanting from a window across the hallway gave a little shiver. Jake thought of his model bomber giving little shivers when Shubin was stomping above him in the attic. What happened in the classroom happened because of Shubin. Because of that thin, gray, nearsighted Russian who had invaded his dad's attic, Jake's life at school was ruined. The words scrawled in red pencil flashed through his mind. *Jake McCauley is a Communist!* He? A Communist? How stupid it was and how unfair.

The long hand of the wall clock twitched toward the hour. Twenty minutes to recess. Clapping and cheering came from the gym. One of the teams must have scored. Jake cared little for basketball, but suddenly he felt like weeping. Who would want him now on the basketball team? Who would want to play with him, sit next to him, laugh at his jokes?

He sprung to his feet with a sudden urge to run away from here, away from his shame, away from his swelling tears. The dust motes inside the sunbeam sparkled and reeled before his face. He swiped at them and bolted up the hallway.

"Halt!" someone cried as Jake pulled at the door. "Forbidden to exit!"

Startled, he turned, letting the doorknob slip from under his hand. The door slammed closed, resounding through the hallway. Principal Hirsch emerged from the sunbeam, charging at Jake with a hurried and menacing stride.

"I can explain, sir—" Jake began, but the principal yanked him away from the door.

"Not to me, yes? They're waiting!"

"Who's waiting?"

Mr. Hirsch grasped Jake under the upper arm and dragged him back up the hallway and up the staircase, barking at each step, "Right! Left! Right! Left!" as if he were an army sergeant drilling a private.

"You're hurting me, sir!"

"Hurting?" Mr. Hirsch cackled and drew Jake across the second-floor landing, using him to bust the hallway door wide open.

"Ouch!"

Two eighth graders sauntered out of the boys' room, saw Mr. Hirsch hauling Jake toward his office, and ducked back in.

Mr. Hirsch had come from Germany after the war. Once, when he rolled his shirtsleeves to wash his hands in the schoolyard, Jake saw something written on the inside of his forearm. Blue numerals, five or six in a row. Duane said that the number was tattooed on his arm when the Nazis put Mr. Hirsh in a death camp. Jake couldn't make up his mind whether that was really true. If Mr. Hirsch made it out of the Nazi death camp, he should have been happy. Instead, the principal was the angriest person Jake had ever met in his life.

Mr. Hirsch swung Jake toward the door to his office. Holding him flat against the wall at arm's length, he said,

"I have this school to answer for? Yes? My pleasure to expel you."

"Why, sir? I didn't do anything wrong."

"He makes me laugh," Mr. Hirsch said, not laughing. "Did Principal Hirsch miss today the Pledge of Allegiance or did student McCauley?"

"Well, you see, sir—"

"Don't tell me, McCauley. Tell them."

"Tell who, sir?"

Ignoring the question, Mr. Hirsch planted his ear against the door to his office and stood, listening, with his eyes closed. His droopy, clean-shaved face was purple and drenched in sweat. It hit Jake that Mr. Hirsch was not angry at all. He was scared.

"You want to stay in my school, McCauley," whispered Mr. Hirsch, rapping on the door, "prove to them that you are a loyal citizen."

"Enter," a voice said inside the office.

Mr. Hirsch opened the door just wide enough to squeeze Jake in, nudged him through the gap, and shut the door behind him.

17

The electric fan atop a steel cabinet lurched side to side with sudden clucking jerks, pushing the overheated air back and forth across the room. The American flag in the corner stirred and flapped against the wall each time the whirring blades swung in its direction, then drooped again when the fan lurched away. Mr. Hirsch's office was small, but the two square-shaped fellows sitting shoulder to shoulder behind the principal's desk made it look even smaller. The fellows looked remarkably alike, with their matching buzz cuts, matching square jaws, and matching suits stretched tightly across their massive matching chests.

When Jake was shoved into the room and the door behind him closed, two sets of matching X-ray eyes bored right through him. He flinched and quickly looked away, and while the matching fellows studied him, Jake studied his broken-down high-tops. The silence in the room seemed to go on forever until the chair creaked under one of the fellows. "Care for some chewing gum, McCauley?"

Jake glanced up at him quickly, then looked down again. "No, sir. Thank you, sir."

"I'll take one," the other fellow said, and while they unwrapped the gum, and folded the sticks over their tongues, and worked their massive jaws in silence, Jake felt their X-ray eyes fixed squarely on him. A sharp scent of Doublemint made him a little sick.

"Name's Bader," said the one on the left. "Agent Bader. And this here is Agent Bambach."

"Federal Bureau of Investigation," the fellow called Agent Bambach said. "Grab a seat, son. Let's have a chat."

Jake's knees gave out under him, and he dropped into a chair. They were G-men. That's what the FBI agents were called in the comics, G-men, short for *government men*. The Communist hunters.

"Chat about what?" Jake said in a small voice.

"If you are a loyal citizen, as we think you are," said Agent Bader, "you ought to know."

"If it's about what Duane says . . . he's full of it. I'm no Communist. He's the one who's a traitor."

"Duane who?" Agent Bambach said.

"Duane Armbruster, who else?"

Agent Bambach scribbled something on a square pad before him. "That'd be Major Armbruster's son. Correct? Your neighbor?"

"You didn't talk to Duane? How do you know about the Russian, then?"

"It's our job to know such things," said Agent Bambach smugly. "What did you say that Russian fellow's name was?"

"I didn't say."

"So what is his name?"

"Why ask me? Ask my mom. She rented him my dad's room."

"And where's he, Jake?" said Agent Bader.

"Where's who?"

"Your father."

Jake glanced at him quickly. Could these G-men get his dad out of Russia? They were government men, were they not? Fighting the threat of Communism? It was worth a try.

"My dad didn't come back from the war, sir. Went MIA, missing in action somewhere in Europe. That's what the letter from the air force says." He paused and looked from one G-man to the other. "Only I don't think it's true."

Both fellows glared at him severely, and Jake lowered his eyes, worried that he should not have said that. He was staring at his high-tops and yet somehow he also saw the G-men, weighing heavily upon him with their massive chests, both huge and still and solid, as if they were chiseled out of rock like those presidents on Mount Rushmore. Nothing moved on their flat, clean-shaved faces, not a twitch of a muscle, not a blink of an eye, and when the fan whirred in their direction, not a hair stirred in their flattops.

"So what are you saying, son?" Agent Bambach said fiercely. "The United States Air Force is lying?"

"No, sir. I didn't say the air force was lying, sir. They just don't know where he is, that's all."

The G-men seemed to relax a little.

"Fair enough," agreed Bader. "Let's go back to that Russian fellow. What's your take on him?"

"Why don't you talk to my mom, sir? She took him in."

"We've talked to her, Jake," said Agent Bambach. "And now we are talking to you."

Jake looked up, interested. "Oh, yeah? What did she say?"

"She said she was expecting your full cooperation with the FBI," said Agent Bader.

"You don't want to disappoint your mother, now, do you, Jake?" said Agent Bambach.

To disappoint his mother? No matter what he did, his mother always seemed to be disappointed in him. *Well, guess what, Mom?* It was Jake's turn to be disappointed.

"Okay," Jake said. "What do you want to hear?"

"Just how much do you know about that Russian fellow?"

"The Russian fellow?" Jake repeated, and scratched his head. "Well."

His mother said not to talk about Shubin to anyone, but thanks to Duane, the whole school knew about him by now. And did his mother lie to these fellows when they asked *her* about Shubin? No, not his mom. Besides, cutting up Shubin's suitcase and hiding his stuff under the porch was stupid and childish. It would hardly make him move out. If Jake really wanted to get rid of the Russian for good, he should be smarter than that. Jake looked up at the G-man and said a little too loud, "His name is Victor Shubin, sir. He's a Russian spy."

For the first time since Jake had entered the room, the agents shifted their X-ray eyes off him to exchange glances, and Jake knew he had them now. He quickly followed with, "You better arrest him, sir, before he starts stealing our secrets. We live next door to the air force base, sir. That's why he moved in with us, see?"

The G-men looked at him severely again, and Jake began to worry that he had gone too far again. He could not meet their gaze. His ears were burning.

"This is a serious allegation, Jake," said Agent Bader. "Do you have evidence of Mr. Shubin's subversive activities in the United States?"

"You want evidence? Sure. I can find where he hides his stuff."

"What stuff?" said Agent Bambach.

"His spy stuff, sir." He tried to remember what Duane had told him. "A shortwave radio, and an umbrella that's like a gun that shoots bullets, and poison, and cameras, and film, and stuff like that. Well, isn't it your job to know such things?"

The G-men were silent, and Jake knew that he definitely went too far this time. The hole from the missing tooth in his mouth began to hurt him so badly, he stuck his tongue inside it to soothe the pain. It did not help.

"Let me give you a piece of advice, son," said Agent Bambach, leaning with his massive chest across the desk. "You want to be helpful to the FBI, you stay away from Shubin, you hear?"

"Do not talk to him," said Agent Bader, "and talk to no one about him."

"And don't go into his room again," said Agent Bambach. "What did you ruin his suitcase for?"

Jake looked up at him in astonishment. How did he know?

"Quit playing detective, son," Agent Bambach went on, peering fiercely at him. "You're not cut out for the job. Keep to your homework and leave the grown-up business to us."

"Okay, okay," said Agent Bader. "You're scaring the pants off him." He smiled at Jake. "You are a clever boy, right? Clever? So just stay away from the Russian, that's all you have to do."

"Stay away?"

"Yeah, that's it," Agent Bambach said. "You got it."

"Naturally, if you see or hear anything suspicious," said Agent Bader, "you report to us at once."

"About the Russian?"

"About anything," said Agent Bader.

Anything? How about the black Buick following him today? How about the gold-toothed fellow snooping around the house?

"You heard the man," snapped Agent Bambach. "Whatever comes up, you tell us. Is that clear, or do you want me to draw you a picture?"

Jake looked at the two matching bullies with their matching flattops and their matching suits and knew that he was going to tell them nothing. Let them figure it out if they were so good at it. They figured out the suitcase, right?

"Call this number," said Agent Bader, "or come see us in person."

As if on cue, the agents whipped out two matching cards engraved with their names and lined them up along the edge of the desk. The electric fan lurched toward them, and the hot air current lifted the cards off the desk and sent them spinning and fluttering back into their faces.

18

When Jake stepped into the hallway, the principal caught him by the arm, drew him away from the door, and whispered, "What was said, McCauley?"

"Not sure, sir." Jake looked up at Mr. Hirsch's sweat-drenched face. "They gave me these cards."

He offered the principal the cards, but he would not touch them. The cards were as identical as the men themselves, but one had SPECIAL AGENT A. A. BAMBACH engraved on it and the other, SPECIAL AGENT B. B. BADER. Both said FEDERAL BUREAU OF INVESTIGATION.

"If I see or hear anything suspicious, sir, I have to report to them at once."

"Report to them?" Mr. Hirsch wrenched a handkerchief

out of his breast pocket. "Naturally, McCauley, naturally. It's your duty as a loyal citizen to report, yes?"

For a moment, Jake thought that the principal was about to start crying. "Will they stay in there a while longer or were they about to go?" he said, mopping his face with a handkerchief.

"Why don't you go in and ask them yourself, sir? It's your office."

"Why interfere, yes? I'll wait here awhile."

Mr. Hirsch tried to shove the handkerchief back into his breast pocket but missed, and the handkerchief slipped through his trembling fingers. He lunged after it, staggered, spun his arms in two large circles to regain balance, buckled at the waist, and sat down hard on the floor.

Jake squatted next to him. "Are you okay, sir?"

Mr. Hirsch's eyes rolled up in his head, showing yellowish whites spiderwebbed with blood vessels, and he began falling backward. Jake caught him.

"You look sick, sir. Should I call the nurse?"

The principal blinked, and his eyeballs slid down. He looked at Jake, as if surprised to see him, and then he looked at the wall, no more than three feet away.

"It's all right, McCauley. I'll just rest here a minute."

He tried to scoot toward the wall and began falling, sideways now, but Jake managed to catch him again.

"Thank you, McCauley." Mr. Hirsch gripped Jake's hand. "Thank you kindly. Just help me to the wall, my boy."

Jake dragged Mr. Hirsch toward the wall. He was not as heavy as Jake thought he would be. The principal clutched Jake's hand, and when they got to the wall, Mr. Hirsch glanced over his shoulder to judge the distance, cautiously leaned back, and only when his shoulders were propped safely against the wall did he let Jake's hand go.

"I also have to say, McCauley," he whispered, "last week they accused the janitor at Las Vistas Elementary of being a Communist, and they fired him and the principal. At Palo Verde, the English teacher turned out to be a Communist, too. They said that she was poisoning the minds of our youth. They fired her and two other teachers, friends of hers, and they fired the principal."

"But we have no Communists here, sir. They won't fire you."

"I'm just a little worried, my boy, that's all," he said, searching Jake's eyes. "That's how it all started in Germany, you know."

"What started, sir?"

Mr. Hirsch smiled weakly. "Never mind, McCauley. You run back to your class, yes? And don't miss the Pledge of Allegiance tomorrow, you promise?"

19

By the time the bell exploded for recess and the classroom doors burst open, resounding through the hallways like cannon fire, Jake was speeding away from the school on his roadster. To go back to the classroom was out of the question. Not after the interrogation by the G-men, and not after the beating by his classmates, and above all, not after that A-bomb movie. The hatred in his classmates' eyes watching him leave the room on his way to the principal astonished him. It was as if *he*, Jake McCauley, had dropped the A-bomb on New York and not those Commies in the stolen American bomber.

And then there was Mr. Hirsch. What did he mean when he said, *That's how it all started in Germany*? In

Germany, the Nazis had tattooed a number on his forearm and threw him behind the death camp's barbwire. Such a horrible thing could never happen in America. Or could it?

In moments like these, Jake missed his father terribly. His dad, who had fought the Nazis in Germany, would have explained to him what Mr. Hirsch was talking about.

Maybe Jake should have asked the G-men to help him find his dad. He could have told them about the radio program he heard, and about his dad being imprisoned by the Russians, and about the letter Jake wrote that went unanswered. But would those G-men, with their faces carved out of a rock and their X-ray eyes, believe him? And suddenly the story about his dad in the Russian mines seemed unbelievable even to Jake. Why was he lying to himself? He made that story up just to keep hoping his dad was alive. The thought stunned him. His heart was racing, and something happened to his vision. The mountains, the desert, and the blacktop began to throb in time with his violently beating heart. The same nagging feeling he felt in the morning that the worst was yet to come overwhelmed him, and before he even looked over his shoulder, he knew that the black Buick was following him again.

He glimpsed two dark shapes behind the dusty windshield. Who they might be or why they were tailing him, he was too scared to think about. He rode faster, knowing the Buick would speed up, too. It did. The distance between them did not change, about a hundred yards apart.

The cards that the G-men gave him were in the right front pocket of his jeans. He felt the cards fold and unfold as his foot pushed on the pedal, then rose with it. At least, he should have told the G-men about the Buick. Report, they said, anything suspicious. If he could take a closer look at the Buick's license plate and try to memorize it, he could telephone the G-men's number on the card and report the vehicle. Whatever Mr. Hirsch might have said to him, Jake lived in America, not Nazi Germany. It was the G-men's duty to protect him.

Abruptly, he wrenched the bars to the side and skidded to a halt to face the Buick. Squealing brakes, the Buick fish-tailed, blue smoke billowing from under the tires. Someone ducked out of sight behind the side glass, and when the Buick sped away in reverse, Jake's eyes shot to the front of the bumper.

The license plate was missing.

At about a hundred yards away, the Buick came to a stop with its engine running and the sun blasting at its windshield. Jake leaned over the bars, dry spat at the scorched asphalt, and wiped his mouth with the back of his hand. In the distance, the mountains shimmered in the heated air, and in the sky above the shimmer, a tiny bomber shone so far away Jake could not hear the sound of its engines.

He rode home slowly, not looking over his shoulder even once. The Buick growled steadily behind him. When at last Jake saw his house, the garage door was open, but his mother's car was not inside. Afraid that the Buick might follow him into the driveway, he shot up the buckled concrete, turned the house corner, and leapt off the bike without braking. The roadster fell on its side, sliding through the dusty weeds. When its wheels whacked into the fence, Jake was already in the house. He locked the kitchen door, flew through the hallway, and locked the front door, ramming the chain guard inside the keeper. He dashed to the window and, panting, peered in between the lowered slats. The street was empty.

20

Jake found the trunk with his father's things that his mother and Shubin had removed from the attic under an old canvas tarp behind the garage. The trunk was heavy, but he decided to haul it upstairs instead of carrying a few pieces at a time, worried that he might drop and damage the precious things. It took hard work to drag the trunk into the house, and through the hallway, and up the steps into the attic, but he did it in record time and he felt proud of himself.

The door to his father's study was wide open the way Jake had left it. He heaved the trunk over the threshold into the empty room, opened the lid and took out his father's books, his maps, his jacket, and his glass globe with the light inside, and carefully placed every object exactly where it used to stand. He swiveled the desk calendar to the day his dad went to war and one day before Jake's first birthday and set it on the chair by the cot where it had always stood. He dragged the trunk out onto the landing, went back inside the room, and stood, looking around with a sense of great accomplishment until he saw a pair of Shubin's shoes peeking from below the cot that he must have missed in the morning. Jake's sense of great accomplishment instantly vanished. The shoes looked suspicious, huddled together with their scuffed toes pointed inward. Jake thought of Major Armbruster's oxfords cut from American mirror-like leather, squeaky clean and honest, while Shubin's shoes looked as if they had something to hide. No wonder the Commies had to steal American-made bombers. They could not even put together a decent pair of shoes. He was about to kick Shubin's nasty pair out of the door and down the steps when he remembered what Duane said: *Check the heels of his shoes for secret compartments.*

The shoes reeked of sweaty socks and something else Jake decided was the smell of melted Russian snow. The heel of the first shoe was scraped and well worn, and no matter how hard Jake yanked at it, the heel stayed attached. He dropped the shoe, picked up the other, and turned it over. A clump of chewing gum was stuck to its sole. When he pulled at the heel, his fingers slipped and broke through the hardened shell of the chewing gum, which was still soft inside. The gooey stuff packed under his fingernails, and he yanked his hand out in disgust. The strand of gum sagged between his fingers and the shoe. He shook his hand to toss the gum aside, but the strand only stretched thinner and, making a loop in the air, stuck to the side of his jeans. Angered, Jake flung the shoe to the floor. It clomped against the floorboards, bounced off, and vanished.

He kneeled on the floor and looked under the cot. The shoe was not there, but he saw a long, narrow gap at the edge of the flooring he had not remembered ever seeing before. One board was missing. He wondered if the shoe fell in below the floor. He moved the cot away from the wall and crouched beside the gap. He could not see into the opening because the angle where the ceiling joists met the rafters was too steep, but if he stretched flat on the floor, he could stick his arm in up to his elbow.

"Easy now, McCauley," he said aloud. "Don't get bit by a black widow."

He moved his hand in slowly, wary of webs and exposed nails. He felt around for a while but could not feel the shoe. He rose to his knees, grasped the edge of the board beside the gap, and yanked. The board buckled, groaned, and, slipping off the rusted nails, splintered in his hands. He tossed aside the pieces, sharp as arrows, and grabbed the second board. The dried-up timber cracked and splintered.

The opening was wide enough *for him* to fall through now. He cautiously leaned into the murky space between the attic floor and the ceiling of his room below. He saw the shoe at once stuck behind a tangle of electric wires. Carefully, he lifted up the shoe, wrapped in threads of spiderweb dotted with mouse droppings. He wiped it clean against the leg of his jeans and tried to detach the heel again, but it was firmly attached to the shoe. He should have known better than to listen to that traitor Duane Armbruster. Neither the Russian's suitcase nor his filthy shoes had any secret compartments.

He tossed the shoe to the floor and lifted the cot to move it back over the gaping hole. But then he stopped. He stood with his knees bent and his back in a curve, holding one end of the cot off the floor, thinking. Then he set the cot down, squatted at the edge of the hole, and looked in again. A satchel, the kind doctors use for house calls, was wedged in deep behind the rafter. He had almost missed it while fishing out the shoe because the satchel was made of dull black leather nearly invisible in the murk. But he saw it. He paid attention. The G-men had told him to quit playing the detective. They had said that he was not cut out for the job. Well, he would show them.

Jake leaned into the gap, pulled the satchel out, and drew it into the light. The leather was scuffed at the edges and along the strap, and there was a brass clasp below it

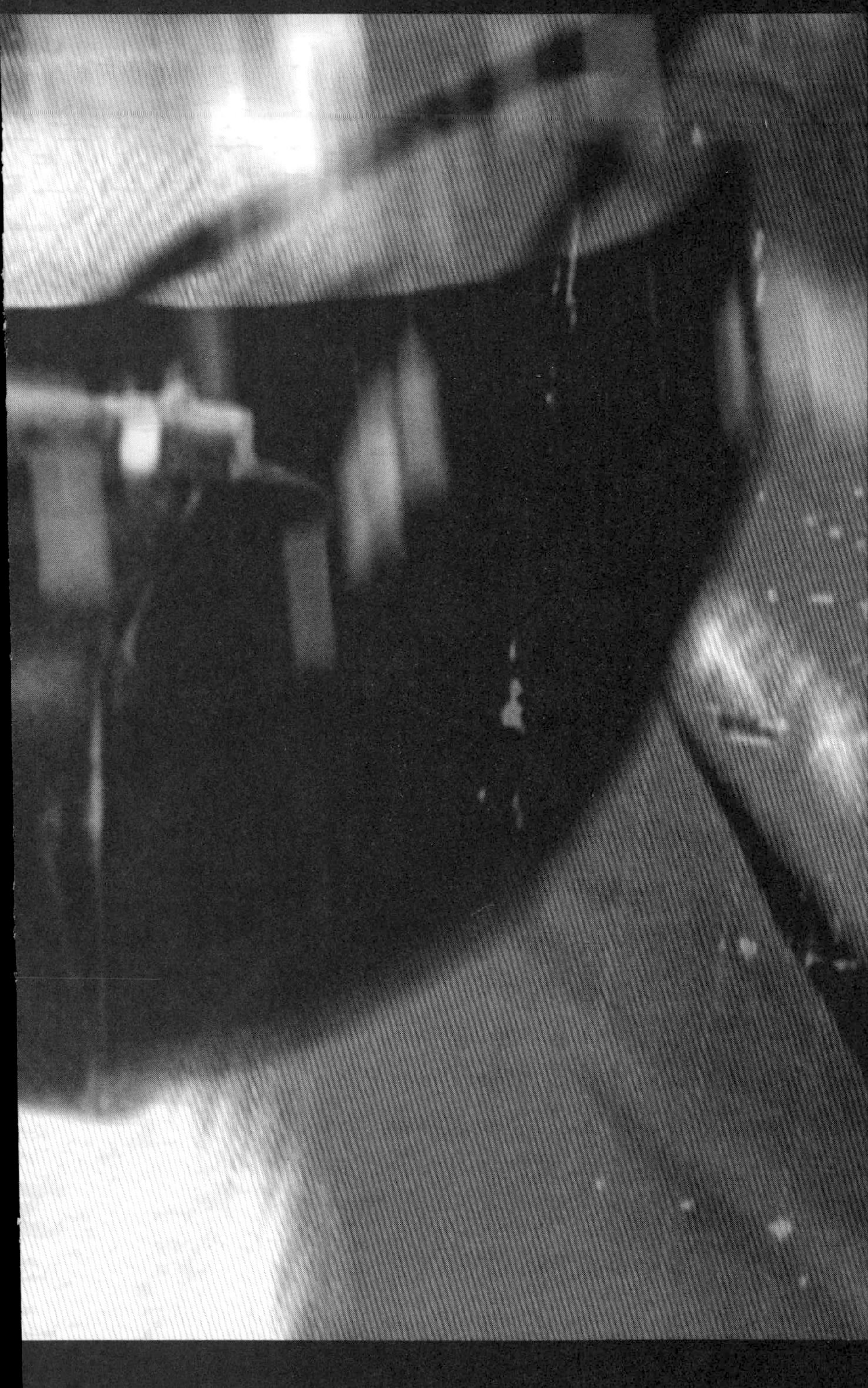

that locked with a key. The clasp had something engraved on it in blocky letters that were probably Russian. The satchel could not have belonged to his dad, so it must have been Shubin's. He thought the clasp would be locked, but it was not, and when he clicked it open and looked inside, he could not believe what he saw. He turned the satchel over and dumped what was in it on top of the cot.

He stared at about a dozen cameras. A few looked like anyone could buy them in the store, but most were smaller than a deck of cards, some smaller than a matchbox. There were also black cylinders with glass tops and bottoms, no bigger than a pinky, and he wondered if those were special kinds of lenses. There were dozens of film cartridges, some with twin chambers. There were other things in there, too, but he could not tell what they were for. He leaned in close and cautiously lifted one of the cameras, the whole thing no thicker than his two fingers pressed together. He held it in the palm of his hand, studying the tiny glass eye, the tiny knob, and two tiny dials on the tiny body in silver finish. He knew he had seen it before, but where? Then he remembered the spy in the movie he watched at Duane's house taking pictures of the top secret pages.

"The Minox," Jake said aloud.

The instant he named the thing, a string of grainy pictures from the movie flickered before his eyes. He saw the spy leaning over the pages stamped TOP SECRET. He saw the spy's face lit by the desk lamp from below. He saw a line of beaded sweat glistening above his upper lip, and on his bristly chin he saw each tiny hair casting an upward shadow. He saw the spy holding in his black-gloved hands a tiny camera. The tiny glass eye, the tiny knob, two tiny dials. The camera exactly like the one Jake now held in the palm of his hand.

The grainy images appearing before his eyes brought forth the movie's jittery music. The screech of high-strung violins surging through his ears hushed all other sounds: his mother's Chevy turning up the driveway, doors slamming, his mother's voice, her laughter, footfalls in the hallway, footfalls up the steps. Then suddenly—

"Well, well, well. What do we have here?" came Shubin's voice. "A burglar in the house?"

Startled, Jake dropped the camera and wheeled around. Shubin was coming at him from the doorway. Jake backed away from him. Shubin kept coming. Jake stepped around the cot. Shubin followed, closer, looming over, reaching out to him. Jake took another backward step, knowing ahead of time that there would be no floor below his foot. He fell into the gap.

Something slammed against his back and pitched him forward. He brushed against a web of wires, and crackling, they fired sparks. The fall must have taken a quarter of a second, but out of time, the fall was endless. Jake's mind was reeling. He tried to recall the position of the bed in his room below. If he fell through the ceiling, would the mattress break his fall or would he miss it and strike his head against the dresser? He saw himself crashing through the ceiling in the shower of dust, splinters, and plaster, tangled in the fishing line that used to hold his model bomber to where now gaped a jagged hole.

But Shubin did not let him crash. He snatched Jake before he broke through the ceiling, yanked him upward, and held his body dangling over the hole. Jake peered in horror at Shubin. His face was so close that he could see a line of beaded sweat glistening above his upper lip, and on his bristly chin he saw tiny hairs casting upward shadows.

"You ought to be more careful when you go through other people's stuff, kid," Shubin rasped. "You might get hurt."

Jake's heart clamored so loud that when his mother's voice called to them from below, it seemed to reach him from a million miles away: "Mr. Shubin? Jake? What are you two doing up there? Come help unload the groceries."

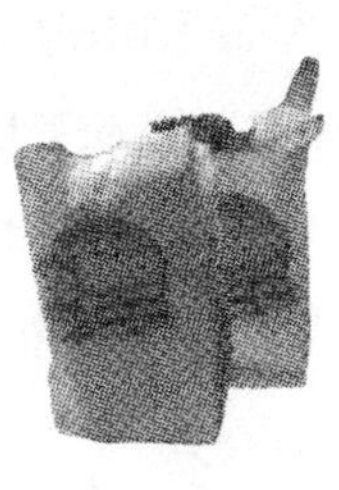

21

Jake scrambled down into the garage and saw his mother smiling at him over the raised trunk of her Chevy.

"Hello, sweetie pie. Look what Santa brought us."

Two paper bags full of groceries crowded the spare tire inside the Chevy's trunk. When he lifted the bags out of the trunk and turned to go, his mother's hand fell on his shoulder. "Wait a minute, mister. How did you get so dirty?"

Jake looked at her, surprised. What a question. How was he supposed to stay clean after what had happened to him today? First, a truck nearly ran him over and then the bus, he flew off his bike into the ditch and lost his tooth, half of his class gave him a thorough thrashing, and just now he nearly crashed to his death through the hole in the floor. He knew it was unfair to blame his mother for having no idea of all the horrors he went through—how could she know?—but still he felt upset with her.

He wriggled from under her hand, hurried out of the garage, hauled the bags into the kitchen, and set them down on the counter. The bags held expensive things. His mother would only splurge like that for holidays, Thanksgiving or Christmas dinners, which meant that Shubin must have given her the money. Lifting the groceries out of the bags, Jake tried to memorize each item, so as not to eat anything Shubin had paid for. He took a brick of cheese out of the bag, and then another, and another, each with a different smell, and set them down on the counter.

Shubin scared Jake as no one had ever scared him before, but also left Jake utterly confused. In the attic, when Shubin swung Jake away from the hole to set him down on the floor, he noticed that Jake's dad's things replaced all of his ugly belongings and, glancing back at Jake hanging limply in his arms, Shubin burst into a peal of merry laughter.

Obviously his laughter made no sense, so Jake guessed right away it was spy cover. He knew from the comics that spies were trained to pretend. Most likely, he would not even tell Mrs. McCauley what Jake had found in the attic because that would be as good as confessing that he was a spy. What Shubin would do instead was to keep Jake silent, but how he would go about it Jake was too afraid to even think about.

He heaved a hefty chunk of meat wrapped in butcher paper from the bottom of the bag and turned to put it in the icebox. Shubin stood right behind him. Jake gasped and dropped the package. Shubin caught the package in midair and held it, squinting at Jake through his spectacles. Jake gazed up at him, openmouthed, shocked that he did not hear Shubin's footsteps. Instinctively, he glanced down at Shubin's feet. No shoes. His hat was gone and his coat, also. His necktie loosened. His gray crumpled shirt was wet under the arms. He reeked of tobacco. He held the package wrapped in the butcher paper, blood-soaked from the freshly cut meat, blood oozing brightly through his knobby fingers. Jake felt light-headed, staggered, and grabbed the edge of the counter to keep from falling.

"What's wrong, kid?" Shubin said. "Are you all right?"

Jake could not speak.

Shubin's lips stretched into a mocking grin. He walked away and said, cramming the meat inside the icebox, "What do you say we give your mom a little hand with all these goodies?"

When he returned to the counter, Jake scrambled out of his way.

"Take it easy, kid," Shubin said, smirking. "I won't bite you."

Shaking his head, Shubin went on putting away the groceries. Everything went to the wrong place, of course, not where Jake's mother would have wanted it. Sorting out groceries was Jake's chore, one in the million his mother made him do and maybe the most boring, but watching Shubin taking over his job, Jake's terrible fear of him began to fade a little. He could not stand the fact that the Russian spy was meddling in *his* business. Handling groceries was Jake's duty, and Shubin had no right to do it.

Jake took a deep breath, detached himself from the counter, and, pretending that Shubin was not even in the kitchen, began taking foodstuffs from where he had put them and instead put them where they belonged. Shubin did not say a word but went on, smirking and shaking his head and doing the job all wrong. In this way, not speaking, not looking at each other, the two of them kept shuttling between the counter, the icebox, and the cupboard, Jake giving Shubin plenty of room as he passed.

Jake felt proud of himself for his defiance of the enemy, but ever since he had crashed into that dusty hole in the attic, his throat felt itchy and dry. He desperately needed a drink of water. For a long time he refused to pause, worried that his mother might come into the kitchen at any moment and see Shubin doing Jake's chore by himself. Finally Jake began to choke. He darted to the sink, spun the faucet open, and stuck his mouth under the gushing water.

His mother walked in.

"Good job, Shubin," she said cheerfully. "Ain't nothing like having a man in the house."

She laughed and threw her purse on the counter and tossed her keys in. She missed. The key ring clanged to the floor. Jake made a move to fetch it, but Shubin beat him to it. He swiped the keys off the floor and dangled them in front of Mrs. McCauley. She tried to snatch the keys away from him, but he withdrew them.

"Come, Shubin, don't be a fool," she said, laughing. "Give me the keys."

Shubin grinned and jingled the keys. She lunged at them and missed again. Jake dashed in from behind and yanked the keys out of Shubin's hand. Mrs. McCauley blushed and glanced at Shubin. Jake dropped the keys into her purse.

"Thank you, honey," said Mrs. McCauley. "Mr. Shubin's just being silly." She went to the sink and shut off the running water and said over her shoulder, "Why don't you boys go sit in the parlor, where it's cooler? I'll bring you two Coca-Colas in a jiffy."

"Much obliged, ma'am," Shubin said, grinning, and brushed past Jake on his way out. Jake leapt aside.

"Why are you so jumpy, honey? Go sit with Mr. Shubin. I'll be right there."

Instead, Jake went back to the counter and lifted a jar of strawberry jam. He was about to set it on the shelf in the cupboard when his mother snatched the jar out of his hand. "Please, Jake, go to the parlor," she said, and set the jar down in the wrong place, beside the canned pea soup.

"Why should I?"

"Because I'm asking you, okay? You should get to know Mr. Shubin."

"I know plenty about him already."

Mrs. McCauley gave him a suspicious look. "What do you mean, you know plenty?" And before he could tell her what he had found below the attic floor, she said, "You don't have to make it complicated, you know."

"I'm not the one who's making it complicated."

"Fine! Suit yourself, Jacob McCauley!" she said, and began frantically looking for something in her purse. "Why should *you* care what your mother might need?"

Jake stood beside her, watching her yank things out of the purse and fling them on the counter until she swung the purse upside down and slammed it down hard. Loose change bounced off the tiles. He looked at her thin fingers, white from grasping the purse; at her small, delicate ear; at the side of her face; and at a thread of her hair the color of roasted chestnuts, shaped like a question mark hanging upside down. He felt angry with her and sorry for her at the same time, and he wanted to tell her that, but he did not know how, and so he turned away and went out of the kitchen to do as she had asked him.

22

To be alone with Shubin made Jake feel sick with dread, and although it could not have been thirty feet down the hallway from the kitchen door to the door of the parlor, he took plenty of time covering the distance. When at long last, he reached the parlor, he halted in the doorway, stunned at the sight of Shubin rocking in the rocking chair, as if such a thing were perfectly natural.

To be fair, Shubin could not have known the unspoken rule that prevented Jake and his mother from rocking in that chair. That creaky old rocker, with elbow-polished armrests and the rocker tips gnawed off by some long-gone Labrador retriever his dad had owned, used to be Jake's dad's favorite seat in the house. The rocker was waiting for him to return, and it was unthinkable for anyone else to use it.

"Don't just stand there, kid," Shubin rasped. "You're making me nervous. Come in and sit down, will you?"

Jake shuffled in and dropped onto the sofa as far from the rocking chair as he could. He sat half turned away from Shubin, listening to the chair squeaking under his weight. Each squeak stabbed into Jake's heart like a knife. He could not look at Shubin directly, spying on him instead in the old murky mirror hanging on the wall opposite the sofa. Shubin's reflection moved in and out of the frame in which his cracked spectacles flared each time he rocked back toward the quarter-shuttered window. Jake waited anxiously for him to say something about what had happened in the attic, but Shubin kept rocking in silence, as if Jake were not even in the room. When Shubin spoke at last in that voice of his that grated Jake's ear like a rusty nail scratching a piece of rusty tin, he said not at all what Jake expected him to say.

"What grade are you in, kid?"

"Who? Me?"

"Who else? Me? You go to school, right? What grade?"

"Seventh."

"Already?" He seemed amazed. "Got a girlfriend?"

Jake glared at him.

"Okay, okay, don't get mad now. Just kidding." He shifted in the rocking chair, forcing such a pitiful squeal out of the aged timber that Jake winced in pain. "You've got pals though, right? Who's your best pal?"

Jake shook his head. Listen to him. Best pal. Duane Armbruster was until a certain Commie spy showed up and ruined everything.

"What about that neighbor kid? Armbruster, is it?"

Jake quickly glanced at Shubin. Can spies read people's minds?

"Oh, yes," said Mrs. McCauley, sweeping into the parlor with two Coca-Cola glasses and a kitchen towel slung over her shoulder. "Duane. Duane Armbruster. Nice boy. Jake and Duane are inseparable. Right, honey?"

She seemed to be talking to Jake, but she was looking at Shubin. She handed him the Coca-Cola first, too.

"Jake is very popular at school. Eddie Cortes is a good friend, and Tony Gonzales, and Dean Wheeler, and that new boy, what's his name, Vernon something. Isn't that so, honey? You have many friends."

Jake felt again Eddie Cortes's small hard fists kneading his belly in the classroom today, but he said nothing. And neither did Shubin. Mrs. McCauley stood halfway in between the two of them, smiling and twisting the towel in her hands and waiting for Shubin to speak, but he kept rocking in silence, and the rocker squealed under him, and the ice cubes rattled in his glass.

The shutters were down to keep the parlor cool, but even in the semidarkness of the room, Jake could see the changed expression on his mother's face. Shubin was clearly a jerk, not to mention an enemy of the United States, but for some unknown reason, his silence seemed to be upsetting to his mother. Jake watched her closely. By all signs, she had made up her mind to make Shubin feel nice and cozy in their home, and Jake knew that if his mother had something on her mind, she was not the kind to quit trying.

"What am I standing around for?" she exclaimed cheerfully. "It's near dinnertime. What do you boys want to eat? Mr. Shubin?"

She asked *him* first.

"I ain't particular, ma'am. Whatever's less trouble."

"But I love cooking, Mr. Shubin," she lied without blinking an eye. "Jake, honey, what would you like for dinner?" And without giving him any time to think of something, she added, "It'll be a surprise, then," and turned to go.

"I'll give you a hand in the kitchen, ma'am," Shubin called after her, pushing up to his feet.

"No!"

She had all but screamed that *no*. Seeing that both Jake and Shubin were gaping at her in amazement, Mrs. McCauley blushed. "Please stay where you are, Mr. Shubin.

You too, Jake. Try to make Mr. Shubin feel at home." She stepped into the hallway and twirled back to face them, adding brightly as if it were a joke, "If you run out of things to say, boys, there's a wireless in the room. Why don't you tell Mr. Shubin about your favorite radio program, honey? What's it called again? *I Was a Communist for the FBI*, right?"

23

Keeping his eye on Shubin's reflection in the mirror, Jake was frantically searching his brain for something clever to say when Shubin asked him about his favorite radio program. He could not come up with any clever insults in answer to Shubin's question, but it made him furious that Shubin did not even bother to ask.

The radio set, an old Zenith left over from Jake's dad, stood on the rickety chiffonier beside the window. Reflected in the mirror, Jake saw Shubin trying to reach the on and off knob on the wireless without getting up from the rocker. He leaned far back, stretching his hand farther and farther behind him until his pointy knees rose higher than his spectacles. The rocker was just about to crack under his gymnastics.

The reflection of Shubin's knees cocked up toward the ceiling gave Jake a very bad idea. He knew it was a bad idea, but he had no time to talk himself out of it. He scooted along the sofa toward the rocking chair, slid his foot below the rocker blade nearer to him, and gave it a slight push upward. He missed seeing Shubin go down because he was scooting back to where he sat before, but he did hear the crash. Only when his mother rushed in shouting, "What happened?" did Jake look in Shubin's direction.

Shubin was on the floor, still in the sitting position, L-shaped, with the soles of his socked feet stuck up in the air and his back flat against the spindles of the chair pressed to the floorboards. He looked ridiculous. Mrs. McCauley clapped her hands and burst out laughing.

Startled, Jake looked at his mother. He had not expected such a reaction from her. With all her annoyingly predictable flaws, Mrs. McCauley could really surprise Jake sometimes, surprise him in such unexpected ways that he often wondered if there was more to his mother than he could ever possibly know. But this time, it was the neat little trick Shubin pulled next that surprised Jake even more than his mother's laughter. In fact, it left him openmouthed.

Wedged in the overturned rocker, Shubin doubled over,

bringing his knees to his chest, and all at once, as if a wound-up spring had released within him, leapt into a backward flip. His socked feet arced below the ceiling, just missing the overhead fixture, and—*wham!*—he landed on the carpet like a circus gymnast.

Mrs. McCauley shrieked with pleasure and began clapping. With one hand pressed to his heart and the other hand making a grand gesture, Shubin took a deep bow, first to Mrs. McCauley and then to Jake, trying to look very serious, but soon grinning ear to ear.

Jake loved Shubin's trick, he loved his bow, and to be honest, he loved that he was not angry about falling off the chair. Instead, Shubin was smiling and ogling Jake's mother, as if she were the most terrific thing he had ever laid his eyes on. That part Jake did not love. Watching Shubin looking at his mother that way gave Jake such a sick feeling, he had to do something about it quick. He dashed to the wireless and twisted the on and off knob all the way up.

"Our Washington correspondent reports," a radio voice bellowed, *"that the director of the Federal Bureau of Investigation, J. Edgar Hoover, issued the following statement . . ."*

His mother and Shubin did exactly what Jake wanted them to do; they quit looking at each other and turned to the wireless.

"We can successfully defeat the Communist attempt to capture

the United States by fighting it with truth and justice. Further, Mr. Hoover said . . ."

"Oh, what baloney." Shubin stepped up to the wireless and snapped it off.

Mrs. McCauley glanced uneasily at Jake. "But, Mr. Shubin—"

Shubin flipped the rocker in the upright position and eased himself into the seat. "Justice and truth have nothing to do with fighting Communism, and J. Edgar Hoover knows it better than anybody."

"What is he saying, Mom?" Jake said, stunned. "He doesn't believe in truth?"

"Whose truth, kid?" Shubin said. "There's more than one."

"Mom?" Jake moved closer to his mother, turning his back to Shubin. "We have only one truth in America, right? Tell him, Mom, tell him."

"Please, Jake, Mr. Shubin is joking again."

"No, Mom, he's not joking," Jake whispered, glancing over his shoulder at Shubin. "Something is either true or untrue, right? And as for justice, maybe they don't have any in Russia, Mom, but in America there is liberty and justice for all like in the Pledge of Allegiance."

Shubin burst out laughing.

"Please, Mr. Shubin," said Mrs. McCauley nervously. "Jake is still very young, and perhaps—"

"No, ma'am, he's old enough to know that these days lies are sold as truths, and as for liberty and justice for all, there are plenty of suckers in this country who get neither."

"What is he talking about, Mom?" Jake said, horrified.

"I'm talking about your fellow Americans, kid, those who choose to think differently than J. Edgar Hoover wishes them to. They get their share of spying and snooping same as they would in Russia. It could make your head spin, kid, plus it's perfectly illegal, so don't you talk to me about justice."

"Mom?" Jake pleaded. "I don't understand."

"What's there to understand?" Shubin said, rocking faster and faster and smirking a nasty, menacing smirk. "If you're ever suspected of being a Communist, kid, you'll understand just fine. It won't be pretty, I guarantee you that."

Everything that happened today at school, the note tossed at him, and the beating he got, and the hatred with which everyone stared at him rose so vividly before Jake's eyes that he instantly verged on tears. He spun around to face Shubin and screamed at the top of his voice, "Shut up! Shut up! Shut up!"

Mrs. McCauley pulled Jake away from Shubin and held him tight in her arms. "Please, honey, please."

"Who does he think he is, Mom?" Jake shouted. "Sitting in my dad's favorite rocker!"

24

At Duane's house, Major Armbruster's face was everywhere, beaming from every wall and out of dozens of neat little frames crowding the side tables, but Jake had only one tiny snapshot of his father. About a year ago, he found it in the attic, stuck between the pages of the atlas from which he had torn the foldout world map. In the snapshot, Jake's dad in his air force dress was standing in their backyard. Behind him, a portion of the fence and a limb of a hackberry tree were in sharp focus, but his dad's face was a little fuzzy. The camera must have clicked when he looked down at a baby wrapped in a blanket he held in his arms. The baby was Jake.

Now under the cover of the night, Jake kneeled before

the dresser in his room, slid out its bottom drawer crammed full of spy comics, and noiselessly set it down on the floor. He trained the beam of his Eveready into the open space at the back of the dresser, flashing out of the gloom the very baby blanket from the snapshot, carefully folded. He reached in, pulled out the blanket, and shook it open. His dad's snapshot fluttered to the floor. Jake took the blanket and the snapshot to his bed and sat, propped against the pillows, studying the picture under the Eveready's light.

Jake could explain neither why they had no pictures of his dad nor why Jake had never told his mother about the snapshot he had found. Somehow he had a strong suspicion that it was his mother's fault Dad's pictures were missing from their home. Once, a terrible thought came to him that maybe there were no pictures of his father because his mom had stopped loving him. It frightened Jake so much that he had never thought about it again. Not at least until Shubin showed up in their house.

Jake was so absorbed in studying the snapshot that he nearly missed the sound of the opening door. He clicked off the flashlight, dived below the covers, and faced the wall, covering his head completely. His mother must have been walking without shoes again, because he could not tell if she had come into the room until he heard her voice beside him.

"I know it must be awfully confusing, honey," she said, as if she knew that he was only pretending to be sleeping.

"But please, Jake, I beg you, try to be patient. Mr. Shubin is—"

"He hates America, Mom," Jake said from under the covers.

"Oh, honey, but he doesn't." She sat at the edge of the bed, and he felt her hand on his shoulder. "Do you want to talk about it? About what he said in the parlor?"

Jake flung the covers aside with such force that his mother leapt to her feet and backed away from the bed. He sat up and, trying to make her out in the dark, shouted, "Know what he's hiding under the floor in the attic, Mom? A whole bag full of photo cameras! He's got a Minox. A spy camera! Don't you get it, Mom: he's a spy!"

"I wish you'd stop reading those spy comics, Jake," she said calmly. "You're beginning to imagine things. And please keep your voice down."

"Why, Mom? So *he* won't hear? I don't care, okay? I cut up his suitcase. Duane said it would have a false bottom, but it didn't. I hid the suitcase under the back porch with all his stuff in it, but you know what? The G-men knew it, Mom; they knew about the suitcase. They must be watching our house! We have to get rid of him! Ever since you took him in, bad things have been happening. Really bad things. You don't even know!"

"You went into Mr. Shubin's room without his permission?"

"It's not his room, Mom! It's Dad's! Why do you always defend that Russian? What, are you in love with him or something?"

He sunk his teeth into his lower lip until it hurt, terrified of what had just come out of his mouth. His mother was silent, and he strained to see her in the dark, a slight shape against the dimly lit hallway. She lingered inside the door frame, neither out of his room, nor still in it. Her voice came to him flat, without any feeling.

"I love your father, Jacob. You shouldn't worry."

"Oh, yeah? Why don't we have any pictures of him, then?"

"He didn't like pictures, Jake. The one you're hiding behind the dresser is the only one we have in the house."

Stunned that his mother knew about the snapshot, Jake watched her disappear into the hallway.

"As for Mr. Shubin," she said before the door behind her softly closed, "at least try to be civil, that's all I'm asking. Good night, honey."

And then she was gone, while he, with the baby blanket and his dad's snapshot held tightly to his chest, remained still and speechless and overwhelmed with confusion. The window in his room was open, and for a long time he listened to the drone of crickets outside. The sound rose and fell in evenly timed waves. Each time a wave of sound rose, its pitch seemed louder and higher than the one before.

Soon, the pitch was so high that it began to hurt his ears. Pained, he let the blanket and the snapshot fall into his lap and slapped his hands over his ears. There was a momentary quiet, but when he moved his hands away the crickets' shrill was louder; its pitch was higher. He covered his ears, waited for a moment, then opened them. This time, the noise pierced his eardrums, as if some supersonic jet were roaring through his head. He fell onto his sheets, folding the pillow twice over his ears to escape the terrible sound.

25

The muffled shrills of the telephone ringing in the hallway reached Jake through the pillow crushed over his ears. Who could that be? His mother rarely had anyone calling the house, certainly not in the middle of the night. The phone operator must have made a mistake; such things often happened.

He waited for the telephone to stop, but its urgent shrills continued to resound throughout the house. At last, he heard footfalls in the hallway. The ringing ceased abruptly. He had expected his mother to answer the phone, but it was Shubin's voice he heard. Jake tossed the pillow aside and bolted up in bed, listening intently. He could not understand a word. Shubin was speaking in Russian, or whatever those growling noises were, but one thing was clear: the caller made Shubin terribly angry. His voice trembled with rage.

Careful not to make any noise, Jake climbed out of bed, tiptoed to the door, listened for a moment, then cracked the door open. At the far end of the hallway, Shubin stood with his back to him, framed in the doorway of the moonlit kitchen. His angular shadow stretched down the length of the entire hallway, brushing against Jake's bare toes at the threshold of his room. Instinctively, Jake stepped back to avoid the shadow touching his skin.

Shubin slammed down the handset. Jake ducked back into his room. He waited by the door for Shubin to stomp up the steps to the attic, but the staircase remained quiet. Cautiously, Jake peeked out again. Shubin was stooped over the telephone, unscrewing the mouthpiece from the handset. He took the receiver cap off and felt with his fingers inside the handset, then turned it around and unscrewed the transmitter cap. He put both caps in his trousers pocket, let the handset drop, and, stepping silently on his gray-socked feet, disappeared into the kitchen.

The handset swung off the cord along the wall, catching a blue glint each time it rose toward the kitchen. It swung five times back and forth before Shubin silently returned. Something flashed in his hand. When Jake saw the knife, he ducked back into his room. He stood, listening with his ear pressed against the door. The hallway was quiet. When he peeked out again, the telephone box had been taken off the wall and was lodged between Shubin's knees. With the knife he had brought from the kitchen Shubin was prying the backing off the box.

Jake closed the door and crept back to his bed. How could his mother be so blind? Obviously Shubin was a Communist spy. Hiding all those cameras under the floor, criticizing America, talking to someone in Russian in the middle of the night, and now taking their telephone apart, no doubt looking for a listening bug the G-men who watched their house must have planted.

A coyote barked outside, very close, a sharp urgent yap. Several others responded in a frenzied chorus. Jake tiptoed to the window and peered out, but could not see the coyotes. He looked over the hackberry hedge at the Armbrusters' house looming dark against the darker mountains. The brilliant moonlight mirrored in its windows made the house look spooky. The invisible coyotes went on yapping, but nothing else stirred under the cold, harsh light, not a leaf on a tree, not a blade of grass. He inhaled a breath of chilled air, and it seemed to him that among the scents of hackberry and creosote and sweetbush, the same sick-sweet smell rose faintly from somewhere near him. The face of the man with gold teeth shaped itself in Jake's memory, and a shiver of dread ran through his body.

The coyotes' chorus ceased abruptly, and in the ringing silence, Jake heard a growl of an engine. A motorcar with its headlamps off was slowly coming down the street, creeping like an alligator through a moonlit swamp. The reflection of the moon slid across its windshield when the vehicle drifted past the Armbrusters' house.

Jake stepped to the side, concealing himself behind the opened windowpane, and watched the approaching motorcar through the angled glass. For a moment, the motorcar vanished behind the hackberry, and when it showed up again, passing their driveway, Jake saw that it was that very same two-door black Buick.

Jake dropped to the floor, crouching below the windowsill. His heart was pounding. He waited until the hum of the engine faded in the distance, then cautiously rose to peek into the driveway. A set of gold teeth glinted inches away. Jake pulled back in horror. The man with gold teeth was standing right outside his window, so close that Jake gagged on the stench of his sick-sweet aftershave.

Jake wheeled around and ran straight into the door, banging hard against it. His hand, trembling wildly, groped for the doorknob but could not find it. He gulped for air in half sobs, shaking with fright, deafened by the clamor of his heart. At last, the doorknob was there. He spun it, forgetting which way it had to be turned. When the door finally came open, he shot into the hallway and slammed it behind him. He pushed with all his strength against the door, expecting the man with gold teeth to ram into it from the inside of the room. He did not, but Jake held the door for a long time, chilled from the cold sweat streaking in between his shoulder blades. When at last he gathered his will to dislodge himself from the door, the floorboards creaking underfoot spooked him. He switched to tiptoeing on his quivering legs, creeping silently along the hallway, as if *he* were the intruder in his own home and not those others: Shubin in the attic, the man with gold teeth outside his window, and the thugs in the Buick.

Expecting the telephone to be gutted, he was surprised to see the box hanging on the wall intact. It confused him, but also eased his panic a little. Now his mother could put a call through to the police or to the G-men or both. He felt enormous relief when he saw a bar of soft yellow light below the door to her bedroom. His mother was awake, probably reading. All at once, he remembered what he could not remember last night, remembered coming into his mother's bedroom as a little boy and watching her sleep, while the imagined airplane outside his window was waiting to take them both to Russia to look for his dad.

He took a deep breath and cautiously opened the door, just the narrowest chink so as not to frighten his mother. A lamp under a yellow shade glowed on the low table beside her vacant bed. A large pearly-winged moth fluttered beside the lampshade, tapping it repeatedly with short hollow taps. A shadow slid across the wall, and suddenly she was there, leaning over the lampshade with her hands cupped over the moth.

"Open the window," she whispered softly.

Surprised that she knew he was watching her, Jake almost stepped into the room, but another shadow crossed the wall, and it was Shubin—Shubin was in her room!—who passed silently toward the window and silently returned.

Jake watched, astonished, as Shubin and his mother, bent side by side over the glowing lampshade, tried to shoo the moth toward the open window. The moth kept escaping and returning to the shade. In passing, Shubin's hands brushed against Mrs. McCauley's, and the two exchanged quick little smiles.

Jake couldn't bear looking at them smiling at each other. He lifted his eyes to the ceiling, where their shadows swayed together as if dancing in time to the sound of the soft hollow tapping of the moth and of his heart beating hard against his rib cage and wanting to explode.

26

By the time the sun had finally begun to rise at the east end of Congress Street, Jake had been cruising downtown for hours. The squeaking of his bike's rusted chain echoed between the walls of the locked-up shops and the empty office buildings. Dry desert wind swept loose newspaper sheets along the sidewalks. When Jake's bike printed a black thread across yesterday's front page, he circled back to read the headline, THE RUSSIANS TEST A NEW ATOMIC BOMB! On a grainy picture below the headline, a boiling ball of flame and smoke was swelling to a giant mushroom, and remembering the movie he saw in Mr. Vargas's class, Jake imagined himself the sole survivor of the atomic

TEST A NEW ATOMIC

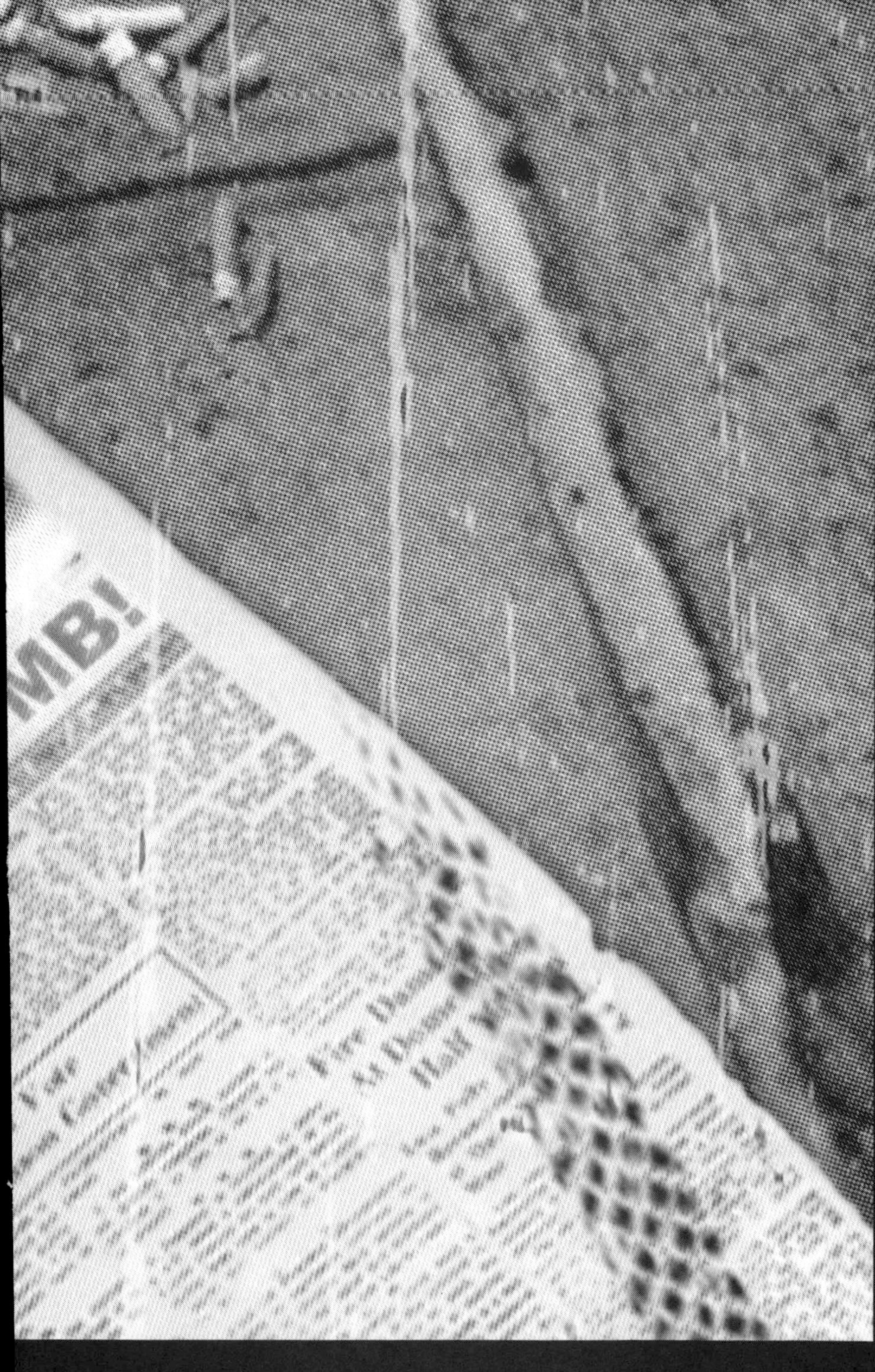

blast, destined to ride the desolate streets of his town forever and ever and ever.

He turned off Pennington to Arizona, riding past the east-facing buildings blushing in the rising sun. Returning to Congress again, he saw the first delivery van and then another. Soon the trucks appeared. The buses began their morning runs. A B-29 droned past the fading moon still visible above the rose-colored clouds. Somewhere a wireless was tuned to a bouncy Mexican ranchera, and in a second-story open window someone said, "I'll be a monkey's uncle! The Commies test a new atomic bomb!"

Jake's legs were sore from the all-night riding, and comforted by the sounds of the waking city, he climbed off his bike for the first time since he sped away from his house. It had been hard fleeing his home in the middle of the night with that gold-toothed fellow lurking outside and that Buick patrolling the streets, but it would have been harder staying home after the horrible thing he had witnessed in his mother's bedroom.

Jake propped his roadster on the kickstand beside the J. C. Penney entrance and, leaning against the streetlight post, sat on the sidewalk to rest his legs. Behind the glass of the storefront window, three dummies—a man, a woman, and a boy—stood facing one another. The man, his hand strangely cocked at the elbow, supported a two-tone Schwinn

Phantom, the same bike Duane had. The man and the woman were supposed to be smiling at the boy, but their heads were turned oddly, birdlike, with their painted eyes looking not at him but elsewhere, just over his shiny head.

Jake studied the dummies for a while, certain that they were meant to show a happy American family. It was the boy's birthday and his dad was giving him the Schwinn as a present. Jake stared at the dummies, but the longer he stared at them, standing together but also somehow apart, he began feeling terribly sorry for himself. Would *he* ever get to see his own father, let alone get a Schwinn from him for his birthday?

Jake heard a bus rumbling to a stop across the street and looked up at the plate of glass, dark over the dummies' heads. There, in the clear reflection, he saw the downtown bus lurching away to reveal Shubin standing on the sidewalk.

Jake leapt up and spun around in panic, looking for a place to hide. A mailbox squatted at the corner ten paces to his left. Jake dashed behind it. He crouched, clinging to the cool blue metal, hoping that Shubin did not see him. He listened to the bus wheezing away, other vehicles passing, then cautiously peeked out around the edge of the mailbox. He could not see Shubin, and he rose to his feet, craning his neck up and down the street. The sidewalks were busy with people hurrying in all directions. He felt relieved that

Shubin had vanished, but then he spied his hat above the crowd flowing west on Congress. The hat, dirty gray like every stitch of Shubin's clothes, bopped cheerfully above the other hats. Jake stood watching it until in a brief gap between the briskly moving bodies he spied what he had missed before—the secret satchel clutched in Shubin's hand.

27

Pedaling eastward, in the opposite direction from which Shubin was heading, Jake thought about life. In general, life was unfair. Take Shubin, for example. A foreigner, a Communist, a spy, Shubin was walking American streets in broad daylight as if *he* owned them, while he, Jake McCauley, the honest American who pledged allegiance to the flag and to liberty and to justice for all, had to hide behind the mailboxes with no place to go. He could neither go back home to his two-faced mother, nor could he return to school, where his best friend betrayed him.

In the meantime the sun, oblivious to Jake's tragic mood, kept climbing merrily, and soon was in his eyes. He could hardly see where he was riding. Having no particular direction to follow, Jake made a loop in the middle of the street, pedaled westward, and before he knew it, found himself within a short distance of Shubin's nasty hat, bouncing above the moving crowd.

Worried that Shubin might spot him, Jake hunched low over the bars and rode against the traffic, close to the motorcars lining the curb. The trouble was the doors kept opening, the people kept getting in and out of their vehicles, and close to his right, other motorcars kept speeding by in the opposite direction.

Abruptly, the driver's door of a parked sedan was flung open in the path of Jake's roadster, forcing him to swerve into the moving traffic. A horn blared. A delivery van thundered past, blasting him with heated air. Jake swung back toward the sidewalk. Turning into a narrow gap between two parked vehicles, he yanked on the bars and hopped over the curb. A group of office clerks scattered, cussing him. Jake whirred away and, to avoid colliding with a woman pushing a stroller, nearly rode through the swinging doors of the Valley National Bank.

"Hey! You there!" A thick reddish hand of a policeman reached for the bars of Jake's bike. He spun the bars away and smashed into a waste can. The can flipped over, spilling, and Jake sped off the sidewalk back into the traffic.

"Watch out!" someone shouted. Jake looked up quickly,

but there was no time to swerve. A truck was bearing down on him. The bugged-out headlamps and the toothlike grille were so close, the stench of gasoline stung Jake's nose. A woman screamed somewhere. The policeman blew his whistle. The truck veered off, screeching brakes. The tires whined on rubbed-out treads. Blaring its horn, the truck barreled by within a foot of Jake. The empty flatbed bounced past, expelling a cloud of exhaust. Jake stood up on the pedals and, catching an opening in the constant flow of traffic, darted to the opposite side of the street.

On the corner of Congress and Pennington, he saw a break in the wall of the buildings, hopped off, and walked the bike into the narrow sunless space between two brick walls. A Davis & Son Hardware trash bin stood crammed with sawdust and sawed-off lumber. He heaved the trash bin away from the wall. A scrawny cat hissed and scampered down the alley. Jake pushed the bike deep into the cranny and moved the trash bin back into place. He stood for a moment, squinting into the darkness between the wall and the bin. He could not see the bike. He turned and ran out into the street.

Keeping close to the walls and pausing now and then to take cover, Jake tailed Shubin. Because that was what he was doing, tailing him. He realized it now. In spy language that Jake had learned from the comics, he was *in command of the target*, which meant that Shubin, *the target* of the observation, was under Jake's surveillance. In other words, Jake was undercover, following the Russian spy. And what else was there to do but to get Shubin arrested and charged and imprisoned, so he would never step into anyone's mother's bedroom again!

Ignorant of Jake's secret plan, Shubin strolled leisurely, as if he had no care in the world, turning his head this way and that, and swinging his satchel and even, it seemed—though at such distance Jake could not be certain—whistling a silly and cheerful tune. Jake tried to stay focused, but Shubin's obnoxious way of walking was so irritating that soon Jake made a mistake.

At the corner of Congress and Church, he nearly bumped into Shubin. When he lost sight of him behind a newsstand, Jake stepped away from the wall to look around the stall. He stepped out too far. Shubin was loitering not five feet away, leafing through a magazine. Jake gasped and ducked behind the stall. He crouched under the sidewall hung with the overlapping rows of freshly printed comics. Above Jake's head, tough, square-jawed, trench-coated men, brandishing tommy guns and pistols, eyeballed him from the covers of the latest issues: *Deadly Intrigue! Daring Action! Spy Runner Smashes the Communist Spy Ring!*

Spy Runner was Jake's favorite action hero. In every issue, he defended American democracy from gun-toting

Commie thugs, often with his bare knuckles. The only trouble was, Jake never had money to buy Spy Runner comics and had to borrow them from Duane. Since Duane turned out to be a dirty traitor, Jake could never ask him for comics again, and for an instant, he had the bizarre idea of asking Shubin to buy him a couple. That was crazy, he knew it, and he closed his eyes to concentrate on what was important. With Shubin around, who needed comics anyhow? Jake's life now could match any Spy Runner adventure and more.

"Somebody call his mother," a scratchy voice came from above. "The child has been found."

Shubin loomed over him with the satchel in his hand and a rolled-up magazine under his arm.

"Your mother was worried sick when she couldn't find you this morning. What are you up to, kid? I've been watching you since I got off the bus. Still playing detective?"

Jake felt his whole face go hot and then, instantly, cold. Shubin had been watching *him*, while it was Shubin who was supposed to be under *his* surveillance!

"Don't sweat it, bud," Shubin said. "I won't tell her. It'll be our little secret. You seem to like secrets, huh?"

Jake looked up at Shubin, whose face was in complete shadow save for the sunlight igniting the outside curves of his spectacles. Jake could not be sure, but it seemed that Shubin was laughing at him.

"Why don't you walk me to work?" he said. "It's nearby. On Stone."

"Why?"

"Why what? I'm giving you a chance to solve a mystery."

"No, thanks. I got to get my bike."

"Get it later. Come along."

28

On the corner of Congress and Stone, a troop of mounted policemen blocked the traffic, escorting a red Ford semitruck piled high with folded flags and canvas banners. On both sides of Congress Street, men in hats and overalls stood high on ladders, stringing lines festooned with Stars and Stripes between the lampposts. The intersection vibrated with red, white, and blue: flags were everywhere, hanging in between the buildings, off the storefront awnings, and out of the open windows.

"What's this?" Shubin said, looking around. "Why all the flags?"

"Don't you have parades in Russia?" Jake snapped.

"What are you so sore about?" Shubin said, thrusting the satchel at him. "Hold this a minute."

Jake's eyes flickered over Shubin's face and narrowed at the satchel. "You want *me* to hold it?"

"Yeah," Shubin said, grinning. "*You* can hold it. Sure."

While Jake held the satchel by the strap, Shubin snapped it open and took out a camera—not his spy Minox, of course; he wasn't that stupid—but a regular camera anyone could buy at the J. C. Penney. He stepped off the sidewalk and, squinting at the sun for a moment, clicked the camera dials and swiveled the lens with quick, confident fingers. Next, he began snapping pictures of the flags, the men on the ladders, the mounted policemen, and the banner unfurling right over his head: EVERY COMMUNIST IS A MOSCOW SPY!

Jake watched him from the sidewalk, wondering if, and maybe even hoping against his better judgment that, Shubin was not a spy at all but a photographer, someone who took pictures for a magazine, for example, or a newspaper. But if he were a photographer, those magazines or newspapers were surely Russian, and what evil use the Commies might put such pictures to Jake did not even want to know. Just then, Shubin turned around and snapped a picture of him.

"Hey!" Jake cried. "Don't take pictures of me!"

"Why not? Your mother would like one."

"I don't care what she would like."

Shubin seemed surprised. "You don't?"

"No. I don't." He spun away from Shubin and began walking.

"Hold your horses, partner," Shubin called after him. "Where do you think you're going?"

Jake kept on marching away, fuming for letting Shubin defeat him so easily. Jake was supposed to be tailing the Russian spy, not the other way around. If Shubin was not lying, if he was really watching him since he got off the downtown bus, then Jake was no Spy Runner, not even close.

That last thought made Jake feel so bad that it took him half a block down Stone to notice that Shubin's satchel was still clutched in his hand. Startled, he glanced at it out of the corner of his eye. What would those G-men say if Jake showed up at their office right now? *You asked for the evidence of Shubin's subversive activities in the United States, sir? Here it is, sir. A bag full of evidence.*

The satchel was heavy, and when it banged against his knee, Jake realized that he was running. He lifted up the satchel and, pressing it against his chest with both hands, ran faster. He thought he heard Shubin running after him, but he did not look around, keeping his head sunk low between his shoulders and weaving along the sidewalk like a wild hare running away from a bullet.

Jake was a fast runner, the fastest in his grade, and when, a quarter of the block down Stone Avenue, Shubin had still failed to catch him, Jake knew he had gotten away. He quickly glanced over his shoulder, kept running, glanced over again, then slowed down and halted altogether, scanning the sidewalk behind him in confusion. Shubin was nowhere in sight.

At that moment, at the blocked intersection of Stone and Congress, the same black, two-door Buick screeched a sharp left onto Stone. The mounted policeman shouted for the driver to stop and began turning his horse. Instead of stopping, the Buick sped up, cut in front of the Ford truck loaded with flags, and squealed to where Jake stood on the sidewalk.

Jake bolted instantly. The creeps in the Buick and Shubin were in cahoots, that much was clear. Failing to catch Jake himself, Shubin called on the Buick to lend him a hand. They had those neat two-way radios to talk to each other. Jake knew about things like that because the Commies had always used two-way radios in the Spy Runner comics.

He heard the Buick gun its engine and, turning to look at it on the run, bumped into some fellow strolling out of a nearby doorway. The satchel slipped from under Jake's hands and fell to the ground.

"What's the hurry, soldier?" the fellow said, bending to pick up the satchel.

The Buick swerved to the curb beside them, grinding the brakes, and someone hollered Jake's name out of the passenger's window. Jake snatched the satchel from the fellow's hands and darted up the sidewalk. The Buick screeched away from the curb. Behind the noise of the revved-up engine, Jake heard the mounted policemen blowing their whistles, and then the hooves of their horses clopping the pavement at a gallop.

He ran by a gap between the buildings, caught sight of a shadowy alley, but kept running until the Buick passed it. When it did, Jake took a sharp one-eighty, slipped, nearly fell, caught himself, and dashed back toward the alley. The brakes grated behind his back, and the Buick sped in reverse.

Jake swung into the alley, leaping over a pile of flattened cardboard boxes. Someone snagged him in midair. Yanked him toward the wall. A large hand slapped over his mouth, stifling his scream. The Buick burst into the alley. The person squashed Jake against his body and stepped into the shadows. The Buick roared by. In the flashing windows, Jake glimpsed the reflection of himself and the man who held him.

It was Shubin.

29

Shubin held Jake until the Buick sped the length of the alley and, turning onto Convent Avenue, screeched out of sight. The horses' hooves clopped to their left, and three mounted policemen galloped past the entrance to the alley.

When he was let go, Jake's shaky legs gave out under him, but Shubin caught him just in time. "You okay, buddy?"

Jake drew a deep breath and pulled away from him. "Who are those creeps?"

"What creeps?"

"In the Buick."

"How should I know? I just didn't want you to be run over, kid. May I have my bag, please?"

Avoiding Shubin's eyes, Jake thrust the satchel back at him.

"Thank you for lugging it for me, my friend," Shubin said brightly. "And now, as promised, Jake McCauley is about to solve a mystery. This way, if you please."

Defeated, Jake followed Shubin out of the alley and southward on Stone. As before, Shubin strolled ahead of him as if he had no care in the world, turning his head this way and that, and swinging his satchel, and even—Jake had been right!—whistling a silly and cheerful tune. Thankfully, this torture was short: at the corner of McCormick and Stone, Shubin halted abruptly, and Jake bumped into him from behind.

"Take it easy, kid," Shubin said, nudging Jake with his satchel toward a glass door shadowed under a faded green awning. "Right through there."

They approached the door on which PHOTO & REPAIRS was written in flaking gold letters. Shubin put his hand on the dusty glass and pushed. The door swung open. A thin bell chimed.

"Welcome to the spy lair, kid."

Jake glanced up at him quickly, but could not tell by Shubin's mocking grin if he was serious or joking. He turned away from Shubin and peered into the murky space. Faded photographs of sunsets, weddings, and kids playing baseball hung haphazardly on the darkly paneled walls. Below the pictures, a glass display case held boxy photo cameras, the kind that had not been in use since the war. Beside the case, an advertisement for Kodak film leaned against the wall: a full-size cardboard cutout of a pretty woman about to snap a picture with a slick camera aimed in Jake's direction. At the sound of the bell, a brown drape hanging from a rod behind the counter moved aside, and a young woman, who looked remarkably like the Kodak cutout, stepped out and said in a pleasant voice, "Please come in. We're open."

Shubin gently pushed Jake in, and the door thumped closed behind them. The bell chimed again.

"You're thirty-seven minutes late, Mr. Shubin," the young woman said. "I was beginning to worry."

"Sorry, darling, I was held up saving this young fellow's life from a reckless motorist." Unexpectedly, Shubin slapped Jake on the shoulder. "This is Jake McCauley, Kathy, my landlady's kid. I'm warning you, he is extremely curious. Watch out what you say to him."

"I better be careful," the woman said, smiling. "Hello, Jake McCauley."

Jake blushed and nodded awkwardly. She was much

prettier than the woman on the Kodak cutout, and her hair was even redder than Trudy Lamarre's.

"Meet my boss, Jake," Shubin said. "Kathy Lubeck, a perfect slave driver. Makes me work around the clock. Isn't that so, sweetheart?"

The woman laughed. "Well, Mr. Shubin, it is hardly my fault everyone wants their pictures developed and printed and their cameras fixed by the best photo expert around."

"Photo expert?" Jake breathed in astonishment.

"The *best* photo expert," Shubin corrected him, and flipped open a section of the counter beside the glass display case. "Get in there, kid."

Shubin pushed Jake into a cramped space behind the counter in which he stood, embarrassed and confused, while Kathy Lubeck asked him what grade he was in and what school he went to, and while Shubin kept bumping into him from behind, changing out of his jacket into a soiled white lab coat.

"The moment we were all waiting for!" Shubin cried, pulling aside the drape. "The mystery solved! Spy Runner triumphs!"

Amazed, Jake looked up at Shubin. How did he know about Spy Runner?

"Spy Runner?" Kathy Lubeck said. "You like spy comics, Jake?"

"Who? Me? No," Jake mumbled. "They're for kids."

Shubin burst out laughing. "Indeed, indeed, we're all adults here. Excuse us, Kathy." He drew Jake past the curtain and let it drop behind them. "Take a look."

He punched the light switch beside the door frame. A naked lightbulb flickered, mutely lighting a low workbench, tin cans filled with tools, and cardboard boxes full of spare parts along the racks of raw and sagging plywood. The stagnant air reeked of cigarettes and chemicals and dust. The room was windowless, dead quiet, but somewhere in the shadows Jake heard the buzzing of a fly.

Whistling the same silly tune, Shubin set the satchel atop the workbench, snapped it open, and began taking the cameras out and placing them carefully onto the yellowed newspaper sheets with which the workbench was covered.

"So you are . . . ," Jake began but halted.

"Hate to disappoint you, kid," Shubin said. "A photo technician. Not a spy."

Jake peered into Shubin's face, inspecting it for signs of lying. "Why did you hide your bag under the floor, then?"

"I didn't, my friend, I didn't," said Shubin brightly, sorting out the cameras. "One board happened to be missing below the cot, and the bag must have fallen in. In fact, I'm much obliged to you for retrieving it. I was afraid it was lost for good. I'm terribly absentminded." He winked at Jake. "It seems I also lost my suitcase with all my clothes."

Jake felt his face burning and quickly looked away. So Shubin was not a spy after all. He was a photo technician, the best photo expert around. Jake felt almost giddy, almost wishing to thank him for not being a spy. Ashamed for his feelings and anxious that Shubin might read what he felt on his face, Jake turned away and, with a nod toward a narrow door in the corner, said, "What's in there?"

"You're going to love this, kid," Shubin said. "It's a darkroom."

He pulled the door open, stepped into a tight closetlike space, and yanked on a chain dangling from the ceiling. A red light came on.

"Besides fixing cameras, the charming redhead slave driver that you just met makes me process film and print pictures. Sunsets. Weddings. Kids playing baseball. Family folks' day-to-day, regular lives." He sighed, as if he were envious of someone having a regular life. "I can pull a half-decent print from a lousy negative, but you see, my problem is . . ." He lifted a tray piled with snapshots out of the sink, set it on the splattered tiles below the shelving unit, and shoved it out of sight. "My problem is that on occasion, I put pictures in the wrong envelopes and make the customers angry." He laughed and motioned for Jake to enter the tiny room. "Want to learn how it works? I can teach you."

Jake looked attentively at Shubin's stooped body, which filled the narrow space, and at his face, completely dark save for his thinning hairline, bloodred below the lightbulb, and said, "Sure. Maybe. Not now."

Shubin leaned forward against the door frame, and his face came into the light. He seemed disappointed. "Oh, well, I thought this was something we could do together." He hesitated for a moment, as if turning something in his mind, then said, "Do you ever think about your dad?"

"What?" Jake said, caught by surprise. "Why?"

"Why?" Shubin repeated. He also seemed to be surprised.

At that moment, the doorbell chimed. Shubin looked up quickly at the drape separating the front of the store from the workshop. Behind the drape, two voices were heard. One was Kathy Lubeck's, the other, a man's low grumble. Shubin froze, listening intently.

The drape moved aside, and Kathy Lubeck's face appeared. "Excuse me, Mr. Shubin? When will Mr. Bull's prints be ready?"

Shubin brushed past Jake, patting his shoulder briefly, and looped around the workbench toward Kathy Lubeck. With their heads close together, they spoke in hushed voices. Jake watched them for a moment, then all at once, ducked into the darkroom, squatted, and slid out the tray that a moment ago Shubin had pushed out of view.

The snapshots piled in the tray must have been taken in a quick succession. What they captured astonished Jake, and yet somehow did not, as if he was expecting to see what Duane had warned him about. On the snapshots, Duane's father, Major Armbruster, was (1) climbing out of his Cadillac, and (2) shutting the door, and (3) looking around, and (4) walking up the steps to (5) a restaurant entrance with (6) a sign above it that read in flashy neon letters EL MATADOR. All the snapshots were slightly fuzzy, taken from somewhere across the street, clearly without the major knowing that he had been photographed.

The drape swooshed along the rod. Jake leapt up, spun around, heeled the tray below the shelving unit, and stepped out of the darkroom. He saw three things at once: Shubin hurrying toward him, Kathy Lubeck pulling at the drape, and in the brief instant before the drape was closed, the man with gold teeth peering straight at him from behind the counter.

"You better run on to school, kid," Shubin said. "She's giving me more work than I can handle."

The doorbell chimed again. The gold-toothed fellow must have left.

"Promise you'll come back," Shubin said. "I'll show you the ropes. This photo business can be fun."

Jake did not answer, studying his face intently.

"What? Still suspicious?" Shubin smiled. "Tell you what. We'll have a nice heart-to-heart in the parlor tonight, just you and me, without your mom. You can ask me anything you want. But promise not to flip my rocker over again, will you?"

Startled, Jake took a quick step back.

"That's all right. I've done such things myself." Shubin's crooked smile lingered on his face as if forgotten, while his unsmiling eyes peered at Jake from behind his spectacles. "We'll talk about your dad, too. I knew him well."

30

On the way back to Congress and Pennington where he had hidden his bike, Jake tried hard to figure out what had just happened in the photo shop, but he could not make any sense of it. What were those snapshots of the major that Shubin was hiding from him? Why had that gold-toothed fellow they called Mr. Bull suddenly appeared? What were Shubin and that redhead Kathy Lubeck whispering about? And the hardest thing to understand, the hardest thing to even think about, was the mind-boggling discovery that Shubin knew Jake's father.

Lost in thought, Jake missed Davis & Son Hardware by a good block and a half, and had to retrace his steps. He ducked in between the buildings and found the trash bin just as he had left it. He heaved it away from the wall and reached in for his roadster. The bike was not there. Jake peered into the dark space between the wall and the bin, blinking to keep from crying. Someone had stolen his dad's bike.

The working day had begun, and there were fewer people on the sidewalks, fewer vehicles on the street, but many more flags everywhere. Jake emerged from the passage into the blazing light and stood on the sidewalk, watching the men in overalls high up on their ladders, hanging flags and shouting to one another. Their voices reached him from afar as if through a thick layer of wool. What would he tell his mother? That his bike was stolen? Downtown? When he should have been at school? He could just see her face, stern, cold, as she pretended that she was not angry. *Sure, Jake, such things happen. Things get stolen. Not everyone is honest.* And then, sighing, *We don't have money for a new bike. That's all. You can go.*

When the image of his mother slowly faded, he remembered that something much worse than having his bicycle stolen had happened to him already. How could he go back home after what he had witnessed last night between her and Shubin? The thought that he might never see his mother again had not occurred to him before, and now, frightened and confused, he looked around, not understanding where he was.

"What seems to be the trouble?" A mounted policeman was looking down at Jake from his impossible height. "Are you all right, son?"

Jake squinted up at the policeman past the enormous head of his horse, and past its great teeth and past its glazed eye the size of a baseball that reflected Jake's tiny figure back to him and mumbled, "I'm fine, sir."

"You don't look fine to me, young man," the policeman said, pulling on the reins to keep his horse from sniffling at Jake's hair. "But you must smell good to Buddy. You eat oats for breakfast, or what?" The saddle creaked under him as he began turning the horse. "You're a bit early for the parade. Shouldn't you be at school about now?"

"Yes, sir. I was just on my way."

Jake began walking away from the policeman, but then he stopped and looked over at him again. "Excuse me, sir? Do you know where El Matador is?"

The policeman peered down at Jake for a moment, snapped his bubble gum, and said, "You mean that Mexican joint on Herbert? The restaurant?"

"Yes, sir. I think so."

The policeman worked his chewing gum in silence, but if he was at all suspicious why a boy who ought to be at school was looking for a restaurant, he did not mention it.

"Why, it's seven blocks east up Congress and then a

block south on Herbert. Northeastern corner. Can't miss it. They've got a neon sign going all day."

"Thank you, sir."

Then, all at once, in some inexplicable way, everything around Jake came into motion. The policeman and his enormous horse were swept away, the lampposts with the American flags began to flicker past him, the storefronts sparkled and flashed in the sun, and when the parked vehicles to his left merged into one madly billowing streak, Jake realized that he was running. Noisily inhaling and exhaling the scorched air and pounding the soft concrete, he ran for seven blocks east on Congress, a block south on Herbert, and stumbled to a sudden halt at its northeastern corner before Major Armbruster's Cadillac, parked below a sign flashing in red neon letters, EL MATADOR.

31

Jake peered in astonishment at the major's Cadillac, then, suddenly alarmed, he spun around, half expecting to see Shubin standing at the corner, snapping pictures. He was not there now, but he was there once, that much Jake knew for certain.

He slipped around the Cadillac toward the restaurant's window and leaned into the glass, shielding his eyes from the sun. Red leather booths, ceiling fans, waiters in starched white jackets. In the last booth against the wall occupied by a group of air force officers, Major Armbruster was making them howl with laughter by swooshing a bread roll in the air as if it were a fighter aircraft performing a risky maneuver. Two waiters, shouldering loaded trays, sailed out the

swinging door in the back and approached the table. The officers turned, cheered, and began moving water glasses around, making room for the plates.

Jake had not eaten since yesterday and, watching the officers gobble fried eggs and tacos, he felt the hole from the missing tooth in his mouth quickly fill with saliva. He swallowed hard, turned away from the window, and bellied up to the Cadillac, pressing his nose against the passenger-side glass. The thing was beautiful inside: white leather, spotless, roomier than his mother's parlor. Squeaking a sweaty slug trail across the glass, Jake slid his nose down until he could make out the speedometer behind the steering wheel. He whistled respectfully at what the gauge was promising.

A sharp crack came from around the corner and then another, closer. Jake looked up and saw, distorted through the Cadillac's windshield, a brown pickup truck grinding to a stop across the street. The muffler fired, spewing a burst of smoke. The engine cut. The driver's window slid down. A thick, meaty arm sagged over the ledge. Glowing in the blazing sun, that naked white arm made Jake think of some exotic jungle snake, and he felt a sudden cramp in his throat, imagining being strangled in its slimy coils. He shifted his gaze away from the arm up into the shadowy cabin where at that very moment, the driver's head rotated slowly in his direction. Jake ducked down. How could he not recognize the truck? It was that gold-toothed fellow, Bull.

Jake waited for a moment, then cautiously peeked out above the rim of the door. Bull was looking at the Cadillac, holding something up to his face with both hands. Two even dabs of light flared briefly side by side. Binoculars! Jake plunged behind the door again.

Bull was a spy, another spy in the Russian spy ring along with Shubin, Kathy Lubeck, and those invisible creeps in the Buick. Their target was Major Armbruster, exactly what Duane had predicted. Jake glanced over toward the restaurant. He had to warn the major that he was under surveillance by the Russians, but the distance between the Cadillac and the restaurant's front door lay in Bull's plain sight. If Jake tried to make a dash for it, Bull would see him, binoculars or not. With his sneaky two-way radio, he would let the others know, and then the major and Jake would both be in trouble.

Jake squatted behind the Cadillac, sorting out his meager options. To alert Major Armbruster was Jake's duty as a patriotic American, but there was some other thought that began to stir in his mind. The thought was this. The major had come to Mr. Vargas's classroom to share his method for fighting the threat of Communism. If Jake could help the major now, he, too, would be fighting that threat. Then

Jake could return to the classroom to share *his* method of fighting, so that no one would ever call him a Commie again.

The Cadillac was parked by the entrance to the restaurant at the northeastern corner of Herbert Avenue and Twelfth Street. Bull's truck was parked across the street on Herbert. If there was another entrance to the restaurant along Twelfth Street, say a kitchen entry, Jake could try to sneak in without Bull spotting him. Jake turned around to scan the length of the buildings, looking for the passageway that might lead to the kitchen door, but there was none. He looked away, kept still an instant thinking of what he just saw, then turned and looked again. He was not mistaken.

Shubin was heading his way.

32

The sun, directly above the Cadillac by then, beat down mercilessly. To stay out of Shubin's sight Jake clung to the rear door, scorching his skin against the overheated metal. The creases behind his knees and elbows were filled with sweat. His shirt was soaked. Panting like a thirsty dog, Jake watched Shubin coming closer. He did not know what to do.

Shubin had promised to tell Jake about his father tonight, but Shubin was an enemy of the United States, a Russian spy, a Communist, and clearly a liar. How could Jake trust him? Besides, the arrogant way in which Shubin was walking, strutting along as if he owned the streets, irritated Jake so much earlier that he became careless and made a mistake. This time, Shubin's arrogant walk made Jake cautious.

He had no way to escape in either direction without being seen by either Shubin or Bull, let alone warn the major that he was under surveillance and not by one spy but by two. He thought of slipping under the Cadillac, but it was parked so near the curb that even as skinny as Jake was, he could have never squeezed beneath its shiny trim. Jake glanced around one more time. There was no way out. Meanwhile, Shubin was rapidly approaching, and Jake could already imagine Shubin making fun of him when he would discover Jake hiding again. Desperate to get away from Shubin's mocking grin and from his sarcastic, grating voice, Jake reached up to the Cadillac's rear door handle. With a soft click the door came open. Jake ducked inside and shut the door behind him.

The Cadillac was oven-hot. The smell of brand-new leather near melting point burned Jake's nostrils. Folding himself into a neat little bundle, he cowered on the rubber-matted floor below the door. It was ridiculous, Jake knew, but his heart was hammering so hard, he was afraid that Shubin might hear it while passing the vehicle. Besides, if he decided to take a look at the speedometer the way Jake did, he would see him inside for certain.

Jake waited.

Then suddenly, the front passenger door swung open. Someone got into the car. The door thumped closed. Jake held his breath. Beside him, the back of the seat sagged under the person's weight. Jake leaned away a little. The leather creaked, as if the person was shifting in the seat. Something was lifted and opened. There was a rustle of paper. Pages of a book or a magazine were turned methodically, without hurry. After each page turn came a metallic—

Click.

Click.

Click.

A camera, Jake guessed at once. From where he was hiding behind the seat, Jake could not see the person taking pictures, but when the whistling came, that same silly tune that Shubin had been whistling all day, Jake knew who was taking pictures with his Minox.

Every sound in the well-sealed Cadillac's interior seemed extraordinarily loud. Shubin's whistling, the rustle of the pages, the Minox's clicks, the creaking of the leather, and Jake's wildly beating heart all merged together into a crashing clamor pressing painfully upon his ears. Drenched in sweat and holding his breath as if he were underwater, Jake began adding up the clicks but soon lost count. He was afraid of suffocating. He needed air. He did not know how much longer he could stay without breathing or without

moving, when suddenly the clicking and the whistling stopped. He heard Shubin shifting in the seat, as if he was putting something away. The door opened, and the street noises flooded the interior, cars passing, footfalls, someone laughing. Shubin climbed out, the door thumped shut, and dead silence fell again.

Jake exhaled and, gulping the scorching air, peeked over the bench out of the rear window. Shubin was strolling away the way he had strolled in, carefree, as if nothing unusual had happened. While watching Shubin, he remembered Bull with his binoculars and plunged to the floor. Had Bull seen him? He lifted himself off the floor and cautiously peered above the bottom rim of the window. The truck was gone.

He clambered over to the front bench and looked under the seats and above the dashboard. There was nothing in sight, no papers. What was he taking pictures of? Jake yanked the glove compartment open and stuck his hand inside. His fingers thumped against a solid object. He felt a cross-hatched grip. His index finger slid around a metal curve. A handgun!

Jake was not surprised that Major Armbruster carried the handgun in his vehicle. After all, he was the head of security at the air force base; he had to be armed. At home, Jake had a Red Ryder BB carbine with a plastic stock, good at shooting empty Coke bottles in the desert, but he had never held a real gun before. Jake could not tell what kind of gun it was, but it felt warm and heavy in his hand, heavier than his Red Ryder carbine. Jake studied the gun for a minute. He did not know how to check it, but the gun must have been loaded. Careful to keep his finger off the trigger, Jake glanced around for a target, raised the gun, squeezed one eye shut, placed the restaurant's door inside the gun sights, and—phfff!—blew air through his folded lips in a perfect imitation of a gunshot.

The restaurant's door flew open, and a headwaiter stood to one side, holding the door for the air force officers on their way out. Still aiming the gun, Jake froze, watching the officers file out one by one, blinking into the sun and squaring blue hats over their flattops. Jake ducked down, tossed the handgun back into the glove compartment, slammed the lid shut, and cautiously peeked out at the restaurant's entrance. In the doorway, Major Armbruster was whispering something into the headwaiter's ear. Laughing, the waiter threw back his slick, shiny head, and the major, also laughing, slapped him on the shoulder.

Minutes ago Jake had wanted to warn Major Armbruster about the Russian spies, but seeing him now, he suddenly was not so sure. He had not found any proof of what Shubin was taking pictures of, so the major might not even believe him and get angry that Jake snuck inside his Cadillac without permission. No, it would be better to tell him later, taking the time to explain in detail what had happened in the car while he was having breakfast. This was a national security matter, not something Jake should be doing in a hurry in front of other people.

Crouching below the steering wheel to stay out of sight, Jake clicked the driver's door open and slipped out of the car. On the way out, he was amazed to see what had been in plain sight the whole time he had let himself be distracted by the handgun. A slim leather briefcase with the major's initials embossed in gold below the handle sat in the driver's seat. The briefcase had been shut in such a hurry that the edge of a blue cardboard folder got caught below the lid. Squatting on the pavement outside of the car, Jake stared in astonishment at a bright red stamp clearly visible on the folder's right upper corner—TOP SECRET.

"*Hasta mañana, amigos!*" Jake heard the headwaiter calling from the doorway.

"*Hasta mañana!*" Major Armbruster's voice bellowed back. "*Mismo tiempo!*"

The officers were approaching the Cadillac. Their voices and their laughter were getting nearer. Having no time to decide what to do next, Jake snatched the folder out of the briefcase, slammed the door, and took off at a run.

33

Inside the blue cardboard three-ring folder: charts and diagrams and drawings of an aircraft, probably a bomber. Swept-back wings Jake had never seen before and six slick engines tucked under the wings in pods that made him think of race cars. All the pages in the folder, and there were many, were stamped TOP SECRET in the upper right corner, even pages with no pictures but blocks of impenetrable words like *nacelles*, *airfoil*, *subsonic*.

Squatting in the shade against the wall in the alley off Fourth Avenue, Jake leafed through the folder from the first page to the last, and then back again from the last page to the first, frowning at the pictures and words and struggling to understand their meaning. He snapped the folder shut and read the cover: THE UNITED STATES AIR FORCE STRATEGIC AIR COMMAND, and above it in red ink, TOP SECRET.

He knew he should not have taken it. What was he supposed to do with this thing clearly beyond his understanding? But what if he would show it to someone? To the G-men, say, to Bambach and to Bader? They told him to stop playing detective. They said he was not cut out for the job. Well, maybe *they* were not cut out for the job. He had managed to catch the spy in the act. Not only was he in the car when Shubin was snapping pictures of the folder, he *had* the folder. That should be enough for Bambach and Bader to put the cuffs on Shubin. But if Jake handed over the folder to them, would that not get Duane's dad in trouble with the FBI? The G-men might wonder why he had left his Cadillac unlocked. Of course, no one locked cars in the city, but how many were driving around with top secret folders in their vehicles? Besides, even though Shubin was clearly a liar, why would he lie to Jake that he knew his father? That made no sense at all. Jake should have interrogated him then and there, but he had lost his nerve, and now, if Shubin was arrested, the G-men would not let Jake ask him anything at all.

His head began to hurt from too much thinking, and when he heard the horses' hooves clunking along Fourth Avenue, he hopped up to his feet, eager for distraction. Not that he cared to gawk at the mounted policemen patrolling the streets before the parade the way little kids do, but he was glad to give his head a break from trying to figure this spy thing out.

He skipped out of the alley and—what a surprise!—instead of the policemen, a procession of cowboys, about a dozen in all, trotted by single file. Shielding his eyes from the sun with the top secret folder, Jake admired the beautiful horses, clomping a pretty Western tune out of the softened asphalt. The silver-plated saddle horns, spurs, and belt buckles dazzled, and the American flags, with their glossy staffs propped inside the silver stirrups, billowed and rippled in the sun. The cowboy bringing up the rear, silvery-white from his hat to his spurs, spotted Jake marveling at his pony with the braided mane and tail. Flashing his teeth below the droopy mustache, he called out, "Coming to the parade, son?"

"Yes, sir," Jake called back. "Wouldn't miss it for the world."

The cowboy nodded, tipped his Stetson, and spurred his pony to catch up with the others. The American flag behind him snapped and fell away, clearing Jake's view of the opposite side of the street. The black Buick, nearly invisible in the shadow of the Federal Savings building, sat growling at the curb.

Jake glanced at the top secret folder he was holding in

plain sight and quickly snatched it behind his back. Across the street, the driver gunned the engine. The wheels spun away from the curb. When the reflection of the cowboy's flag rippled across the Buick's windows, Jake was in a dead run already. Deliberately, he took off in the opposite direction from where the vehicle's grille was facing. He heard the Buick screech a U-turn and kept running, quickly overtaking the cowboy procession. The horses, the riders, and the flags streaked to his left as he ran.

"Where's the fire, amigo?" one of the cowboys called after him.

The squeal of the tires drowned out the cowboys' laughter. Jake glanced over his shoulder at the Buick coming out of the U-turn, skidding, screeching, blasting its horn, barely missing the pretty pony in the rear of the procession. The pony snorted, lurched, and reared. The cowboy's white Stetson flew off his head, jumping and bouncing across the street. The Buick crushed it under its tires. Surging wildly and bumping flanks, the horses stomped over the sidewalk, rolling their panic-stricken eyes. Jake darted through the confusion of the reeling horses and the tangled flags, made a right on Broadway and right again on Herbert. At Twelfth Street, he ducked into the alley. A moment later, the Buick shot right by the alley's entrance.

Panting, Jake clutched the top secret folder in his teeth, unbuttoned his jeans and yanked his shirt out, stuck the folder next to his boxers, and stuffed the shirt back in and buttoned up his jeans. He squatted a couple of times and hopped up and down, testing whether the folder would stay put. It did fine.

Moving down the narrow alley, Jake came across an empty Coke bottle and began kicking it as he walked, glancing over his shoulder in between the kicks. He knew he had a little time to catch his breath before the Buick would double back to look for him. The bottle rolled and spun along the rough and rutted surface, and Jake decided that if he could kick the bottle to the end of the alley without breaking it, the Buick would never find him.

He picked up speed and kicked the bottle forward. It spun, flashed in the sun, and knocked against the wall, shattering to pieces. The Buick roared in from the far end of the alley and bore head-on toward Jake. Startled that the vehicle had not come from behind as he had expected, he halted, gaping at the Buick gunning straight at him. Halfway down the alley, someone began opening the back door of a shop.

"Watch out!" Jake screamed.

A slight man under a hat folded out of a newspaper glanced at him from the doorway. "*Qué?*"

The Buick sped by, ripping the door clean off its hinges. The man leapt back inside. The door sailed up, spinning in the air. By the time it came down, splintering to pieces against the rear bumper of the Buick, Jake was running out of the alley.

A bus rattled by, blocking his way. He took a sharp right. The Buick came after him, slamming into the side of the bus. Jake heard a dull thud, metal crumpling, glass shattering against the pavement, but he kept running without looking back.

34

One thing Jake had never done was take other people's stuff without their permission. He had never stolen a thing in his life. Taking the major's top secret folder from the Cadillac made him feel uneasy, but was it stealing? It was collecting *evidence of Mr. Shubin's subversive activities in the United States*, the way the G-men had put it. The trouble was what to do with that evidence now.

What helped him decide, and he was ashamed to admit to his weakness, was this: he was becoming a little desperate managing this spy thing on his own. The last high-speed chase against that Buick, how it bore toward him through the alley, how it took that door clean off its hinges, and how it crashed into the bus had much to do with his decision. He had the G-men's cards stuck in the pocket of his jeans, he knew the number to call, but a telephone call cost a nickel, a nickel Jake did not have. As awful as it was, he had no choice but to try his hand at stealing.

Crossing Ochoa Street, Jake came upon McGhee's soda shop. It had the best ice cream in the city, but he tried not to think of it. The important thing was that McGhee's had a phone booth in the back of the shop. Past the marble counter and past the soda fountain, it was a narrow, ill-lit cubicle with numbers scribbled on the paneled walls and a wobbly door that folded twice to open and to close.

Leaning casually against the wall beside McGhee's window, he eyed the customers inside. The newly polished glass reflected a patch of sky, a dentist's sign across the street, and Jake himself. The soda shop was crowded. Hiding from the heat, folks who had come to the city to watch the parade swarmed the marble counter. Jake scanned the crowd and, trying to ignore the nasty feeling this whole business gave him, carefully chose his victim.

A thin, blue-hatted lady of indefinite age perched atop a stool nearest the window sucking on a straw from a bottle of pop. Jake fixed his eyes on the lady, encouraging her in his mind to hurry up and finish the pop. It was unbearable loitering by the soda shop in the brutal sun with lots of important things to accomplish while she was sipping her icy pop in no hurry whatsoever. But his plan required patience, the hardest thing for Jake. He had to wait for the lady to finish her pop and lay her nickel on the counter, and then, and only then, he was to make his move. A worry that he might be caught stealing money did not cross his mind. The blue-hatted lady's nickel he was planning to take was not just any old nickel but a matter of national security.

At last, the lady pushed the bottle aside and dabbed at her lips with a napkin. Jake entered the shop. He entered leisurely, as if he had no worry in the world, softly whistling some silly tune that came to him out of nowhere. Strolling along, he glimpsed his reflection in the tilted mirror above the counter and halted, horrified by what he saw. His phony way of entering the soda shop was a perfect imitation of Shubin's arrogant walk.

The blue-hatted lady dug a nickel out of her purse, placed it on the marble top, slipped off her stool, and smiled at Jake. "Hot out there?"

Jake looked away from his reflection in the mirror. "What?"

"I said, hot out there?" the lady repeated. "Think they're still aiming to have the parade in such a heat?"

Jake's eyes darted to the nickel gleaming on the marble top, then to the soda clerk drawing a glass of pop from the

soda fountain, then to the back of the blue-hatted lady pushing through the door on her way out. In one smooth and rapid motion, Jake swiped the nickel, cut through the crowd, and before the clerk turned back to set the glass of foaming pop before the customer, Jake was inside the phone booth, folding the door closed and dropping the nickel into the coin slot and shouting into the receiver, "Operator?"

"What number?" a woman's voice answered.

"Number? Oh yeah. Hold on." Jake dug inside his pocket and yanked out the two matching cards the G-men had given him. The one on top was Agent Bader's.

"Number, please," the woman repeated impatiently.

Jake read the number off the card, two letters followed by five numerals.

"Connecting," the woman said.

While the receiver hissed and crackled, Jake was turning over in his head the best way to put it all to Bader, but before he could decide, the hiss and the crackle cut abruptly and in the hollow silence that followed, a man's voice whispered, "Jake McCauley?"

Jake stood, pressing the handset to his ear, his mouth oval-shaped. How did they know it was *him* calling?

"Jake McCauley?" the voice insisted. "Did they lose you? Are you alone?"

Jake stood, speechless, holding the handset.

"Jake McCauley? Do you hear me? Stay where you are. We are coming to get you."

Jake slammed the handset into the cradle so hard, the phone box shuddered, a bell rang, and the lady's nickel popped back out and jingled into a shallow aluminum bowl.

"Hey, brother!" the soda clerk hollered when Jake raced out of the phone booth.

"Who? Me?"

Several customers bellied up to the counter turned around to look at Jake.

"What did I do?" he mumbled, glancing toward the door.

"Not you, brother, not you, but listen up, folks!" the clerk hollered, looking around at the customers with a grin on his shiny face. "Did you all see the old gal who sat over there? In a blue hat? Respectable-like?" He leaned back and burst out in a fit of merry laughter. "Skipped the joint without paying! How do you like that? Drank the Coke, but didn't leave her nickel! Where does she think she's at, folks? Communist Russia?"

Jake looked around at the wildly laughing faces, slammed the lady's nickel onto the marble top, and hurried out of the shop.

35

In the comics, the Communists watched Spy Runner's every move with secret TV cameras hidden in the most unusual places. The phone call in the soda shop left Jake so bewildered that he was beginning to believe the Communists were watching *him* with those cameras. He even thought that the G-men who gave him their cards were not G-men at all, but Russian spies in disguise. That was how they knew that Jake had cut up Shubin's suitcase and that was why the fellow who had answered the phone knew it was Jake calling.

He kept glancing all around for any sign of hidden cameras, and when, without realizing where he was headed, he found himself on the corner of Stone and McCormick, he stared in surprise at PHOTO & REPAIRS written in gold flaking letters on the dusty glass door. Jake leaned into the glass, shielding his eyes from the reflection of the street. The murky space was empty. The lights were off, and the brown drape was tightly drawn, concealing the entrance to the workshop.

Jake had no doubt that Shubin was inside. He even knew what he was doing in the darkroom now. Jake imagined Shubin under the dim red light, stooping over a thick and heavy liquid rippling in the cracked enamel tray. Below the surface of the liquid, Shubin's tobacco-stained fingers held a sheet of paper on which a picture began to appear, faint at first, pale, then deep and rich and dark. It was a picture of a bomber with six slick engines tucked below the swept-back wings, a picture that Shubin's Minox stole from the pages of the top secret folder, the very same folder concealed below Jake's sweat-soaked shirt.

While Jake was peering through the glass, he saw the brown curtain move aside, and someone entered the murky space behind the counter. Jake wheeled around, looking for a place to hide. He ducked behind the lamppost on the corner, and when a faint sound of the doorbell reached his ears, he saw a large potbelly thrusting out of the Photo & Repairs doorway. The gold-toothed Bull emerged through the door, but the blaring horn of a passing motorcar alarmed him and Bull stepped back in quickly. The two of them stayed that way for a moment, not twenty feet apart yet invisible to each other, Jake behind the post, Bull inside the doorway.

At last, Bull ventured out on the sidewalk, looking in all directions and mopping the rolls in the back of his neck with a hankie. Jake did not have to be Spy Runner to figure what was inside a large manila envelope tucked under Bull's other arm. Shubin had just handed Bull the pictures of the top secret folder.

Bull stuffed the hankie into his pocket and charged down the street. The moment his back was turned, Jake stepped out from behind the lamppost, watching Bull's burly shape cut through the crowd. The manila envelope swung under his arm.

What terrible trouble Major Armbruster had gotten himself into by leaving his Cadillac unlocked. Not just himself but every American. The moment Bull smuggled Shubin's pictures to Moscow, the Russians, using stolen American know-how, would build their own aircrafts with swept-back wings and six slick engines. They would load those bombers with A-bombs and fly them over here. *Duck and cover all you want, Mr. Vargas. If Bull gets away with that envelope, everyone in America is as good as dead.*

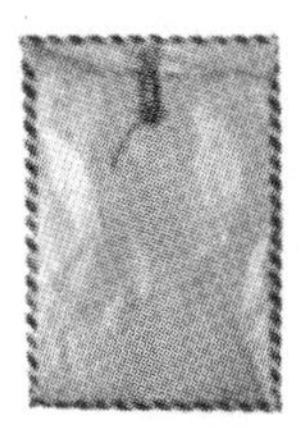

36

Bull stomped south on Stone Avenue and made a left on Cushing, moving in and out of the shafts of sunlight, slanting in between the buildings. Each time Bull stepped out of the sunlight, Jake could not see him in the shadows. Worried that he might lose Bull, Jake tailed him closely until the corner of Sixth Avenue, where Bull stopped so abruptly, Jake nearly bumped into him. Thick folds in Bull's neck rolled above his sweat-stained collar, and like a giant ball, his massive head rotated in Jake's direction.

"What you want?"

"Who? Me?" Jake said, nervously glancing at the manila envelope under Bull's arm.

Bull noticed Jake's glance, frowned, moved the envelope

under his other arm, blocking it from Jake with his bulky shape, and stepped off the sidewalk to cross the street. The moment he turned, Jake rushed at him from behind and snatched the envelope from under his arm. Then all at once, a sharp pain shot through Jake's chest. Somehow he was not standing anymore but lying on the sidewalk, and Bull was looming over him, and the envelope was under *his* arm again.

Jake reached out and grabbed the envelope. Bull snarled a confusing word, "*Doorak*!" and yanked the envelope away. Jake yanked it back. "*Otdai, doorak*!" Bull pulled it harder. They tugged the envelope back and forth until the flap burst open and glossy snapshots fanned out to the pavement. Bull flung Jake a murderous look, came down to his knees, and, muttering to himself in Russian, began collecting the snapshots.

Jake sat up, gazing at the pictures in bewilderment. No charts and diagrams and drawings of the bomber, but men in overalls on ladders, and mounted policemen, and flags strung between the lampposts. These were not the pages of the top secret folder at all but the pictures Shubin had snapped while they were walking up Congress toward his workshop.

Confused about what he should be doing now, Jake rolled over to his knees and picked up one picture on which he saw himself glaring at the camera. Bull slapped the picture out of his hand.

"Ouch!" Jake cried, rubbing his hand. "What's the big idea?"

"Go away!" Bull growled, the rolls in his neck turning purple.

"What's your problem, mister?" Jake finally exploded. "You should go away, not me, okay? What if I came to Russia and stared into your window at night, huh? Would you like that?"

Bull turned to check if any pedestrians were in earshot, then scowled at Jake. "What Russia?"

"Well, you know," Jake said. "The Commieland. Aren't you a Commie?"

Bull's left hand did something to Jake again. Sharp pain shooting through Jake's chest made him black out, and when he opened his eyes, he was ten feet away from Bull, flat on his back, wedged between the trash can and the lamppost. Bull stood, wheezing, shoving the snapshots inside the torn envelope. The snapshots would not fit, and a few of them fluttered to the pavement. Bull glanced at Jake with hatred. Squatting on his thick haunches, he began collecting the snapshots but halted suddenly, frowning in the direction of Jake's belly. Confused, Jake followed his gaze. In the fall, his shirt had bunched up to his chest, revealing the top secret folder tucked inside his jeans.

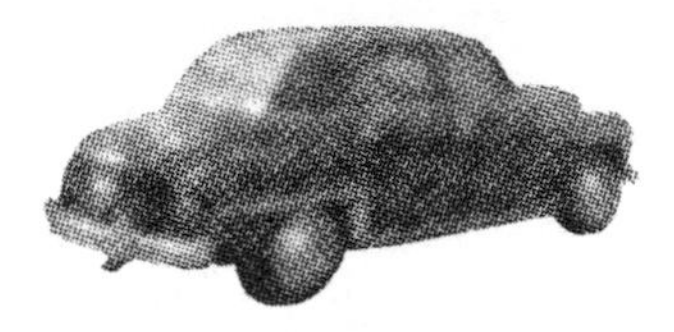

37

Jake tried to scoot away from Bull, but he stomped his foot behind Jake's back to halt his escape and, looming over him like a mountain, reached for the folder: "Give it!"

"Just a moment, sir." A gray-haired man, likely a Valley National Bank employee by the looks of his neat suit, stepped in between Jake and Bull. "What did you hit the boy for?"

"I saw it, too!" A woman kneeled beside Jake, the same blue-hatted lady from whom he had stolen a nickel at the soda shop. "Poor child!" she chirped, patting his forehead with a hankie.

"Is that your father, boy?" a deep voice said over Jake, and a pair of strong hands slid under his arms and lifted him up to his feet.

A small crowd began to gather.

"Give it!" Bull roared, lunging at Jake, but the pedestrians, squeezing in between the two of them and all talking at once, slowed Bull down. Jake spun away, looped around someone standing next to him, and sprinted through the busy intersection. A slick sedan zoomed by, blaring its horn.

At Stone Street, Jake darted behind the corner building and, leaning against the wall, tucked his loose shirt into his jeans to cover the folder. The left side of his chest where Bull had hit him twice hurt, and he leaned forward with his hands propped on his knees, waiting for the pain to subside.

Shouting and screaming came from the other side of the street. Jake edged toward the corner and cautiously peeked out. The lady from the soda shop, her blue hat hanging off one ear, sat on the pavement, screaming. Beside her, the bank employee lay motionless with his head hanging facedown off the curb. The sidewalk was strewn with hats. Growling and grunting, the gold-toothed Russian was in the thick of a half-dozen hatless men, holding on to him in one mad, lurching, grappling, shuffling swirl.

"Danny! Danny!" someone was shouting. "Fetch the sheriff!"

Jake ran again, crossing Sixth and Fifth Avenues and dodging in and out of traffic. Either from too much running or from Bull hurting him, he felt a stitch in his side and had to slow his pace, then switch to walking. At the intersection of Jackson and Stone, he halted altogether and stood, panting, with his hands to his side. If only his roadster had not been stolen, this spy thing would not be so hard. When Shubin and Bull and Kathy Lubeck and those creeps in the Buick were all safely in prison, Jake would report the theft of the roadster to the police. He could not tell why, but he was convinced that his father's old bike would be found.

Jake took a deep breath and looked around, deciding which way to go. Not fifty feet away, Bull was stomping up the sidewalk in his direction. Caught by surprise, Jake froze, watching Bull approach. His hat was gone, his jacket torn at one shoulder, and his crumpled shirt hung open over his white bouncing belly. In a moment, he was within a leap from Jake. For all his enormous bulk, the gold-toothed fellow was remarkably fast.

Jake wheeled around and shot into the traffic, ignoring the blaring horns. Halfway across the street, he glimpsed a motorcar coming at him from the left. He sped up, expecting the vehicle to let him through. Instead, the motorcar swerved into his path, cut him off, and ground to a halt. At full run, Jake smacked against its fender. From the impact, the folder blasted off from under the belt of his jeans. With its blue covers jutting out like a fighter jet's wings, the folder soared high in the air, hung motionless there for an instant, then dived into a corkscrew maneuver and crashed into the pavement.

Jake pushed away from the fender and, looking around wildly, took in several things at once: Bull's gold-toothed scowl behind the flicker of the traffic, the top secret folder on the ground with its pages slowly turning, and the motorcar that stopped him, so badly damaged it took Jake a moment to recognize the same black Buick that had been chasing him all day. The dull noise of the crumpling metal and the shattering glass rang through his mind.

Oh, yeah. The creeps had run into the bus.

Behind the windshield veiled in a spiderweb of cracks, Jake glimpsed two shapes scooting away from each other. The doors flew open. The driver's door slipped off its hinges and clanged to the ground.

Two matching suits stepped out. Two matching flattops. Two matching pairs of X-ray eyes. Agent Bader and Agent Bambach, grinning, talking over each other, moving toward Jake along the sides of the crumpled hood.

"Quit running, McCauley—"

"Look what you've done to the—"

"Government property—"

"Taxpayers' money—"

"Your mother said—"

"To keep an eye on you—"

"Will come out of her salary—"

"The repairs—"

"Will not be cheap—"

"So you know."

Startled, Jake watched the agents closing in on him, saying things he could not understand. His eyes shot toward the sidewalk, but Bull was no longer there. When he looked back at the G-men, they were towering over him.

"Looks like you dropped something, McCauley," said Agent Bader.

"Could be important," said Agent Bambach.

"Let's take a look at it," said Agent Bader, squatting beside the buckled bumper under which the open folder turned its top secret pages in the gust of wind raised by the passing cars.

If not for the phone call he had made in the soda shop, Jake would be relieved to see them. He badly needed help, but these twin thugs seemed dangerous and frightening to him. Jake needed time to think this over, but the nasty smirk on Bambach's face and Bader's hand reaching for the folder sent him into action. Jake darted forward, snatched the folder from under Bader's fingers, and, ignoring the agents shouting for him to stop, the motorcars flying in both directions, and the pain from the stitch in his side, he tore across the street.

38

Exhausted, Jake slumped in the shade beneath a rusted tin wall of an abandoned warehouse. To his left, a large truck tire lay smoldering below the abandoned bonfire's dwindling flames. Through the smoke-filled air, gray specks of ash twirled down upon Jake's sweaty high-tops and his sweaty socks drying on the flattened cardboard box beside him.

For close to an hour after he had escaped Bambach and Bader, he had pounded the sunbaked alleys desolate in the dead glare of the high noon sun. He had passed machine shops, warehouses, garages; once leapt over a pile of oil-stained rugs set afire; and gulped the arid air that stung his eyes and made his throat itchy. The sheets of corrugated tin had extended for a long time to his left, and when they had stopped abruptly, a guard dog had charged him from behind a chain-link fence. Jake had lurched aside, catching his foot in a hard clay rut. The dog, flinging long strands of saliva from its snapping jaws, had hurled itself into the bulging chain links long after Jake limped away.

Now his ankle had begun to swell. He poked at the tender skin with his dirty fingers, then leaned toward the bonfire and spat into the flames. Not a drop of spit came out. His mouth was dry. He undid his jeans and, pulling out the top secret folder, flipped once again through its smudged, creased, and sweat-soaked pages. Just as before, its diagrams and its complicated words confused him. Why had he taken it? He became terribly angry with himself, but in a moment or two, he was sorry for himself instead. He felt completely alone. Nobody cared about him except for the Russian spies who wanted to hurt him. He was sick of secrets and he was sick of spies and he was sick of running. He wanted to be home with his mom. One of those fake G-men said that his mother asked them to keep an eye on him. But was it even true? Jake did not know. He did not know anymore how to tell truth from lies.

He heard the soft tinkling of a bell, but soon the sound stopped. He listened. All was quiet. Just as he thought he

had imagined it, the bell chimed again. He leaned away from the wall and, squinting through the blue-gray smoke drifting off the smoldering tire, saw a ghostly figure drawing toward him. A man in a loose white shirt and loose white breeches, pushing ahead of him a white ice cream cart. The man and his cart and his loose clothes were so sun-bleached, they looked transparent. The man was old and frail, and it was hard for him to wheel the cart over the rutted ground. Now and then he had to stop to rest, and when he did, the bell ceased tinkling.

It took the old man a long time to come level with Jake. He paused and, wiping his old face with a threadbare bandanna, looked openly at Jake, studying him through his watery eyes without hurry and without judgment.

"*Helado de frío, hijo?*" creaked his barely audible voice.

Jake shook his head. "*No dinero.*"

The old man nodded and tied the bandanna round his withered neck, then flipped open the lid on his cart and stuck his hand up to the elbow into the opening. Through the drifting smoke, Jake watched him grope inside the cart. At last, the man took out an ice cream bar, closed the lid, and shuffled over. Jake quickly swiped the folder off his lap, hiding it behind his back.

"*Vainilla,*" the old man said, holding out the bar to Jake. "*Cortesía de la casa.*"

Jake looked at the ice cream in the old man's trembling fingers, nodded, and carefully took the bar. The old man peered for a moment at Jake's swollen ankle and shuffled back to the cart and returned with a chunk of ice.

"*Hielo*," he said. "*Bueno para el pie.*"

Jake felt tears scalding his eyes. He wanted to cry. Bawl his eyes out, as if he were a little kid again. He clenched his teeth and, lifting his chin up so that tears would not spill down his cheeks, he leaned forward and took the ice. He wanted to thank the old man for his kindness, but had he tried to speak, he would have broken into sobs. The old man did not seem to expect any thanks. He shuffled back to his cart, and the tiny bell began tinkling again until the man, his cart, and soon the tinkling of the bell faded away behind the hazy smoke-filled air.

Jake held the melting chunk of ice against his ankle with the toes of his other foot and ate the vanilla bar greedily and quickly. The ice cream ran through his fingers and down his chin, and when a big chunk of it plopped onto the folder in his lap, Jake licked it off, smudging the TOP SECRET stamp into a curved reddish smear.

By the time he finished the ice cream, the ice over his swollen ankle melted, and his foot felt pleasantly numb. He licked his fingers one by one, sucked clean the wooden stick, then leaned away from the wall and looked over the way the old man had gone, but he could neither see him nor hear the tinkling of his bell. If not for the ice cream stick in his hand, Jake would have thought that he had imagined that man. He studied the stick for a moment, then slipped it into the pocket of his jeans next to the tooth he had lost when he had fallen into the ditch. He was not sure why he was saving the stick. Maybe he wanted to keep it in case he was in trouble again and needed to think of someone being kind to him for a change.

Jake pushed himself up to his feet, and the top secret folder fell from his lap onto the flattened cardboard box and slid, spinning toward the bonfire. He did not try to stop it when the folder bumped against the smoldering tire. In an instant, the blue covers caught the flames, and Jake stood, watching the pages curl and blacken until they turned to ash.

39

The American Legion parade began at the Federal Building on the corner of Congress and Granada, moved east on Congress, turned north on Arizona, and doubled back via Pennington. The parade commenced at four P.M., but by two, all of the downtown parking lots had been packed with motorcars. The patriotic citizens had gathered early to stake a spot along the curb for a better view of the passing floats. They brought iceboxes and foldout chairs and umbrellas, adorned their headgear with miniature flags, and lined the curbs in colorful clusters of white, red, and blue.

The deep hollow thuds of the bass drums and the shrill of trumpets reached Jake in the alley behind Toole Avenue. By the time he caught up with the parade, the marchers, sunbaked and worn out, were tramping down Pennington, following a twelve-foot-tall Statue of Liberty fastened to the flatbed truck at the head of the procession.

Jake kept his eyes on the statue's torch, with long red silky ribbons that stood for flames, floating above the hats and the umbrellas of the crowd. When he finally squeezed his way to the curb, the statue had passed and the Veterans of Foreign Wars were marching by in pairs, lugging canvas banners stenciled with FIGHT THE RED MENACE, and DOWN WITH GODLESS COMMUNISM, and EVERY COMMUNIST IS A MOSCOW SPY.

Everyone cheered and clapped and shouted the slogans, reading them off the sagging banners. Behind the veterans clip-clopped the procession of cowboys that Jake had seen earlier on Fourth Avenue. The silvery-white cowboy was now heading the procession, and Jake felt a quick pang of guilt at the sight of a black smudge across the crown of the cowboy's Stetson. It was a tire print left by the Buick chasing after Jake in the morning. The cowboy was making his pony trot circus-like, kicking up its front legs, bowing its neck, and swooshing its plaited tail. The crowd began to clap. Jake clapped, too, smacking the palms of his hands hard together. The cowboy looked up, smiling under his droopy white mustache and, recognizing Jake, whipped off his damaged Stetson and waved it at him. Jake waved back, smiling. Smiling for the first time since he could not remember when, since before Shubin had ruined his life. It felt good to smile again.

A lady in a polka-dot blue dress standing beside Jake peeked at him from under her umbrella. "Looks like a friend of yours?"

"Well," Jake said, not wanting to lie, "I saw them all pass on the way here this morning, ma'am."

"A grand parade, ain't it?" the polka-dot lady said. "Them foreigners better think twice before they fool with us."

"Which foreigners, ma'am?"

She looked at him, surprised. "Communists, who else?"

"Yes, ma'am," Jake agreed. "They better think twice."

"I can just see you're a real patriot, young man."

"Yes, ma'am," Jake said. "Proud to be an American."

And having said that, he felt his heart swelling with a glorious feeling of pride. Jake *was* proud to be an American, and he *was* proud to rub shoulders with honest folks, not spies and foreigners and liars but other Americans, folks just like him. It felt good to clap and to cheer and to have a good time at this dazzling display of loyalty, freedom, and truth after all the terrible things that had happened to him.

Then, in the wide clearing between the Valley National Bank's float hauling the enormous Chains of Communism and the blue-and-gold marching band that followed in its wake, he saw Trudy Lamarre, the redhead from his class.

With a glittering smile fixed on her face, she bounced ahead, twirling a baton. She tossed the baton into the air, and caught it without effort, and kicked her legs so high her tiny spangled skirt shimmered, as bright as the sun.

Spellbound, Jake watched her approach. What had happened yesterday in the classroom, the beating he had endured and the hatred with which Trudy, among others, had stared at him, seemed far away to him now and unimportant. It was one giant mistake, and to show her that all was forgotten, that he was not angry with her, he shouted as Trudy tossed her baton high in the air, "Good job, Lamarre! Way to go!"

She saw Jake before the baton came down. Her eyes opened wide. She paused, staring at him in panic. The baton fell, just missing her head, and bounced off the pavement. Jake pushed through the line of people and limped to her help. He was right beside Trudy now, at the very heart of the parade. Everyone could see him and everyone cheered when he snatched the baton off the ground. Smiling, he waved the baton at the crowd, but when he tried to hand it back to Trudy, she would not take it.

"Get away from me!"

"What?" Jake said, smiling, and he kept smiling until with a deafening blast, a sea of blue and gold swept over him, pounding drum skins, crashing cymbals, and blaring shiny brass. Jake spun around, looking for Trudy to return the baton to her, but she had vanished, and instead it was Eddie Cortes, one of the boys who beat up on Jake yesterday, who bore right down on him behind an enormous tuba.

"Hey, Eddie!" Jake cried over the din. "Over here! Over here! Jake McCauley!"

Eddie's eyes flickered over him, his cheeks puffed and collapsed, and he looped around Jake without skipping a beat. Figuring that Eddie must have not heard him in such racket, Jake reached out to grab at his elbow. Eddie swerved wildly, bumping his tuba into the rest of the brass section. Instantly, there was confusion in the ranks.

"Get out of the way, Commie!" some trombone girl Jake had never seen before hollered at him, and a boy from his class, Ricky Morton, strapped to the bass drum, pointed his mallet at Jake and shouted over the noise, "There's a Communist, people! Right there!"

Bewildered, Jake glanced over his shoulder, expecting to see some crazy Communist who had wandered into the midst of this parade by mistake, but all he saw were the backs of the blue-and-gold jackets marching away.

Ricky was pointing at him.

It went fast after that. Some kids hollered, "Commie!" and some, "Go back to Moscow!" and some whacked him with their instruments on purpose. The band roared like a mighty river, pulling him along, and he could neither break

away from it nor stop moving, as if he were a toy sailboat drawn by a powerful current.

Clutching Trudy's baton, Jake tried to march in time with the others by skipping a step and adjusting his stride, but he was limping badly, and while everyone around him stomped the pavement as one living thing, he was hopelessly out of step. He pushed his way to the curb, but a trombone slide bashed him from behind and he dropped the baton and went down. The concrete throbbed from the stomping feet, the air vibrated with crash and clamor, and after the last of the marching musicians stumbled over his crumpled body, Jake sat up, hurt and confused. His ears were ringing. On either side of the street, people were shouting from the curbs and pointing at something behind him. He could not understand what they wanted, and he turned around to where everyone was looking. An enormous float rolled down on him.

It was a giant model of the B-29 Superfortress built of planks and stretched canvas painted glossy silver, a million times bigger than the model hanging from the ceiling in his room. From wingtip to wingtip the float spanned the width of the entire street, and in the deep shadow below the cockpit, he glimpsed the grille of the army truck, its colossal tires turning slowly but surely in his direction.

When Duane told him about this float being built at the air force base, he said that it was humongous, and he was right. It *was* humongous. And there he was, too, his former best friend, Duane Armbruster, in a real pilot's helmet and a pair of goggles, clutching the handrail atop the Superfortress float. Behind him in crisp air force blue, his father, Major Armbruster, beamed his beautiful smile and waved majestically at the crowd.

Jake sat on the pavement, overwhelmed by the sight of the float, while its cross-like shadow crept steadily toward him. The people in the crowd were screaming at Jake to get out of the way until he understood what was wanted of him. He rose to his feet and hobbled toward the curb, but halfway there, he turned around to look again at Duane and the major. They soared high up above him, a proud boy and his proud father, etched darkly against the blinding sun like a magnificent statue raised to honor the American fathers and sons.

As they passed, Jake felt something rapidly coming at him from the right. Out of the corner of his eye, he saw the edge of the Superfortress's wing closing in on him like the blade of a monstrous knife. He watched it, enthralled, until the edge was inches away from his face. An instant before it whacked into his forehead, someone's hands snatched him from under the swooshing wing.

"What's wrong with you, kid?" Shubin rasped angrily. "Are you nuts?"

Jake was neither surprised that Shubin was there nor

grateful to Shubin for saving him. He felt numb, and while Shubin lugged him to the curb, Jake slumped over his arm like a rag doll. Before they could reach the sidewalk, something blocked their path, and Jake stared in a daze at a shiny black boot pressed against the shiny flank of a horse.

"Don't you know not to cross a street closed to foot traffic?" the mounted policeman's voice rang from above.

"Apologies, Officer," Shubin answered, holding Jake tightly at his side. "The boy got confused."

"What's there to be confused about? Can't you see it's a parade?"

The horse stretched its neck, sniffling at Jake's hair, and the policeman pulled on the reins to keep it from crowding Jake. "I thought it was you," the policeman said, grinning. "Ever find that Mexican joint on Herbert, son? El Matador? Remember you were asking?"

Jake felt Shubin's eyes on him and kept silent.

"Thank you, Officer." Shubin patted the horse's foamy neck. "I'll take it from here."

"You ought to keep an eye on this kid," the policeman said. "You two are related?"

"Yes, sir," Shubin lied.

"Well, then," the policeman said, snapping his bubble gum. "Why don't you buy your kid a soda pop? Looks like he could use one."

40

Around the corner from Pennington was Ruby's, a clean, bright diner with white-tiled walls, a long marble counter, and rows of ceiling fans whose chrome-plated blades had always made Jake think of B-29 propellers. On the way to Ruby's, Shubin firmly held him by the arm, as if afraid that Jake might try to run away, but when they entered the blinding brightness of the diner, he let him go. A waitress loaded with plates whisked past them.

"How you making it, sweetheart?" called Shubin after her.

"Overworked! Underpaid!" she shouted back. "I ain't complaining."

She brought the plates down in one swoop onto the

table inside the nearest booth: "Careful, gents, the plates are hot!" then turned around to Shubin. "You look familiar. Do I know you?"

"Doubt it, sweetheart," Shubin said. "I'm new in town."

"Don't pull my leg, mister. I've seen you before. I never forget a face, ask anyone around here." She studied Shubin for a moment. "You always had them goggles on?"

"Yes, darling," Shubin said. "Nearsighted, farsighted, you name it. Blind as a bat." He nudged Jake toward two vacant stools at the end of the counter. "Go sit down and stay put."

Jake left Shubin flinging wisecracks at the waitress, limped to the end of the counter, and sagged onto one of those tall and shiny stools that were fixed to the floor and spun around. The last time Jake came here was with Duane, and they had spun and spun, laughing their heads off, until both felt dizzy. That was only last week, but it seemed like it happened ages ago. Jake thought of Duane high up on that float with his heroic dad waving at the cheering crowds while he was kicked around and called a Commie in front of the whole town, but he did not feel bitter or sorry for himself. He felt nothing.

"So what was that all about?" Shubin said, setting a Coke before Jake and straddling the stool beside him. "Throwing yourself under a float?"

Jake did not look at him, watching instead the slivers of

melting ice sliding down the grooves of the Coke bottle. He licked his dry, cracked lips—he was terribly thirsty—but he did not touch the bottle.

"Drink it, drink it," Shubin said. "What's the matter with you? Not thirsty?"

Without looking at Shubin, Jake said, "Where's my dad?"

Shubin's stool rotated away. "You must be hungry. When did you eat last?"

"Where's my dad? You said you knew him well."

"Sure, sure," Shubin said, and shouted toward the front of the counter. "Who do I have to see around here to get some food?"

"Menus on the counter, boys," the waitress shouted back from behind the cash register.

Shubin yanked the menu out of the wire stand and slapped it down on the marble top. "Let's take a look." His bony finger moved up and down the menu. "What are you having? Eggs and bacon? Fries? Sausage? Burger? What?"

"You said you'd tell me about my dad, and now you don't want to," Jake said quietly. "I thought you wouldn't." He waited for a moment, unsure if he should say it, but he said it anyway. "I know all about you. It's not like I don't know."

"Know what?" Shubin said, studying the menu.

"You're stealing our secrets for the Russians. I saw you."

Shubin set the menu down, slowly rotated his stool toward Jake, and cocked his head to one side, studying him. Jake glanced up at him quickly. He could not see Shubin's eyes behind the flickering reflections of the ceiling fan in his cracked spectacles, but he could feel Shubin's rising anger. Jake looked around for the quick way out in case Shubin tried to jump him, but once again Shubin surprised him. He burst out laughing.

"What's so funny, boys?" the waitress shouted.

"This young fellow here." Shubin slapped Jake's shoulder. "He's a riot. He ought to be on the radio."

"Oh, yeah? What did he say?"

"You tell the lady, Jake. Come on. Tell her."

Jake thought again of how well Shubin could pretend to be a regular American. His mother said that he had studied English a little harder than Jake did at school, but the truth was, the Commies knew how to train their spies.

The waitress came over, dropped a little yellow pad on the counter, and took a pencil from behind her ear. "Soup is beans today," she said. "So what's the gag? I can use a laugh."

"The young joker here says I spy for the Russians."

"I thought spies were handsome." She smiled, watching Shubin laugh. "I swear I've seen you here before."

Shubin wagged his head side to side, chuckling.

"But the parade today?" she went on. "A fella said they

caught a foreigner. A Communist. Trying to blow up a float or something. You believe that? Them Communists are everywhere."

"To blow up a float?" Shubin said. "Nah. I don't believe it."

"Don't look at me. The fella said. Why would he lie?"

"I wouldn't know, sweetheart. Seems like lying is the thing to do these days. You read and hear them lies everywhere. Certain individuals are paid good money for it. For lying, I mean."

Jake glared at him. *That's right. You're getting paid for it in Russian money.*

"They spread such lies about the foreigners and the Communists, sweetheart, it'll scare the pants off you," Shubin said, and added quickly, "I don't mean your pants, ma'am—I mean Americans in general."

"You kidding, right?"

"No, darling. Dead serious."

The waitress looked around uneasily. "So what are you saying?"

"What I'm saying is," Shubin went on, "if you are going to forfeit your Constitution so that the government can beat up on folks who think differently than you do, how are you better than the Russians?"

Jake saw that the waitress was gaping at Shubin as if she had been hit on the head with a board and that a little old man in a straw hat seated next to him had carefully lifted his plate, moved three stools away, set his plate back down on the counter, and only then flung a nasty look at Shubin.

"Nah, never met *you* before," the waitress said decisively. "Ready to order or what?"

Shubin began ordering dishes, plenty of them, enough for five grown men. The waitress wrote it all down without once again looking at him. When she left to talk to someone through the little window behind the counter, Jake said, "I don't get it."

"Which part?"

"You're a Russian spy, and you're going around telling everyone that Communism is good."

"I didn't say that."

"But you're defending Communists."

"No, young McCauley, I'm defending the Constitution, and I should hope you'd do the same when you're a grown man. Besides—" He grinned ear to ear. "It looked to me that you could've used some defending yourself when those marching jerks knocked you about with their bugles."

Jake winced. He wanted to say that it was Shubin's fault that everyone turned on him, but it was also his mom's fault for taking Shubin in, and also Duane's fault for telling everyone about it, and so he said nothing.

"Listen, pal." Shubin leaned in close. "I'm sorry that you

got yourself into this mess, but you have only yourself to blame. I tried everything I could to keep you out of it, but you got a bee under your butt. If you don't quit sneaking around and sticking your nose into things you can't even begin to understand, you'll be in much bigger trouble than you already are, get it?"

Jake felt Shubin's tobacco breath warm on his cheek and he leaned away from him a little.

"You know how dangerous this is? Do you have any idea?" Shubin glanced over his shoulder and leaned in closer. "You want to know about your dad? Okay, I'll tell you. You're putting his life on the line, pal. He could've been killed today because of you."

"What?" Jake cried. "My dad is alive?"

"Keep your voice down," Shubin snapped. "He's alive, but not for long, if you don't stop snooping around. And not just him, kid. Other people, too."

He pulled away from Jake and, pretending to read the back of the menu, scanned the people in the diner, checking every face for an instant, then moving on to the next one.

"Hand the B-47 manual over." He dropped his left hand below the counter. "Pass the folder under here, so no one sees it."

Jake looked down at his narrow, ropy hand with tobacco-stained fingers, then back up at his face. "What do you mean, my dad is alive but not for long? And who are the others? What people?"

"Hand me the manual."

"What people?" Jake repeated, straining to see Shubin's eyes behind the reflections in his spectacles.

"You, Jake. You can be killed. It's no joke."

"Who else? My mother?"

Shubin yanked his hand away, snatched off his spectacles, and tossed them onto the marble top. A wad of dirty tape around the bridge of the frame had begun to unravel, and studying Shubin's jagged profile, Jake thought that he, too, looked unraveled somehow. Shubin's face seemed grayer and thinner than it did before, and the lines around his mouth and eyes seemed deeper, carved out like scars from knife fights, or torture, or crawling through barbwire, or just from what was on his mind at that moment.

"My mother could be killed?" Jake said again.

Shubin lifted his spectacles off the counter, set them back over his nose, and said without looking at him, "Yeah. Her too."

"And my dad?" Jake said. "My dad came back, but you want to kill him, right?"

"Careful, the plates are hot," the waitress said, putting the dishes down and trying not to look in Shubin's direction. "Virginia baked ham. Ham and cheese. Homemade chili. Potato salad. Bean soup. What did I forget? Coffee and pie à la mode on its way."

"Thank you, sweetheart," Shubin said, and began moving the plates around the counter. The little old man in a straw hat who had moved three seats away from them after Shubin said something to the waitress about the Constitution slid off his stool and, passing Shubin on his way out, elbowed, as if by accident, the bowl of bean soup into his lap. Shubin cussed and backed off his stool, brushing the steaming beans off the front of his trousers. While everyone in the diner turned to look at him, and while the waitress rushed around the counter with the towels, Jake snatched the Coke bottle and slipped out of the diner.

41

Jake caught up with the American Legion parade in front of City Hall. A voice directing traffic crackled through the PA system, but a long chain of floats jamming the length of Pennington between Church and Congress was not moving, caught in gridlock. The school band in their blue-and-gold jackets, now unbuttoned, sprawled over the City Hall steps amid their brass and their drums, fanning themselves with sheet music. The veterans in the uniforms glinting with medals stood in the sun, crowded by the eager Boy Scouts. The cowboys let their ponies graze on a lawn before City Hall, and here and there, the blue coats of the mounted policemen loomed still as statues over the wandering throng. The air was heavy and dead, and below the two-faced clock jutting out of the corner of the building, the thermometer showed a hundred and twelve.

Having finished the Coke in one long, thirsty gulp, Jake tossed the empty bottle into the trash bin overflowing with paper plates and cups, and hobbled past the floats and the flags until he saw the person he was looking for.

In spite of the heat, Duane Armbruster still had on his goggles and his pilot's helmet, snapped tightly under his pudgy chin. He sat on the edge of the Superfortress float, swinging his legs and chatting with Jake's classmates gathered below him in a half circle. Even from afar Jake could tell that Duane was still puffed up with pride from riding with his dad in the parade, and when Jake pushed his way through the ring of his classmates, snatched Duane's swinging leg, and yanked him off the float, Duane was terribly offended.

"Hey, what's the big idea?" Duane began to protest, but Jake was already dragging him away from the curious eyes to the other side of the float, where he held him against the huge army truck tire and said, "Listen, bud, you've got to help me."

"To heck with you! Let me go!"

"Shut up and listen! You were right, okay? That Russian guy my mom took in is a spy. I can prove it."

Duane struggled to break free, hollering, "Gonzales! Wheeler! Help!" but Jake kept him pinned against the tire. "Quiet, you fool. Don't you get it? The whole thing is for real. He's threatening to kill us!"

"Who?"

"His name is Shubin. Victor Shubin. He said my mom, my dad, and I would all be killed if we get in his way."

"You don't even have a dad," Duane said, and began hollering again, "Gonzales! Eddie! Vernon! Help!"

Jake slapped his hand over Duane's mouth, and with his other hand swiped the FBI agents' cards out of his pocket. "Take a look at these."

Duane stopped thrashing, screwed up his eyes at the cards, and mumbled something through Jake's hand. Jake moved his hand away. "What?"

"These real?" Duane said.

"That's what I'm asking *you*. The G-men gave them to me, but I don't know if they were real G-men or if they only pretended to be. This spy business is really confusing," he admitted. "I need your help."

Duane squinted at the cards, then cautiously lifted one from Jake's fingers. "Special Agent B. B. Bader." He flipped the card over, looked at its blank side, and flipped it to the front again. "Federal Bureau of Investigation. Looks real."

"I know it does, but the phone number isn't. I called, and it wasn't the FBI. The fellow knew it was me calling before I even said a word. Maybe the Commies are watching me with those hidden TV cameras, you know, like in the comics?"

Duane's eyes opened wide. "What comics? Don't you know what that means?"

"What?"

"This phone number is just for you. They always set up a separate number for an important agent. Someone sits by the phone around the clock in case you call. In case of an emergency. Of course the G-man knew it would be you calling. Who else would it be?"

"Oh yeah?" Jake said, uncertain. "So what does that mean?"

"It means that you're an agent now, bud. Undercover, like Spy Runner."

Jake peered into Duane's eyes, huge and brilliant and greener than ever, and knew at once that Duane was envious of him.

"No, no," he said nervously. "I don't want to. I don't want any of this spy stuff anymore. But you can help me, right?" He stuck his finger onto the card in Duane's hands. "See the address at the bottom? You got to get there fast. When you see them, one fellow's name is Bader and the other fellow is Bambach, like on the cards, okay? No matter which one you talk to—they look alike anyhow—this is what you're going to say—"

"Me?" The brilliant light in Duane's eyes began to dim. "Why can't you go?"

"I can't be in two places at once, Duane! No, three places at once! I can't go to the FBI, find my dad, and warn my mom at the same time; don't you get it?"

And all at once in the terrible heat of that afternoon, Jake felt his belly turn ice-cold with terror. "What if Shubin gets to my mom before me? He probably knows where she works." He looked around wildly. "He might kill her, Duane! We have no time to lose!"

"What's going on here, Duane?" someone said in a crisp and powerful voice. "McCauley? What are you two doing?"

42

Major Armbruster emerged from the shadow of the Superfortress's wing, and watching him approach—tall, broad-shouldered, and handsome—Jake felt guilty, as if it was *his* fault that the major had managed to get himself in such a mess with the Russians.

"Let us have it, Junior," the major said, halting in front of the boys.

Duane hid his hands behind his back and let the card Jake gave him flutter to the ground. "Have what, Dad?"

"Pick it up and hand it over."

"It's mine, sir," Jake said, picking up the card. "I can explain it later, sir. We're kind of in a hurry."

“Is that so?” said Major Armbruster. “The two of you are in a hurry?”

The boys answered at the same time: “Yes, sir,” Jake said. “No, Dad,” said Duane.

Major Armbruster held his hand out, waiting for Jake to give him the card. Jake stepped up and carefully laid the card in the palm of his clean and perfectly shaped hand. The major studied the card for a while, then flipped it to the blank side the same way Duane had. “Where did you find this, son?”

“Well, sir. Just don’t get upset, sir. It’s not my fault, I swear.”

The major smiled his beautiful smile. “I know, I know, McCauley. Don’t worry. Did you find this on the street somewhere?”

“No, sir. They gave it to me.”

“Who gave it to you?”

“The name’s on it, sir. There were two of them. Bader and Bambach. Special agents.” He glanced at Duane for support. “It looks like I’m an agent now, too, sir, undercover, following the Russian spy. The phone number on the card, sir? It’s just for *me* to call.”

“*You* are following the Russian spy, McCauley?” The major smiled again.

“Don’t smile, sir. It’s not just my family in trouble. You’re in trouble, too, sir. Big, big trouble.”

Major Armbruster's smile vanished. "Don't you forget yourself, McCauley," he said sternly. "You're addressing a United States Air Force major."

"Please, Dad," Duane said. "It's okay."

"Quiet!" the major barked. "Attention!"

Startled, Jake saw Duane snapped to attention, and then looked back at the major, frightened by the sudden change in his face.

"Now, McCauley. State your concern clearly and simply. What trouble are you talking about?"

"I really don't have time, sir, but—" Jake halted.

"Go on, go on," the major encouraged him. "Nothing to be afraid of."

"Well, sir . . . You had that top secret folder in your Cadillac? Remember? In the briefcase?"

Major Armbruster gazed at Jake in astonishment. "What are you talking about, McCauley?"

"It's kind of complicated, sir. See, this morning while you were having your fried eggs and tacos? At El Matador? You know what he did? That Russian, I mean? The spy? He snuck into your Cadillac, sir. You should have locked the doors, sir."

The major was silent for a moment, peering at Jake intently out of his green eyes, and then he said again, "Go on, McCauley."

"What's that bomber called, sir? Wings swept back? Six

engines? You know what I'm talking about? He took pictures of every page. The spy did. His name is Shubin, sir. Victor Shubin."

Major Armbruster blinked, squinted at the sun, slid a pair of mirrored Ray-Bans out of his shirt pocket, and set them over his nose. "How do you happen to know that, McCauley?"

"I was there, sir. I was in the car behind the seat. He couldn't see me, but I saw everything. Well, I didn't really see it. I heard it. He was whistling and then . . . Click, click, you know? He has a Minox camera. Like in that movie—remember, we watched it at your house? He's got loads of them in his bag. He pretends to fix cameras, but he doesn't."

Major Armbruster glanced at Duane. "At ease, Junior."

Duane did not move, frozen at attention with bulging, unseeing eyes.

"Junior!" the major repeated, louder. "At ease."

Duane exhaled and folded like a deflated balloon, standing there, awkward, slouched, and a little chubby, exactly the way he stood when the major had visited Mr. Vargas's class. Now Jake understood that Duane was afraid of his dad and he understood why that was so.

"Run along, son," the major said. "Your friends have been waiting for you."

"Don't go far, Duane—I need you," Jake called after him, but Duane, with his eyes lowered to the ground, slipped around the float and vanished.

Jake sighed. There would be no help from him.

"So, McCauley—" the major began, but suddenly Duane was back again.

"Don't listen to him, Dad. He's crazy."

"I'm not crazy, Duane, okay?" Jake cried, relieved to see Duane return. "That Russian spy, sir? Shubin? He's not the only one." He was speaking fast now, afraid to be interrupted. "There's another Russian. Goes by the name of Bull. You should've seen him. A big ugly fellow. When he figured out that I had your top secret folder, sir? I took it by accident, sir, I swear. He went after me. But the G-men, sir? The ones who gave me their cards? Bader and Bambach? We don't even know yet if they're real G-men, sir, that's something we still need to find out. Anyhow, they almost ran me over! But I got away with your folder, sir. They couldn't catch me." Jake smiled proudly. "So that's it, sir. That's the whole story. But now Duane and I kind of have to go. We really are in a hurry."

Jake grabbed Duane by the arm, but Duane yanked his arm away and stepped closer to his father. "He's made it all up, Dad," he said nervously. "It's all from the comics he always borrows from me. Spy Runner."

"No need to tell me, Junior. I should know the difference." The major turned his mirrored Ray-Bans at Jake. "That's quite a story, McCauley. Mind if I take a look at this alleged top secret folder?"

"Well, sir. I didn't want to get you in trouble, sir. I mean no more than you already are, so I . . . Well, you see, sir . . . I burned it."

"You burned it?"

"Yes, sir. By accident."

Major Armbruster began to smile again and, lifting his chin, looked over at something behind Jake's back. Following his gaze, Jake glanced over his shoulder.

His classmates had spilled out from behind the front of the float and stood gaping at them: Eddie Cortes in the blue-and-gold marching band's jacket, Trudy Lamarre in her tiny shimmering skirt, Vernon and Wheeler in their Boy Scouts browns, and Ruddy Kissel in store-bought western gear.

"Did everyone hear McCauley's story?" Major Armbruster said, smiling. "Your friend here has got quite an imagination." And all at once, just like Shubin in the diner, the major burst out laughing.

Offended, Jake squinted at the laughing major. He did not take Jake seriously at all. For the head of security at the air force base, laughing was hardly the way to treat such important matters. At least Shubin, a Communist and the enemy of the United States, took Jake seriously enough to want to kill him.

The major's rollicking laughter was so catching that even though Jake's classmates had no idea what was supposed to be funny, they were now laughing, too—not simply laughing, but trying to laugh harder than the next kid just to show off before the handsome major.

"We got no time for this, bud," Jake said, turning to Duane, but Duane, too, doubling over and holding his belly and shaking, was laughing hard, so hard that it was easy to tell he was only pretending to be laughing.

43

Jake's mother worked for a fellow named Hoover, who was in the window shades business—blinds, drapes, shutters—stuff you could not see through. She had often talked about keeping Hoover's files in order and managing reports, but it was so boring that Jake had never paid attention. At home, she kept her office number penciled on the hallway wall beside the telephone in case of an emergency, but there were never any emergencies worth worrying her about, and Jake, who once had memorized the number, had forgotten it by now. He had neither visited Hoover's workshop—who would want to watch blinds being made?—nor ever wondered where the workshop was located, but once, his mother had mentioned that when she went to work she had always parked her Chevy on Fourth below Broadway. Figuring the workshop must be somewhere near there, Jake hobbled down Fourth Avenue, scanning both sides of the street for any sign with Hoover's name on it.

The thought of seeing his mother made Jake uneasy. Since she had let Shubin move into his dad's attic, she had been acting strangely, as if she had learned some secret but had refused to share it with Jake. Of course he knew by now what that secret was. Shubin must have told her that Jake's father was alive and coming back. But why would she keep from Jake such important and wonderful news? Was she not allowed to tell Jake about his father? Was she afraid of Shubin? No, she did not seem to be afraid of him at all. She had tried harder to please Shubin than she had ever tried to please her own son.

Jake waited on the corner for the bus to bounce by, then crossed the street, walking as fast as his bad leg would carry him, turning his head this way and that and reading the shop signs. A barbershop, a laundry, a shoe repair, a garage across the street, but no Hoover anywhere. His ankle was hurting, probably swelling again.

He tried to imagine Hoover's workshop. The floor would be covered in wood shavings and sawdust, and it would be stuffy in there and noisy from the shrill of a circular saw.

Hoover would be working the saw, splitting lumber into narrow planks to make window shutters, and Jake would have to shout to his mother over the noise of the saw. Hoover would glance at them every now and then, eavesdropping, probably angry that Mrs. McCauley had a visitor in the middle of the busy day. Jake imagined his mother's pale and tear-stained face after he had revealed the truth to her about Shubin. How ashamed she would probably feel for all the harm she had done to Jake. Hoover, no doubt, would stare at his mother crying, while Jake would stand there, proud that he had proved his mother wrong.

Jake grimaced, not from the pain in his ankle, but from the embarrassing scene he had imagined. It seemed so phony. He did not want his mother to be ashamed in front of that nosy Hoover and he did not want his mother to cry.

He hobbled for some time looking under his feet, feeling sad about his poor mother, and sad about himself, and sad about his father, who was out there somewhere not even suspecting that his life was in danger. When he crossed Eighteenth Street, the word *Hoover* floated up in his mind, and he realized that he had just missed what he was looking for. He wheeled around and retraced his steps.

Half a block up Fourth Avenue, on the east side of the street, he halted before a storefront, or what used to be a storefront. A sheet of crumbling plywood boarded shattered windows, the splintered door was nailed behind a pair of crisscrossed two-by-fours, and above it, sagging off the wall, a sign so sun-bleached that Jake could barely make it out: HOOVER BLINDS, SHADES, CURTAINS & SHUTTERS MADE TO ORDER.

Hoover must have moved his workshop to a new location and his mother had forgotten to tell him, or she had told him but Jake had forgotten to listen. Dumbfounded, he stood in the hard glare of the blazing sun, gaping at the boarded-up storefront. He did not like the look of that storefront. He did not like the look of it at all. His skin prickled from the heavy static air that crackled with electricity. He shuffled from one foot to the other, unnerved from some eerie expectation, but what he was expecting, he could not tell. That same feeling that nagged at him before, the feeling that much worse things were yet to come, had suddenly returned and overwhelmed him.

A slanted shadow slid across the storefront. As Jake turned to look at the approaching figure, a bright white light flashed inside his head. The gritty sidewalk swung at him and smacked him in the face. Then someone switched off the sun.

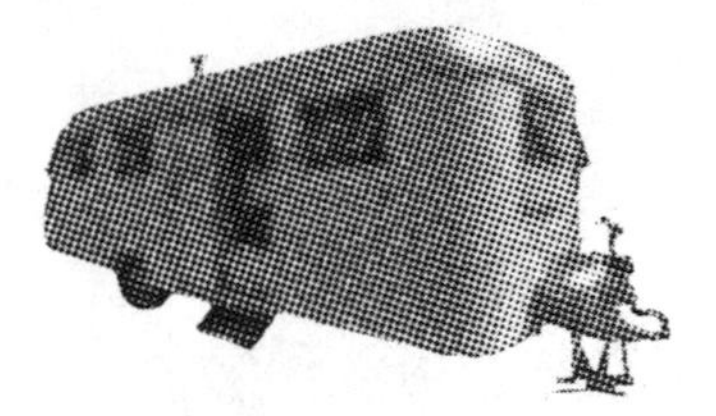

44

When Jake's vision came back, it came back slowly. For a long time, he felt as if he were straining to see through a thick layer of fog. When the fog finally cleared, he saw the riveted aluminum walls curving over him and thought that he was inside the cockpit of a bomber. He looked around for the flight deck with the control wheel and the throttles, but what he saw instead was the cramped interior of an aluminum camper trailer.

The left side of his face was throbbing with pain. He tried to rub at his temple, but could not lift his arm. A thick rope twined around his arms, chest, thighs, and shins bound him to the folding chair.

He tried to scoot the chair forward but lost his balance and nearly tipped it over. He stopped moving and cautiously looked around. Beside him, on a table coated with buckling Formica, the half-eaten remains of some unknown fowl stabbed with cigarette butts was spread-eagled over greasy butcher paper. Overcome with nausea, he quickly looked away.

Drained beer bottles, discarded articles of clothing, and empty food cans moldy-green inside landscaped the trailer's floor. He breathed in a familiar sick-sweet smell and, glancing to his right, saw a set of gold-plated dentures submerged underwater inside a grimy glass. He gasped and, straining at the ropes, rocked side to side, desperate to free himself.

Three rapid knocks on the window behind his back made him stop rocking and cautiously look over his shoulder. Outside the window, Agent Bader, with his nose pressed against the dusty glass, was staring at him. Jake stared back. Bader's right hand came into view gripping a small revolver. He pressed its stocky muzzle against his lips, ordering Jake to be quiet, and ducked out of sight.

The floor swayed under Jake's chair, the trailer shuddered, the door banged open, and Bull lumbered in, bowing the massive ball of his head to fit below the door frame.

When he turned to lock the door, Jake glimpsed rust-colored water sloshing inside the plastic bucket held in Bull's hand. The armpits of Bull's crumpled shirt were stained with dark sweat patches, and his trousers bagged down loose and greasy over his behind. Under his right back pocket, Jake could distinctly make out the shape of a handgun. The door clicked shut, and Bull's enormous body swung around. Jake closed his eyes.

The trailer swayed like a boat on stormy swells under Bull's heavy footfalls. When the sickening motion stopped, Jake heard Bull wheezing beside him. Afraid to raise his eyelids, he was waiting for what would happen next. Suddenly a waterfall drenched his head and shoulders. He gasped and shivered and opened his eyes.

Bull flipped the empty water bucket, placed it close to Jake's chair, and carefully lowered his hefty bulk onto the bucket's bottom. His toothless gums smacked together. "Gve strshet" came out of his mouth, spraying Jake's face with saliva.

Jake wagged his head to shake water off his face. "What?" he said. "I don't speak Russian, sir."

Grunting, Bull leaned across him, fished his golden dentures out of the glass, shook off the water droplets, carefully set the dentures over his gums, and clacked his phony teeth together, testing. "Give Stratojet," he said.

"What's a Stratojet?"

"No lie me. Give."

"What are you trying to . . . Your English is a little . . . I'm sorry, sir, I don't understand."

"I kill you."

That Jake understood. He blinked a couple of times to hold back tears. "You don't have to do that, sir."

"Kill your mama?"

"No, no, no, sir. Please don't do that!"

"Kill your papa?"

Jake paused, searching Bull's bloated face. "You don't know where my father is."

Bull seemed surprised. "How not? No give Stratojet, kill him today."

"Today?"

"Give Stratojet," Bull growled, impatient. "Give it. Give it."

Bull's face with two small slick oily puddles he had for eyes hung so close, it was impossible to look at him. "I don't know what that Stratojet thing is, sir," Jake said, staring down at his knees. "I'm sorry."

Bull leaned over him and lifted the glass that used to hold his dentures and splashed the water into Jake's face. Jake did not move and, letting the water run down his face, bit his lower lip to keep himself from crying. Bull muttered something in Russian and brought the glass down on the Formica table with such force that it shattered to pieces. He yelped and stuck his bloodied fingers into his mouth.

"I no trust you," he said, sucking on his fingers. "In America no trust persons. All lie. No trust him! Need cover, he say. Come customer, he say. Good cover customer. Give me flags and what you call? To go up?"

"To go up? Steps?"

"No. No. Go up." Bull took his fingers out of his mouth and first with one hand and then with the other clawed at the air.

"Climbing? Climbing a ladder?"

Bull nodded. "Larder."

"You mean those pictures Shubin gave you? Men hanging flags for the parade?"

"He say they stop you, you have cover. Regular customer. Give snapshots."

Jake watched Bull for a moment, thinking. "In case you get arrested leaving Shubin's place, you have regular snapshots in the envelope, right? As if you snapped them yourself and brought the film in to be developed? Nothing top secret?"

Bull glared at him in suspicion.

"There was a picture of me, too," Jake remembered. "I didn't want him to take it!"

Bull spat in disgust. "What I do with you? No need you."

"Right! Right!" Jake said in encouragement. "You don't need me."

"Need Stratojet," Bull grunted, bending over his pot-belly. "Gives no Stratojet." He took off his left shoe and shoved it in front of Jake's face. "It he gives!"

"He gave you footwear, sir?" Jake said, lifting his nose away from the stench of the shoe.

"Footvear?"

Bull swung the shoe over his shoulder, as if about to thump Jake on the head. Jake lunged away. The chair keeled over. Bull brought the shoe down, slamming it against the table. Jake crashed to the floor. Something smacked against the wall, bounced off, and clomped beside Jake's nose. He shifted his eyes to the leather heel detached from Bull's shoe. The leather inside the heel was carved out to fit a tiny black cartridge with twin chambers. Duane was right. They *did* have secret compartments in their shoes. The cartridge with the pictures that Shubin took of the major's folder was hidden inside the heel of Bull's stinky shoe.

Bull snatched the heel from under Jake's nose, plucked the cartridge out of the slot with the crook of his bloodied finger, and banged it hard against the table.

"It he gives!" Bull growled. "Send to boss, he say. Is good.

But how to know is real?" He blinked at Jake and added in a low tone, "No real, boss kills me."

"Oh. Oh. I see," Jake said from the floor. "Shubin takes the pictures and gives you the film cartridge, and you ship it to your boss, and if it's not real, your boss would kill you, right?" He waited for Bull to answer, and then added, "But what do you mean *real*, though? Real what?"

"You has real Stratojet! Was in pants! I look. Not in pants!"

"What?" Jake said, horrified. "You looked in my pants?"

"Where Stratojet?" Bull growled. "Give it!"

"You mean the actual folder Shubin was taking pictures of? The one that was in Duane's dad's car? The blue top secret?" Jake looked up at Bull, trying to squeeze a smile out of his trembling lips. "Why didn't you say so in the first place, sir? You don't have to keep me here. I'm no use to you, sir. Could you untie the ropes, please? The folder's gone."

"No give Stratojet?"

"I'm telling you, sir. It's gone. I don't have it, sir."

"Okay," Bull said. "Kill you now."

Bull rose heavily and kicked the water bucket out of the way. Jake glanced toward the window, hoping to see Bader with his gun. He was not there.

When Bull squatted beside him on his massive haunches, Jake's eyes darted from the window toward Bull's thick, stubby fingers, bleeding from the shattered glass, and watched in horror as they closed around his neck.

45

Bull's thumbs kneaded the front of Jake's throat, feeling for something, found it, and began pressing down on his windpipe, first lightly, then harder and harder. Jake shut his eyes, his body crumpling under the steady pressure of Bull's thick fingers. Swooning, he remembered staring at Bull's white arm glowing in the sun when he drove up in his truck to El Matador. His arm looked like an exotic jungle snake, and Jake remembered feeling a cramp in his throat, imagining being strangled in its slimy coils. And so it had come to be. Bull was strangling him.

Somewhere very far away, a voice was shouting. Jake could not grasp the meaning of the words and he stopped trying. He was convinced that he was dead already. He did not feel any pain, not in his throat, nor anywhere in his body. He opened his eyes and, seeing that Bull's fingers were no longer around his throat, looked up, expecting to find himself elsewhere, someplace better than Bull's filthy trailer.

"Put 'em up!" someone shouted. "Step away from the boy!"

Jake's eyes darted toward the voice, but Bull's feet were blocking his view. Jake was still on the floor in the trailer, and Bull's feet, his left missing a shoe, were inches from Jake's face. He looked at Bull's sock, gray like Shubin's but very dirty, slumped down his massive ankle. A big toe with a curled yellow nail was jutting out through the hole in the sock. The stench wafting off that sock and off that toe was unbearable.

"Keep 'em up!" Jake heard the voice he thought he recognized. "Come out!"

Bull's feet pivoted away, and as he shuffled toward the door, Jake looked up at Bull's saggy trousers, his sweaty back, and his arms in the air with spread bloody fingers. In an instant before Bull's enormous body blocked the open door, Jake caught a glimpse of Agent Bambach aiming a tommy gun from the threshold of the trailer.

"Keep moving," Bambach shouted. "No fooling—I'll shoot."

Bull nodded, took another shuffling step forward, and then in a single rapid motion, he kicked the door shut with his socked foot, yanked the handgun out of his back pocket, and fired through the door.

What happened next Jake could only guess because from the moment Bull's gun went off, Jake's eyes were shut. But what he heard was this: the tommy gun barking in bursts of threes, the bullets slugging the walls, shattering glass, single gunshots popping from the direction of the window, shouting and heavy stomping, and when at last the trailer suddenly ceased rocking, Jake heard someone yelling outside, "Bust his tires!" and the tommy gun went back to work. Then there were revved-up engines, squealing tires, more gunfire, and a rumble of many vehicles receding in the distance. And after that was silence.

Jake waited for a long time to open his eyes. When he did, he saw himself bound to the tipped-over chair on the floor covered with shards of broken glass. He thought of pushing himself toward the door, but he kept still instead, lying quietly and watching gun smoke swirling prettily in pins of sunlight streaming through the bullet holes above him.

He heard a motorcar speeding toward the trailer, the sound of the brakes, and while the engine was left running, the floor below him swayed as someone rushed up the trailer's steps. Kathy Lubeck, the young woman from the photography store, entered swiftly and kneeled beside him.

"Oh, you poor baby!" She touched his neck, then looked

at the blood on the tips of her fingers. "Why did they wait so long? We told them he might hurt you."

"Blood's not mine, ma'am."

"Not yours?" she said. "Phew, that's a relief."

Out of nowhere, a knife blade flashed in her hand, and Jake lurched away from her in fright.

"Just going to cut the ropes, Jake, okay?"

"I don't get it," Jake said, watching her sawing at the ropes with the blade. "I thought you and Shubin were—"

"Our people are coming to get you, Jake. Won't take a minute, I promise." She sliced through the ropes that held his feet. "We'll take care of you; just stay put."

And then he was free and the next moment she was gone. He heard the vehicle speeding away outside and after a while, he sat up, cautiously touching his neck where Bull's thumbs had nearly strangled him. He took a deep breath, rolled up to his feet, and, holding himself with care, hobbled to the door. He halted in the doorway and, leaning against the door frame, stood still for a while, watching the desert sun beginning to set.

46

"Agent Bambach is out in the field at the moment," a lady receptionist said, her eyes twinkling behind the large round spectacles. "Is it about a fight, dearie?"

"What fight?" Jake said.

"Your face? Your left cheek is . . ." She paused. "Who did this to you, dearie?"

He touched the left side of his face where Bull had hit him in front of the abandoned storefront.

"I need to talk to someone, ma'am. It's urgent."

"Looks to me like a police department matter." She smiled, and her eyes twinkled again behind the spectacles. "This here is the Federal Bureau of Investigation, dearie, not the police. Do you know the difference?"

Jake snatched Agent Bambach's card, which he had set before her. "Yes, ma'am. I know the difference." He moved away from her desk and stood with his hands deep in his pockets and with his injured foot propped against the wall behind him. "I'll wait."

"Might be a long time, though. They're all awful busy today."

"Yes, ma'am. I know."

"Do you, now?"

The lady's round spectacles were fixed so persistently at him that Jake turned away, uneasy under her stare.

Kathy Lubeck told him to stay in the trailer until someone came for him, but Jake, wary of who that *someone* might turn out to be, decided not to wait to find out. Besides, after what happened there, he did not feel like hanging around that horrid trailer a minute longer. A bus driver who gave him a lift downtown, after taking one long look at Jake's face, did not even ask him for money. Bouncing in the back of the bus on the way to the FBI office, Jake had wondered what he would find. If the phone number was only for him to call, as Duane said, what about the address on the card? Did they put up a special office for him, too? Jake was ready to believe it by the looks of this place.

In the movies and the comics, the FBI offices were always noisy, smoke-filled rooms with whirring ceiling fans, and clicking typewriters, and ringing telephones, and special agents roaming in between the desks with their jackets off

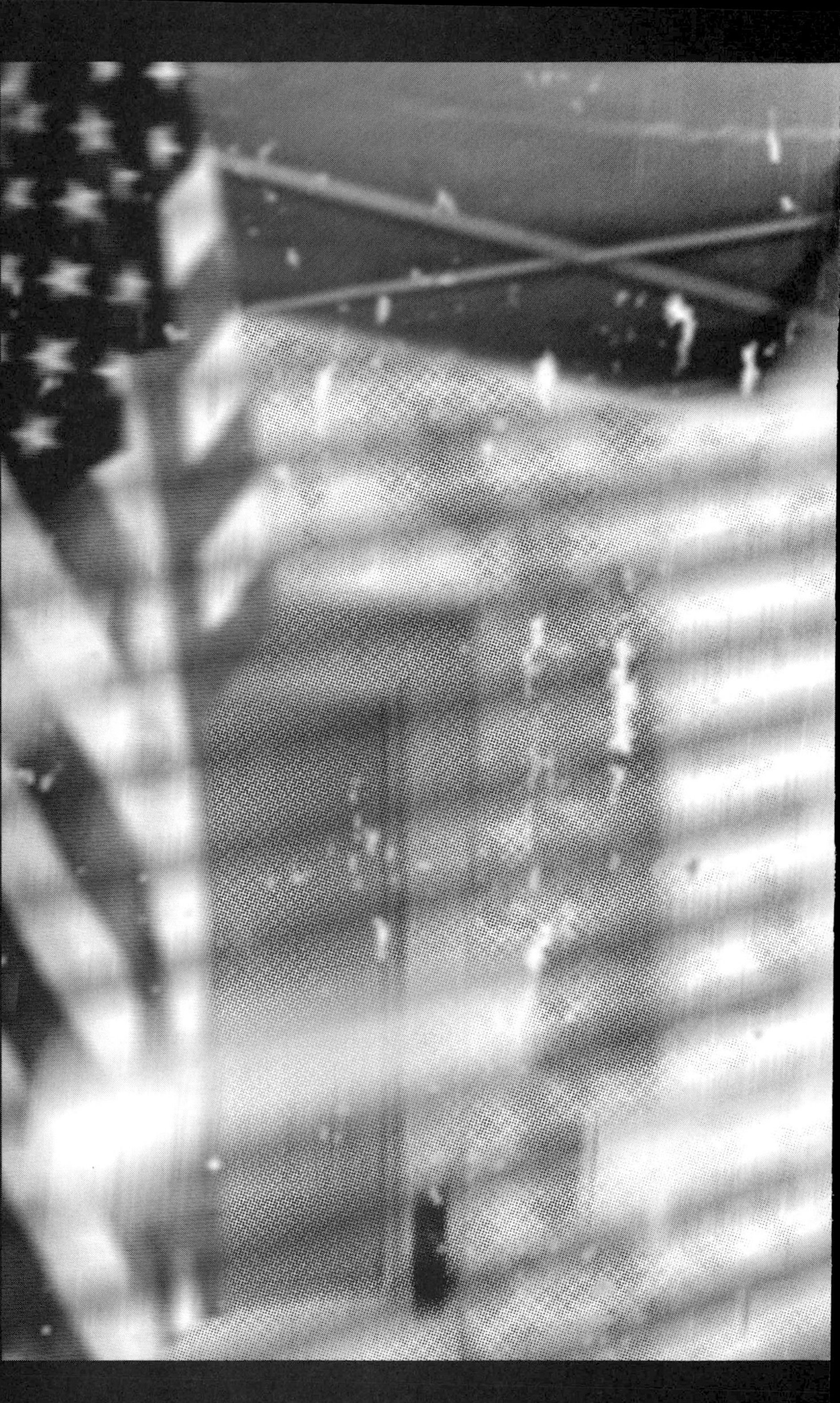

for you to see the pistols in their shoulder holsters. This place was different.

Following the address printed on the card, Jake had found a dreary waiting room with a dust-coated Stars and Stripes drooping from the stand in the corner and a picture of a fat-cheeked fellow hanging above the receptionist's desk. The only thing missing to make it look like any other small-time office in their city was a piece of dusty taxidermy, a stuffed great horned owl, for example—those were always popular.

"J. Edgar Hoover. Our director," the receptionist said, catching Jake eyeing the photograph of the fat-cheeked fellow. "Are you familiar?" She swiveled in her chair and reverently gazed at the picture. "Never met him personally, but some of our men have. An inspiring individual, Mr. Hoover. He said this. I memorized it. 'We can successfully defeat the Communist attempt to capture the United States by fighting it with truth and justice.' Think about it, dearie. Fighting it with truth and justice."

"Yes, ma'am," Jake said. "I heard it on the radio."

He stared at the picture for a moment, then thought of Shubin rocking in his dad's old rocker and he surprised himself by saying, "Only you can't trust everything you hear on the radio, ma'am. Some people think it's all baloney."

"It's what?" gasped the receptionist.

"Some people say there are plenty of suckers in this country who get neither liberty nor justice just because they think differently than J. Edgar Hoover, or something like that, I don't remember exactly, but it's against the Constitution."

Speechless, the receptionist sat under the picture, blinking at Jake through her round spectacles.

"What . . . what are you trying to . . . ," she finally stuttered. "Do you realize where you are, young man?"

"Yes, ma'am, I realize." Jake squinted at the fat-cheeked fellow in the picture. "I just heard someone say it, ma'am. I can't verify it or nothing, but some people, some people in my class, for example, they decided I was different, that I was a Communist, which I am not, and they sure gave me plenty of trouble, ma'am. I can't say what it's like for real Communists, ma'am, but it sure felt lousy to me."

Listening to him talking, the receptionist's face seemed to shrivel into a little crumpled ball, while her spectacles remained the same size, or even grew larger, Jake could not tell for certain, but somehow the spectacles looked so big on her face that she began to resemble a stuffed great horned owl, a piece of dusty taxidermy, perched behind a typewriter.

Then the door to the right of the receptionist's desk came open and another lady backed out, her hands occupied by a tall stack of files. She shoved the door with her hip, and when it did not shut, she gave it a good kick with the heel of her shoe. The door slammed, and the woman turned around. It was Jake's mother, Mrs. McCauley.

47

"File these, Lucy," Jake's mother said to the receptionist. "I cross-referenced every one with the master list, but he didn't come up. He must be here under a different name."

She leaned in to set the stack of files on the desk and saw Jake watching her. The files missed the desk and cascaded to the floor.

"Oh gosh, Mrs. McCauley," cried the receptionist. "Let me take care of that."

She shot up from her chair, scurried around the desk, and, passing Mrs. McCauley, whispered loud enough for Jake to hear, "The boy there? A young Communist."

While the receptionist collected the files off the floor,

Mrs. McCauley and Jake stared at each other in silence. The receptionist rose, set the files on the desk, and said, glancing back and forth between the two, "You all know each other?"

"You need to use the powder room, Lucy," said Mrs. McCauley.

"Do I, now?" replied the receptionist, surprised.

"Yes, Lucy, you do. I'll take care of the files."

The receptionist hesitated, nodded slowly to Mrs. McCauley, and, flinging a dirty look at Jake, minced out of the room.

Mrs. McCauley quickly came over to Jake and with the tips of her fingers touched his right temple. He winced and jerked his head away. She gasped, a sob caught in her throat. "My God, who did this to you?"

"You work here?"

"This is awful . . . I told them . . . I'm taking you to the doctor right away."

"You work here, Mother?"

He had never called her *Mother* before, and she looked at him, frightened.

"You said you were working for the guy named Hoover."

She did not answer. *Oh. Hoover. Right.* Jake glanced at the picture of the fat-cheeked fellow on the wall. J. Edgar Hoover. The FBI director.

All at once, he felt weak. He needed to sit down. He saw a metal folding chair by the wall and made a move for it but stumbled and nearly fell. His mother caught him and, keeping him upright, hooked the chair with her right foot, dragged it away from the wall, and carefully lowered him into the seat.

"I was going to tell you, honey, as soon as this mess settled. I was going to tell you when—"

"How long?"

"How long what, honey? How long have I been with the Bureau?" She could not meet his eye. "Well. A few years. Yes. A few years."

"How long, Mom!"

She began to cry. "I don't know, honey. Since the war. Since your father left for Europe. I took his place here."

"What are you talking about? He didn't work here. Dad was in the air force."

"Ah, yes. In the air force, too, honey. Yes. It's a little complicated."

She kneeled beside his chair and tried to hold his hands as she had always done to soothe him, but this time, he yanked his hands away.

"Why is it complicated, Mom? You have to tell me now."

"He was both, honey."

"Both what?"

"Air force. FBI. Both. You see. The thing is."

Her body began to lean sideways, and all at once, she sat on the floor beside the chair, one leg folded under the other, looking away from Jake and talking very quickly and crying.

"The thing is. I can't tell you. I'm not allowed. But now that he's back, that your father is back—"

"I know he's back, Mom," Jake said. "But where is he?"

Again she did not answer but, crying and looking away, went on in the same flat, colorless voice. "What we have here, you see, honey, we have operational security. *Need to know* it's called. That's the rule. *Need to know.* You didn't need to know, so we couldn't tell you. You see? We had two agents assigned—you met them, Bambach and Bader—they were supposed to watch over you, honey. I wanted to do it myself, but they wouldn't let me. Do you understand? Bambach and Bader were to keep you safe."

"To keep *me* safe?"

"Yes, honey."

"You *lied* to me to keep me safe?"

Jake stood up quickly and, glancing at the picture of fat-cheeked J. Edgar Hoover, saw that the FBI director was staring straight *at him* with the same X-ray eyes that Bambach and Bader were staring at him with at school. Jake paused for an instant, bewildered. He could have sworn that Hoover was not even looking in his direction before.

He turned away from the picture and said to his mother,

"Guess what, Mom. Lying didn't keep me safe. It made it worse."

"Don't go, honey," she cried, reaching out to him. "We have to see the doctor!"

But Jake was already at the door, yanking it open to reveal the receptionist bent by the keyhole, eavesdropping.

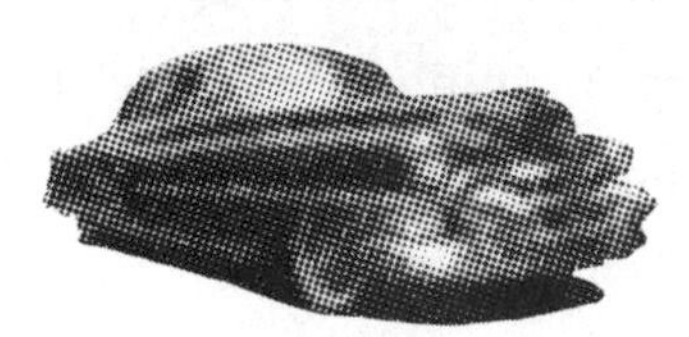

48

He was not a block away from the FBI's office when a shadow of a motorcar slid up beside him. He kept walking without looking over, knowing what he would see if he did, and the shadow of the vehicle and the quiet hum of its engine kept up with him until he reached Arizona Avenue.

That Major Armbruster would be looking for him Jake had no doubt, since he had foolishly given away top secrets in front of everybody at the end of the parade. The major knew where to find him, too, after Jake handed him the G-man's card. Still, it troubled Jake that the major had to look for him. Jake was the one who should have come to him first. Not only did he owe Major Armbruster an apology, but he needed to explain Shubin's spying better to him, not in a rush and not in front of the others. The trouble was that after the shocking truth Jake just learned about his parents, he was hardly in the mood for more explaining. And that was why he kept limping alongside the slow-moving Cadillac without looking at it, just to buy time to calm his nerves.

On the corner of Broadway and Arizona, Jake was about to cross the street when the Cadillac took a sharp right and stopped in his path. Jake halted, watching his reflection in the passenger-side window disappear as the glass slid down and reappear again, doubled and smaller, in the major's mirrored Ray-Bans.

"Get in the car, son," said Major Armbruster.

"I'm sorry about your top secret folder, sir," Jake said without moving. "I'm sorry I burned it."

"I know you are, son. Get in. We ought to have a talk."

"About what, sir?"

"About what?" the major said. "If you're aiming for a laugh, McCauley, you won't be hearing it from me, son, 'cause it ain't funny."

"You did laugh before, sir," Jake objected.

"There were witnesses," the major agreed. "I had to cover for you."

"For me, sir?"

"For you, too, McCauley. Let's face it, son, you got us both in a mess of trouble. Care to sort it out?"

The major sat very still in the darkened interior, watching him through his Ray-Bans. Jake thought of Duane with his bulging, unseeing eyes frozen in terror before his father. Jake glanced over his shoulder. The street was empty.

"What's the problem, McCauley?" the major said. "Scared to go for a ride with me?"

Jake shifted from foot to foot, glanced around again, then looked back at the major. "Why should I be scared, sir?"

He stepped up to the Cadillac, opened the door, and got in beside the major, and while he was still closing the door behind him, the major spun the steering wheel and gunned the engine, swinging the vehicle away from the curb.

The AC was going at full blast. The Cadillac, oven-hot when Jake had been hiding from Shubin in it, was chilled like an icebox. Jake shivered and wrapped his arms around himself to keep warm.

"You got into a fight, son?" the major said, glancing at him.

Jake leaned forward and flipped the sun visor and looked at his face in the clip-on mirror. The left side of his face was swollen as if a bee had stung him, and just below the temple, a nasty bump was glowing purple. Jake flipped the sun visor back.

"Yes, sir. Sort of."

The major nodded in approval. "Thumbs-up, son. Fighting builds character. Junior never fights. He gets beaten. Why is that, McCauley?"

Jake shrugged.

"He got his nose busted yesterday. His mother near had a nosebleed herself when she saw him. Was it you?"

"What, sir?"

"Busted his nose?"

"No, sir."

The Cadillac turned off Twenty-Second Street and crossed the railroad tracks burnished by the glow of the setting sun. When the tires clambered over the tracks, Jake's heart leapt in fright because the gravel spraying the bottom of the vehicle sounded like Agent Bambach's tommy gun spraying bullets.

The major turned onto Alvernon Way, just as something surged from the air force base runway, a couple of miles south. In an instant, the thing grew into a massive bomber that whipped so low over them, Jake ducked instinctively, expecting it to rip the roof right off the Cadillac. The major laughed.

"A beauty, ain't she? B-47 Stratojet."

The aircraft passed over them in total silence, and when it flashed again behind the major's window, Jake glimpsed six slick engines tucked under its swept-back wings.

Gaining altitude, the bomber vanished as instantly as it had appeared, and only then the high pitch of its engines shrieked in pursuit. Jake cautiously touched his throat. So that was the Stratojet. The bomber from the top secret folder the Russians wanted so much that Jake had nearly died for it.

"The fastest bomber ever built," the major said. "Did you know that, McCauley?"

Jake thought of the film cartridge with twin chambers hidden inside the heel of Bull's smelly shoe and said without looking at the major, "Yes, sir. Until the Russians build one just like it."

Since he had climbed into the car, Jake had not looked at the major, keeping his eyes fixed on the road ahead, but he could feel the Ray-Bans linger on his face, and it made him feel uneasy.

"Ever seen the boneyard, McCauley?"

"The what, sir?"

"The boneyard, son. The end of the line. That's where our aircrafts rest in peace. Didn't Junior tell you? I took him there once. It's an instructive sight, McCauley, the boneyard."

Jake thought about it. "Yes, sir. I believe Duane did tell me he saw the B-29s rusting away in the desert."

"Don't say that," the major snapped. "Not rusting

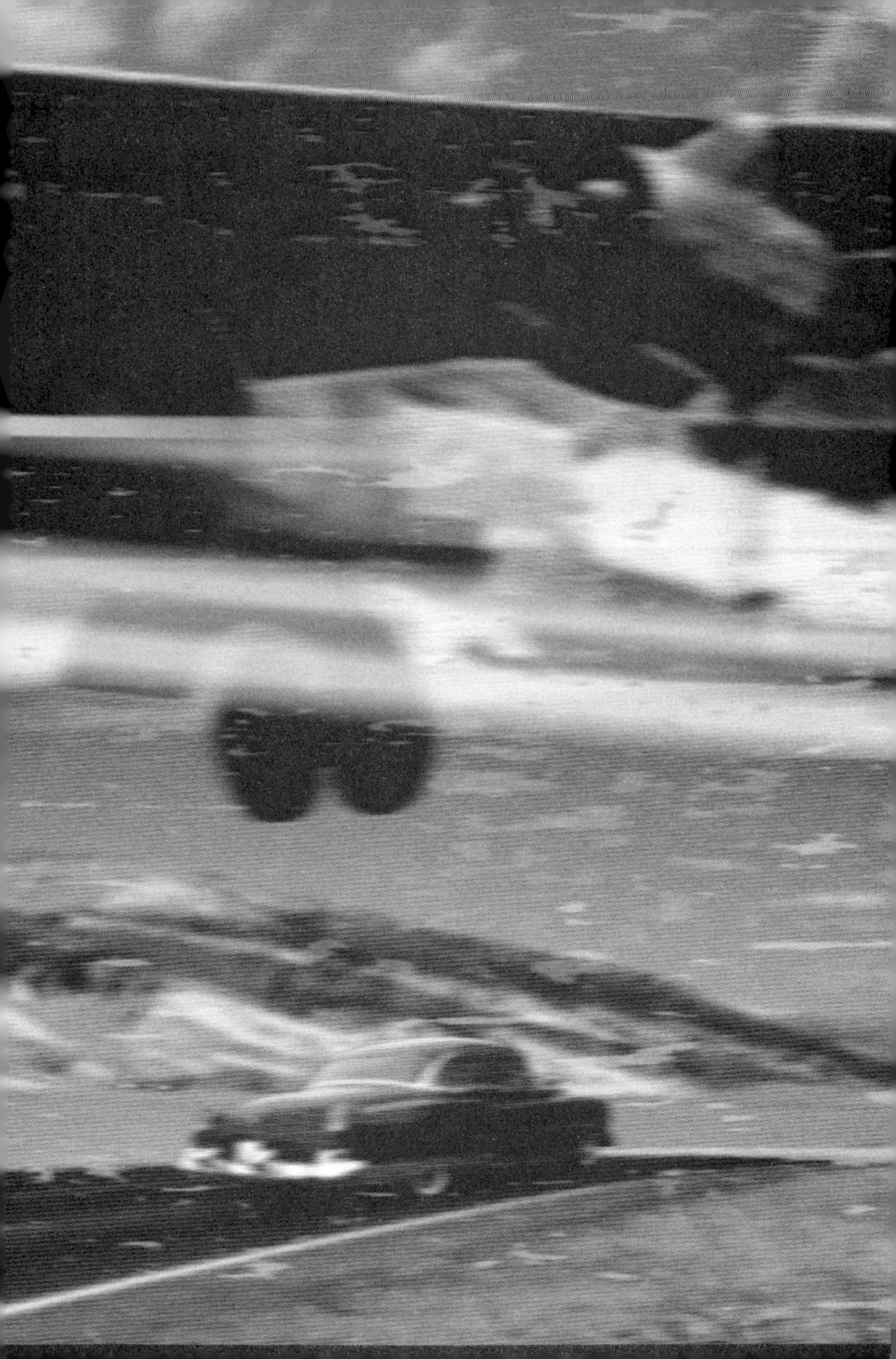

away. Dead aircrafts are like people, son. They need to be buried. No, strike that, the aircrafts are better than people. Better than those morons who are supposed to protect them, that's for damn sure. Let us take a little side tour, son. You'll enjoy it."

And with sudden violence, he spun the steering wheel so sharply to the left that Jake was launched out of his seat, banging his shoulder hard against the door.

49

They were heading southeast toward the desert. The major was silent. Jake, who had never been so far away from the city, looked over his shoulder at the mountains lit by the setting sun, turned back, and said, still not looking at the major, "I always wanted to ask you something, sir. May I?"

"Go ahead, son. What's on your mind?"

"Did you know my dad, sir? Before the war, I mean."

"I knew that was coming." He turned his Ray-Bans on Jake for a moment. "Took you a long time to ask. Can I be frank with you, McCauley?"

"Yes, sir."

"Your old man and I were the best of friends, McCauley. Of all the people and, mind you, I'm well known in the air force, your old man was the only one who knew how to appreciate Major Armbruster. Surprising, isn't it?"

"I guess so. I mean, yes, sir."

"Our friendship goes way back. When our boys were sent to Europe to kick Hitler's butt, I requested to be sent also. The real opportunities, McCauley, were there, not at home. Guess what those morons said?"

"What did they say, sir?"

"We need you at the AFB, Armbruster, and that was that, no excuses." He waved his hand dismissively. "The morons know, McCauley, how to keep a worthy man from feeling good about himself, but do they know how to keep their top secrets secret? You follow me, son?"

"I'm trying to, sir."

"One person who had a true appreciation for my abilities was your old man, McCauley, my best bud by then. So I said to him once over a cold beer, I said to him, and I am paraphrasing, McCauley—it was years back, see? I said, when the dark forces threaten our freedom, the least I can do is to partake in the historical struggle."

The major glanced at Jake to check his reaction. Jake was not sure how to react, so he said, "You said that to my dad?"

"You bet I did, McCauley. Your old man had a friend then in the Russian air force, and I had a hunch he'd know how to appreciate my service. The Russians were our allies in the war, McCauley. Did you know that? I'm talking nineteen forty-three. Everyone loved the Russians then."

Jake was staring straight ahead at the oily black slab of the highway coming fast at them in the twilight, but out of the corner of his eye, he watched the major carefully, straining to understand every word he said.

"I was cleared for security by then," the major continued, "and could, so to speak, let that Russian friend of his peek at some . . . well, nothing important, naturally, a new radar, a couple of manuals. Are you paying attention, McCauley?"

Jake nodded slowly.

"It's important that you're paying attention," the major added sternly. "'Cause you ain't going to hear *this* again."

"I think I am paying attention, sir."

The Cadillac seemed to be going a lot faster now, but faster still were Jake's thoughts rushing through his head. Jake's ears were listening to the major's voice, but his thoughts were coming at him all at once, stumbling, tumbling, crashing into one another, making his head feel very big and full of flashing lights. What the major was telling him about was treason. He had been handing American secrets over to the Russians, and the person who had been helping him was Jake's father. Only Jake's father was more than the major knew. He was not just the major's *best bud* at the base lending him a hand in spying for the Russians, he was also an undercover FBI agent working to beat the Russians at spying. All of it was terribly confusing and scary, but Jake knew that there was no turning back for him now, and so he said, "Did they pay you for that, sir? The Russians, I mean."

The major shook his head in disgust. "I had always wished you were *my* kid, McCauley, but I'm beginning to be disappointed in you. Talking about benefits! Yes, there was cash money from the Russians, but did I do it for cash? No, son. I did it for respect. Your old man respected me, and that can be verified. The United States Air Force failed to appreciate Armbruster, but your old man, he came through."

The western sky, bloodred from the setting sun just a moment ago, faded to blue then to inky blue, and the vehicles coming toward them on the highway were switching on their lights. The major removed his Ray-Bans, carefully folded and slipped them into his front shirt pocket, then clicked on the headlamps.

"The Russian cash, McCauley, paid for the American dream. A comfortable home with a pool? Check. A luxury automobile? Check. A television set, kitchen appliances, a top-notch fallout shelter? Check. Check. Check. This is what every American wants, McCauley."

Jake took a deep breath, held the air in his chest for a moment, exhaled, and said quickly, as if he was afraid to lose courage before he had finished saying it, "So you are a traitor, then, sir? You sold our secrets to the Russians so you could have a house with a pool?"

"Pool has nothing to do with it!" the major shouted so loud that Jake ducked, afraid that he might punch him. "I don't even know how to swim! I'm talking about respect. Your old man was gone, what? Ten years? Eleven? My life was miserable, McCauley. Contemplated suicide. Gave it serious consideration. I'm not talking about the morons at the AFB, McCauley, not a single promotion since the war. I'm talking no respect at home, the man's castle. The wife and Junior are disappointments. They fear me, yes, but where's their respect?"

Jake almost began arguing with him, almost said that the major was wrong, that Duane had so much respect for his father, he could not stop bragging about him. But he did not say anything, worried that the major might get angry again.

"Sure, they kept sending the Russians my way. Each one was dumber than the one before, all morons. Once a fellow showed up with gold teeth, imagine that? Not to be trusted. But when they got wind of the Stratojet, I told them straight out, I'd only deal with my old partner on that one, no one else. And sure enough, they brought your old man back."

"You saw my father?" Jake said, and for the first time, looked openly at the major.

"Saw him? I don't need to see him. Not in person. But

we do have a nice little arrangement how and when the transaction takes place, McCauley, as you had the misfortune to find out."

Jake's thoughts rushed through his head again, flashing like lightning and making bright all that was murky before. Jake's dad was behind this whole operation. He was the one who had arranged the dead drop location, which was inside this very Cadillac. It was not by accident that the major did not lock his car; it was all planned in advance. Jake's dad had told the major to leave the top secret folder in the briefcase and he told Shubin how to find it and when. But it was only a trick to fool the major and Shubin because Jake's dad was a double agent. Shubin found that out somehow and that was why he wanted to kill him. At last, Jake understood what he had gotten himself into. By trying to expose Shubin, he had exposed Major Armbruster instead. Everything became clear to Jake now save for two things. Number one: Where was his dad? Number two . . . Number two was not even that important, but it seemed important enough for Jake to find out.

"Sir?" he said. "I have another question."

"Speak now, son, or forever hold your peace." The major chuckled. "And I mean it literally."

"Well, sir. When you came to our classroom to talk about fighting the threat of Communism, sir? Remember?"

"What about it?"

"Well, it's this, sir. You said that Communism means destruction of the American way of life, sir. But you yourself, sir, you were helping the Russians. Were you lying to us, sir?"

Without warning, the major lunged forward and smashed his fist into the dashboard in a fit of such fury that Jake jumped in his seat.

"What's wrong with you, McCauley?" the major shouted. "Do you have to be so dumb? I'm an American! I love my country! Liberty and justice for all and so forth. The question is how much does my country love me back? I ought to have been a colonel by now. A general. A chief of staff."

The major slammed his foot onto the gas pedal, and the Cadillac growled and leapt forward.

"No, son, don't you confuse me with your old man," the major went on, trying to control his anger. "He's a Russian. Well, sort of. His mom and dad ran away from Russia when the Communists started all that mess over there, but he was born around here. Arizona, I think, New Mexico maybe. Still, to me he's a Russian. He's my best bud and all, but can you trust a Russian completely? No, McCauley, you can't. And that is why you and I will be solving our little problem without him being aware."

"What problem, sir?"

"The problem is *you*, son." The major turned to Jake, smiling his beautiful smile, and his teeth, even and white, flashed for an instant in the brights of the oncoming car. "The problem is *you*," he repeated, and reached over toward the glove compartment.

It was a long way to reach from the Cadillac's steering wheel to its glove compartment, and when the major leaned across Jake's knees, he scooted away and flattened himself against the door. The major flipped the lid of the glove compartment open, took out his handgun, and eased back behind the steering wheel. "Shut the latch, son, will you?"

At the sight of the gun, Jake's whole body went numb, and when he shut the glove compartment as the major told him, he could not feel his fingers touching it, as if his hand did not belong to him.

"This here weapon, McCauley, .45 Colt M1911," Major Armbruster said, thumbing back the hammer, "has been in the US Army service since before the First World War. Ain't nothing, son, more reliable to take care of our little problem. You sit tight now. We're just about to hit the boneyard."

Jake could not see the major clearly in the darkened interior, but he could see the gun in his hand, resting over the steering wheel. It shone brightly, almost merrily, in the beams of the passing vehicles.

So that was it, then. The end of the line, as the major called the boneyard. It would be Jake's boneyard, too. *His* end of the line. Jake imagined his bones bleached by the sun and scattered among the rusted bombers, and he imagined how one day, someone, Duane maybe, or Mr. Vargas with his whole class on a field trip, would come upon Jake's bones, but would not know they were his. How short his life had turned out to be! Jake was in his twelfth year, but he was never to become a teenager. He was never to see his mom again and he was never to meet his dad, the only thing he had ever really wanted.

Jake shoved his hand into the front pocket of his jeans, dug around there for a while, then pulled out two things: the tooth that he had lost when he had fallen into the ditch and the stick from the ice cream bar that the old man had given him for free in the alley. He set both objects on the bench in between the major and himself and said, "Can I ask you a favor, sir?"

"What is it, son?"

"Could you please give these to my mom when you see her?"

"Give her what, McCauley?" Major Armbruster glanced at the darkened bench. "I can't see a darn thing."

When the major leaned in to take a better look, Jake darted away from him, unlocked his door, and leapt out. A gust of wind swiped Jake in the face and the blacktop rushed at him, but it did not have a chance to hit him. The major caught Jake by the waistband of his jeans and yanked him back inside the vehicle. The door slammed behind Jake, knocking him sideways into the major's lap. Cussing, the major shoved him aside and turned to fumble with the wildly spinning wheel.

The Cadillac careened across the center lane. The headlights of the oncoming vehicle flooded the interior. A shudder rocked the car. The windshield buckled, sagged inward, and exploded into a million sparkling fragments. Another vehicle smashed into the Cadillac from the rear. The Cadillac spun in place, flinging shards of glass in all directions. All sounds ceased. The car was spinning. A moment passed in utter silence and in utter darkness.

How long that moment lasted, Jake could not tell, but then there was a jolt, a whoosh, and something whacked hard at his back. Miraculously, he saw the Cadillac from a considerable distance. The vehicle was on its side in the ditch, smoking from under the crumpled hood. Jake looked around in confusion. He was lying on the sunbaked clay about fifty feet away from the ditch. The impact must have pitched him out of the car through the missing windshield. He did not feel any pain, but he could not hear a thing.

He slapped at his ears and shook his head. Tiny fragments of glass fell out of his hair. He tried to get up, but his bad leg gave out from under him, and he sat down hard. He rested for a while, panting, watching the lights of the vehicles lining up along the highway shoulder. Smoke billowed from the wrecked Cadillac. He saw shadows descending into the ditch through the beams of light. He saw people huddle around the Cadillac, force one door open, and then pass the major's body through the gaping windshield.

Jake staggered to his feet and stood, uncertain. His head knew that he should go back to the highway and ask those people for help, but his heart decided otherwise. Mistrustful and suspicious after what he had been through, his heart made him turn away from the highway and limp into the pitch-black desert.

50

When Jake came upon the boneyard, the full moon stood high in the glittering sky. Below it, the retired United States Air Force aircrafts lined wing to wing gleamed in the endless formations. The place was at once beautiful and spooky, and as Jake hobbled in the silence of the ghostly planes, the only sound was that of his breathing and of his beating heart.

He halted below the cockpit of a Superfortress, peering at its dark shape, which loomed above him like an enormous cross. The missing landing gear on one side gave the bomber a sharp tilt so that even with his injured leg, he had little trouble scaling its slanted wing. On hands and knees, he inched along the riveted aluminum still cooling after the day in the merciless sun, reached the fuselage, pulled himself on top of it, crawled toward the sloping nose, and then, feet first, slipped through the glassless windscreen inside the cockpit.

He climbed into the pilot's seat and looked around, awed by the myriad of gleaming knobs and switches. His whole life he had been dreaming of piloting a plane like this to Russia to save his dad. He thought of the pledge he used to whisper to himself at school during the Pledge of Allegiance: *I pledge to save my dad from the Russians and to bring him home so my dad and mom and I can be a regular family like we're supposed to be in America.*

He began reciting the pledge again, but the sound of his own voice in the eerie silence of the decrepit cockpit spooked him, and he stopped. Besides, the pledge seemed silly to him now. At long last, he was in the pilot's seat of the real Superfortress, but it did not matter that he knew neither how to fly it nor how to lift this rusted machine off the ground. What was the use of flying to Russia if his father was back in America?

He glimpsed a radio headset hooked around the throttle beside the pilot's chair, unhooked it, and set it in his lap. He turned the headset over, gazing at the loose mesh threads where the cable had been cut and at the petrified bone-colored foam inside the headphones. Slipping the headset over his ears, he leaned forward and flipped a few random switches.

"Come in, Delta Alpha Delta One," he whispered, calling for his father as he had always done pretending to fly his B-29 model at home. "Off the ground at . . ." He paused, not knowing what time it was, and said again instead, "Come in, Delta Alpha Delta One. Please come in."

He strained his ears, hoping for some faraway voice inside the headphones to reveal his father's secret whereabouts. But there was no faraway voice. There was nothing. He felt tears pooling behind his lower eyelids and lifted his chin up to keep them from spilling. The tears swelled, burst forth, and, plunging down, made two clear channels through the dry dirt caking his face. The channel on the left swerved toward his lips, and he stuck his tongue out to taste the salt.

And while he sat there wearing the useless headset and sobbing his heart out from pain and fear and despair, the darkness that engulfed him made him think of Shubin's darkroom and the look of disappointment on his face when Jake refused to learn how to develop pictures. *I thought this was something we could do together*, Shubin said. His words made Jake feel weird then, but he felt almost guilty now. *Do you ever think about your dad?* Shubin asked him, and when caught by surprise, Jake answered, *Why?* Shubin winced as if he was hurt.

Next, Jake thought of Shubin's cracked spectacles on the counter of Ruby's diner and the wad of dirty tape unraveling off their frame. What Jake saw then in Shubin's unguarded eyes and what he had refused to see was neither anger nor menace nor threat but anguish and worry.

Then Jake thought of the pearly gray moth tapping against the lampshade in his mother's bedroom. He saw again two shadows swaying together in a strange and pretty dance, and tried to understand why watching his mother and Shubin smile at each other made him so furious then but it did not now.

And as Jake thought of his mother's and Shubin's shadows, some other shadows slid from under the cockpit of the bomber. A family of coyotes trotted silently in between the anchored aircrafts. Silvery and transparent under the moonlight, a young pup loped in between two adults. The last in line, the largest of the three, probably a father, paused to look back in Jake's direction. His eyes flared green for one brief moment, then all three vanished into the night.

Jake's heart grew in his chest, expanding to where it could burst. All things he had believed in life, all things he had heard on the radio, and read about in the comics, and seen in the movies—all things about Communists and foreigners and spies—had made him blind to what was so easy to see. After Shubin had moved into their house, Jake had kept looking for his father while he was right beside him. It was Shubin, of course. Shubin was his father.

51

Later, when Jake tried to recall what happened after the air force base guards found him in the cockpit of the B-29, his memory became hazy and confused. The discovery that Shubin was his father had had an extraordinary effect on him. He felt peaceful and content, and for a long time, he sat back in the pilot's seat with his hands folded behind his head, smiling at the stars in the brilliant sky. The stars swarmed and shimmered and fell in long golden arcs until, inexplicably, they began to converge upon him from all directions, drawing nearer and nearer, swaddling him in their soft, luminous glow.

What happened next he could not quite remember. He must have fainted when the stars circling the cockpit turned out to be the flashlights of the guards combing the boneyard searching for him. But later, much later, when he finally came to his senses, he found himself rocking gently to the low hum of a moving vehicle, with his face buried in someone's lap. A thick wad of something, some cotton maybe and some gauze, was taped to the left side of his face. The bandage reeked of medicine, yet he could still smell the faint scent of his mother's favorite soap on the person who held his head in her lap. His skin felt itchy below the bandage, but he fought the urge to scratch it and kept his eyes tightly closed, not wanting his mother to know he was awake.

"Can we swap?" a raspy voice complained. "His sneakers stink."

That was Shubin's voice. His father's voice. Jake knew now that he was stretched along the rear bench of the moving vehicle, his face in his mother's lap, his feet across his father's. Jake smiled.

"Don't wake him," his mother whispered over him.

"But his—"

"Shush!"

During a brief silence that followed, he wondered what his father's real name was and also what was his. Was he still McCauley, or was he now Shubin, or was he now Jake McCauley-Shubin, which was even better, because then neither his father nor his mother would feel cheated.

"You mean stink kind of like rubber burning?" another

voice piped from the direction of the steering wheel. "It's not sneakers, bud. It's us."

This was either Bambach or Bader speaking. The G-men's voices were about the same.

"We had to sift through a mountain of ash and burned rubber," Bader or Bambach said. "Your kid had the bright idea to drop the Stratojet manual onto a burning tire."

"A tubeless Coker number forty-eight, to be exact," another voice chimed in. That was definitely Bambach.

"You should've kept your boy out of the operation," Bader said.

"That was *your* job, Bader," said Jake's mother. "Your assignment was to keep him safe."

"Keep *him* safe?"

Jake guessed by the creaking of the leather that Bader had turned to look at him.

"We should've put a twelve-man team on that kid. No disrespect to his parents, but you got yourself a reckless child."

"I think he's kind of cute."

Jake felt his ears burning. It was that redhead, Kathy Lubeck.

"If you ask me, keeping him in the dark was a dumb idea."

"What would you rather, darling?" Bambach said. "Say hello to your daddy, little boy—he's only pretending to be a Russian spy. He's a double agent."

"Shut your trap," Jake's father snapped. "You talk too much."

"What's the matter?" Bambach said. "The Commies bugged your Chevy?"

"Whose idea was it, anyhow?" Bader said. "I mean the *need to know* and all?"

"We can successfully defeat the Communist attempt to capture the United States by fighting it with truth and justice," Kathy Lubeck sung prettily, as if it were a jingle.

"Truth and justice?" Bader said. "Wait, wait, don't tell me. The boss said it somewhere. I heard it on the radio."

"I'll be darned," Bambach said. "The boss himself ordered you to keep the boy ignorant?"

"J. Edgar Hoover didn't know who he was dealing with," his father said proudly.

"Neither did you," said his mother.

Someone laughed.

"Is that funny to you?" Kathy Lubeck said sharply. "You try to be a woman raising a child by herself while your husband is risking his life undercover in Russia."

"Thank you, Kathy," said his mother.

They were all quiet for a while, and then Jake's father said, as if he was defending himself, "Yeah. Well. It's a dirty job, but someone's got to do it."

"Which job?" said Jake's mother. "Raising a child or staying undercover in Russia?"

Someone laughed again. Bambach or Bader.

His father did not answer, but Jake imagined the kind of look he might have given his mother and the kind of look he might have gotten back. Jake rocked with his face in his mother's lap and his feet in his father's, eager for them to keep talking, but no one said anything for a long time, and there was nothing to listen to but the rustle of the tires and the hum of the engine. He had begun to doze off again when he heard his father's voice: "In that diner—you know, Ruby's, I used to go there before the war—a waitress recognized me and then some creep knocked a plate of bean soup into my lap on purpose."

"Oh, yeah?" Bader said. "I know Ruby's. Good coffee."

"I never made it to the coffee part," Jake's father said bitterly. "I'd kill for a cup."

Jake felt the motorcar making a sharp left, the tires screeched, and his body began to slip off the bench, but his mother and father held him securely.

"Take it easy, Bader," his mother said. "You'll wake up the neighborhood."

"Is that the Armbrusters' house?" Kathy Lubeck said. "A beautiful home. Is there a pool?"

"A pool and a fallout shelter," Bambach said. "Top of the line."

"The Russians have definitely overpaid Armbruster for all that phony film they got from you during the war," said

Bader. "Pity we had to wait so long until he decided to bite again. I guess he only likes you, Shubin."

Bambach laughed. "I'd like to see them building the Stratojet using the crap you handed Bull this time."

So that was it. That was their operation. The major had been paid by the Russians to leave top secrets in his Cadillac to be photographed by Jake's father, who was only pretending to be a Russian spy. He was an American spy instead, a double agent. Bull watched him taking pictures of the real top secret stuff, but what he got instead from Jake's father were film cartridges with fake pictures, not what the major had left in his Cadillac at all. Bull then sent the film cartridges to the Russians somehow, so they would build aircrafts using fake charts, and fake diagrams, and fake drawings. It could never work, but the Russians would not know why. Major Armbruster had no idea, of course. He was a traitor, and he wanted to kill Jake, but still, Jake felt bad for Duane and he felt kind of bad for his dad, too. He hoped the major was not terribly hurt.

"And may I inquire," Jake's father said, "where's my big pal Gold Teeth?"

Nobody answered.

"If my cover's blown, gentlemen," he announced, "the heads will roll. *Your* heads, gentlemen."

"Bull can't get away," Bambach said. "All exits are sealed."

"We'll get him," Bader promised.

"Either you'll get *him*," Jake's father said, "or Hoover will get all of us."

"What do you have to worry about, turncoat?" Bader said. "He's not your boss since the war."

"Shubin is with the Central Intelligence," Bambach said in a mocking voice. "That must make Shubin very intelligent."

"Oh, shut up, Bambach," Jake's father said. "*You* try to freeze your butt in Moscow digging the dead drop from under the snow!"

"I wonder how much phony stuff they're handing *us*," Bader said.

"Just as much," Jake's father said. "It's a lousy game."

"Then why don't you quit it and stay home?" his mother said.

Shubin did not answer, and Jake became worried that his dad might go away again.

"Let me ask you something, Shubin," Bambach said. "We were all here wondering. All that Communist talk of yours? Is it for real or just for your cover?"

"Come on, lads, can't we take a break from the Cold War for a minute?" said Kathy Lubeck. "I've never been invited to their home before."

Jake felt the gears shifting, felt a soft sideways sway, and when the tires bounced over the crumbling slab, he knew that they had turned into the driveway of their house. A lock of his mother's hair tickled his ear as she bent down to whisper, "Wake up, honey. We're home."

Jake waited until the engine cut and the vehicle stopped rocking from the passengers climbing out and then he opened his eyes, looked into his mother's face, and said, "I know, Mom."

52

Jake slipped out of the motorcar after his mother and, keeping slightly behind her, peeked out at his dad. On the far side of the mesquite tree with the tire swing hanging off its branches, his father, Kathy Lubeck, Bader, and Bambach stood close together talking in hushed voices. All four looked a little guilty, but his father looked guiltiest of all.

"Go ahead, Shubin," Jake's mother said, and when his father turned to face them, Jake was struck at the change in his appearance. Shubin's crummy spectacles with one split lens were missing, and his hair was combed in some other, different way. He did not even look that thin anymore, or not as thin as he had the first time Jake saw him, when he seemed so insubstantial that Jake thought he might vanish before his very eyes. Now his father appeared solid and present, but it was hard to miss that he was also terribly nervous.

Shubin glanced at Jake, but instantly his gaze slipped off Jake's face toward Mrs. McCauley. Jake looked up at his mom, then turned back to his father. Shubin hesitated until Kathy Lubeck gave him a little nudge in the back. He nodded and began walking toward Jake, but bumped his knee into the tire swing. The tire swayed away and swayed back, banging into him from behind. Shubin leapt aside and glared at the tire, then over his shoulder at Kathy Lubeck and the G-men, expecting them to laugh. They kept straight faces, watching him. Shubin turned back to Jake and, blushing with embarrassment, continued walking.

Jake's mom gently took him by the shoulders and moved him in front of her, so that Jake would be closer to his father. Jake leaned back into his mom with all his weight, watching Shubin approach. Gone was his easy and carefree way of walking that had so irritated Jake before. Gone was his sarcastic and arrogant smirk. Instead, Shubin dawdled like a kid on his way to the blackboard after he had forgotten to learn his lesson. Not that Jake wanted him to hurry. He, too, needed a little time to sort out how he felt at the moment. There was no anger in Jake, nor fear, but some new feeling toward Shubin, so new he could not even name it yet.

Shubin halted abruptly one step short of Jake and, clutching his shoulder at arm's length, took a deep breath as if he was about to deliver a speech. Everyone waited, but Jake's father stood motionless with his mouth open, unable to utter a sound.

A pearly gray dove flitted from under the eaves of the house, and Jake's eyes followed it to the yellow bird feeder suspended from the hackberry tree in the driveway. When he looked back at his father, he caught the pleading glance Shubin gave Mrs. McCauley. And while the three of them, Jake and his mom and his dad, stood facing one another in that awkward silence, Jake remembered the family of dummies in the window of the J. C. Penney. He remembered the dummy boy standing behind the glass with his dummy mom and his dummy dad, close together and yet somehow far apart. Mrs. McCauley, Shubin, and Jake were just like those dummies with one exception: the dummy boy had been given a bicycle, while Jake's bike was stolen.

By the strangest coincidence, at the very moment Jake had that thought, Bader cleared his throat and said, "Before we forget, Jake," and walked briskly past them to the rear of the Chevy, swung open the trunk, and lifted out Jake's rusted roadster. "Yours, isn't it, sonny?"

"Where did you find it?" Jake gasped.

"Well, we . . ." Bader glanced at Bambach.

"The thing is," Bambach said, "we sort of took it."

Jake looked up at him in astonishment. "You stole my bike?"

"For your own safety," Bambach said, nodding at Bader. "It was his idea."

"We felt it was a bit dicey to follow you on the bike," Bader said sheepishly. "After that trick you pulled with the bus."

"You need to slow down sometimes, kid," Bambach said. "It's not safe."

"Hoover is going to love this!" Kathy Lubeck gave a throaty laugh. "Stealing a kid's bike!"

"Stop dawdling, Shubin," Jake heard his mother say, and he glanced up at his dad still clutching his shoulder. Shubin made a serious face and began in his raspy voice, "So, young man . . ."

"It's okay," Jake said quietly, and slid from under his hand. "Later."

"Later?" his father repeated, searching Jake's face.

Jake shrugged, and when a tiny smile cracked his lips, Shubin exhaled in relief. "Phew," he said, and then, looking around, "Well, what are we standing here for? Let's all go in and have us a little celebration." He rubbed his hands together in excitement. "What do we have that flows, sweetheart?"

"It's seven in the morning, Shubin," said his mother sternly.

"Shubin is still on Moscow time," said Kathy Lubeck.

"I'll make us fresh coffee," said his mother.

"Coffee?" his dad said. "I'd kill for a cup."

53

Jake's father, followed by Kathy Lubeck and Bambach and Bader, went into the house, but his mother halted in the doorway and looked over at Jake. "Coming in, honey?"

"I'll be right there." His mother hesitated, and he added with a smile, "I'll be fine, Mom. Just want to put my bike away."

She watched him for a moment, and then went in, leaving the door wide open.

Jake walked the bike toward the garage, leaned it against the wall, and let his fingers caress its bruised and peeling frame.

His good old roadster.

"Hey, bud? Bud?" he heard a voice behind him. "I brought you something."

Jake's hand halted on the roadster's frame, he hesitated for a moment, and then slowly turned around.

The hedge that separated their properties came just below Duane's chin, and Jake guessed that Duane must have been balancing on his toes, the way his head swayed side to side. "Jeez, bud," Duane said. "What happened to your face?"

"Oh, this?" Jake tapped the bandage with his index finger. "It's nothing." He nodded at his roadster. "Fell off my bike."

"Did they take you to the hospital?" Duane asked, but did not wait for Jake's reply and went on. "My dad's in the hospital now. Mom and I just came back from there. Bad car accident. His Caddy's smashed! We'll have to get a new one."

"Is he . . . okay?"

"Yeah, yeah, he's fine. Sure. Well. I don't really know. We actually didn't see him. The G-men wouldn't let us. Can you believe that? The place was crawling with the FBI." He cocked his head to one side, studying Jake's face. "Know anything about it?" But once again he did not give Jake a chance to reply, as if he would rather not know. "Going back to school on Monday? We'll have a new teacher. They fired

Vargas. Yep. Fired him and fired the principal. Isn't that crazy? Said they were Communists poisoning the minds of our youth. I don't know about Vargas, he might have been a Commie, but Mr. Hirsch? He was in a death camp in Germany! How could he—"

Duane's head disappeared for a moment—he must have lost his balance—then reappeared again.

"What I was going to say, bud . . . I'm sorry about what happened at school. I didn't know they would gang up on you like that. I swear I didn't. Want to talk about it?"

"Not now," Jake said. "I'm kind of busy."

"Right, right. Of course you are, bud. Sorry." His head vanished again, popped up again. "Oh, yeah. I brought you this."

He tossed something over the hedge, and Jake watched the metallic links spin, glinting in the morning light, until the bicycle chain clanked against the buckled concrete in the driveway.

"Brand-new," Duanc said. "I got a couple of spares. My dad was going to buy me a new bike anyhow. Do you want my old Phantom? I'll give it to you, bud, if you want it. I also got a bunch of new Spy Runner comics. Some good ones. Lots of action. Car chases, shoot-outs. You'll like it. Want me to bring them over?"

Jake squinted at Duane, thought about it, and shook his

head. “No, thanks. I’m kind of through with Spy Runner, I guess.”

He left the bike chain where it fell and hobbled to the front door, but on the threshold halted and looked over.

Duane’s head popped up again. “Yeah, bud? I’m still here.”

“Don’t leave without me Monday morning, okay?” Jake said. “We’ll ride to school together.”

54

When Jake entered the house, the grown-ups were still crowding the hallway. The men flung their hats on the hat rack, and stood loosening their neckties and firing wisecracks. Kathy Lubeck was peeking into the parlor, complimenting his mom on her window blinds.

Jake slipped past them and hobbled toward his room. He wanted to show his father the only snapshot he had of him, or maybe he wanted to compare the man holding the baby in the snapshot with the man laughing in their hallway, or maybe he just wanted to be alone for a while to sort out all those strange and scary things that had happened to him.

He put his hand on the doorknob and was about to turn it when the door swung open by itself. Someone was blocking the doorway. Startled, Jake peered at the enormous white potbelly sagging over the handle of a gun stuck behind the trousers' belt. Before he could scream, Bull snatched Jake by the shirtfront, yanked him into the room, whooshed him round, and squashed his neck in the crook of his arm.

"Where did you go, honey?" Jake's mother called from the hallway. "Kathy has a question for you."

Jake began to gag from the neck crush but also from the putrid odor of Bull's body: sweat, sweet-sick aftershave, and something else, death maybe.

"Jake?" his mother's voice rang out again, alarmed. "You okay?"

Moving like a giant crab, Bull stomped sideways into the hallway, squashing Jake's neck and shielding his chest and potbelly with Jake's body. The laughter and the voices ceased abruptly, and in the silence of the hallway, Jake could distinctly feel and hear Bull's meaty heart pumping against his back and Bull's bowels shift and flex inside his massive belly.

"Give Stratojet," Bull growled above Jake's ear. "Or boy dead."

Jake saw his mother's face, white as chalk, rapidly floating toward him through the darkened hallway. Her right arm, rising, came into sight. Bull's right arm jerked up to meet hers. For an instant, Jake thought that they were about to shake hands, but then something glinted between Bull's fingers.

The handgun!

Jake thrashed wildly in Bull's iron grip. A flash. A loud blast. The ceiling globe exploded. Bull crushed Jake's neck harder. "*Teeho, doorak!*"

Choking, Jake grasped Bull's forearm with both hands, trying to push the gun away from his mother. The gun went off again. The window blinds at the end of the hallway burst into splinters. Glass shattered. A shaft of sunlight shot through the hallway from the exposed window, and Jake saw a large chunk of glass sparkle before it split in two over his dad's hitched shoulders.

Blinded by the sun, Jake missed his mother striking Bull in the face. She struck him twice in one continuous motion. Jake felt Bull's body jolt as her fist cracked him just above the ear. She followed with her elbow, smashing it into his jaw. Something bonked the back of Jake's head and lodged below his shirt collar. Bull gave a grunt, swayed, and loosened his grip. Sagging down Bull's potbelly, Jake hit the floor with his knees, then with his chin. The thing tumbled from under his collar and conked the floorboards beside him. Bull's golden dentures, smeared in blood and saliva.

Rapid gunfire popped from several directions. A bullet

whizzed by and slugged into the wall above Jake's head, spraying plaster in all directions. Jake felt his mother's body wrap over his, shielding him from bullets. Through the narrow gap between the floorboards and his mother's elbow, Jake saw what happened next.

The whole thing took no more than an instant, but unfolding out of time in the measured succession of frozen pictures, it did not seem real, as if Jake were leafing through the action sequence in a Spy Runner comic. He may have told Duane that he was through with Spy Runner, but Spy Runner was not through with Jake yet.

He saw Bull on the staircase, firing his gun. Shubin lunged after him, caught him by the ankle, and yanked his leg up. Bull tumbled down. The steps below him cracked and splintered. The entire staircase sunk, leaning away from the wall. Shubin stumbled and reached for the handrail. It came off in his hand. Bull lifted his gun. Fired at Shubin. Missed. Shubin whacked the gun out of Bull's hand with the handrail. The gun cartwheeled through the air. The staircase heaved and gave way. Shubin swayed, flapping his arms. Falling sideways, Bull kicked Shubin's face like a football. Then time sped up and everything came crashing down in the explosion of timber and bodies and dust.

Shubin's head thumped the floor inches from Jake's face. Among the staircase debris, panting and cursing, Bader and Bambach were grappling with Bull. They rolled him facedown. Two matching pairs of handcuffs snapped over Bull's ankles and wrists.

Jake shifted his gaze from the G-men toward a deep gash across Shubin's forehead. His nostrils were bubbling with blood, his eyes were shut. He looked more dead than alive and yet, incredibly, he was smiling.

"Dad?" Jake whispered. "Are you okay?"

One of his father's bloodshot eyes popped open and peered at Jake.

"You know this is not how I wanted us to meet, son?"

"Oh, yeah?"

"What? You don't trust me?"

"No, sir."

His father's smile spread wider. "Fair enough, son. Give it time."

Jake felt his mother's body lifting off him and heard her voice. "You two have plenty to talk over, boys."

"Yes, ma'am," his father agreed. "But what about that coffee?"

"What about it?" his mother said.

"Don't worry, Mom," Jake said. "I'll make it."

"Nah," his father groaned, sitting up. "*I'll* make it."

"We'll make it together," his mother said. "Come to the kitchen, boys."

ACKNOWLEDGMENTS

Spy Runner was conceived at the suggestion of my agent, Steven Malk, to whom I gratefully dedicate this book. He must have been gazing into a crystal ball when he brought up Russian spies in our phone conversation a few years ago. While I was learning about the former Soviet Union's covert actions against the United States in the past, US intelligence revealed that Russia is using the very same tactics in the present. In the meantime, the United States was returning to the politics of division it had already experienced during the Cold War anti-communist crusade. At that time, certain politicians exploited the communist threat against democracy by dividing American people. As a result, Steven's advice—and the work that went into creating *Spy Runner*—seemed not only necessary but urgent. I wish to thank my editor and publisher, Laura Godwin, for her unwavering belief that my books testify, often from personal experience, to the damaging effects of ideology on the lives of ordinary children.

I would also like to thank the talented team at Godwin Books: April Ward, Julia Sooy, copyeditor Ana Deboo, and proofreader Regina Castillo, as well as everyone at Macmillan Children's Publishing for their tireless efforts to connect young readers with my books.

My deeply felt thanks to my fellow authors, librarians, and educators for their comments on innumerable drafts: M. T. Anderson, Viki Ash, Olga Bukhina, Anna Katsnelson, Kristen Kittscher, Hannah Mann, Alec Sokolow, Chris Sturdevant, and Sylvia Tag.

And last, without whom not only my art but my adult life would be inconceivable, my greatest thanks to my wife, Mary Kuryla.

FALLOUT SHELTER
SPY
HUNTER